SPACE PLAGUE

By
GEORGE O. SMITH

I0541425

ARMCHAIR FICTION
PO Box 4369, Medford, Oregon   97501-0168

*For more information about Armchair Books and products, visit our
website at…*

www.armchairfiction.com

Or email us at…
armchairfiction@yahoo.com

CHAPTER ONE

I came up out of the blackness just enough to know that I was no longer pinned down by a couple of tons of wrecked automobile. I floated on soft sheets with only a light blanket over me.

I hurt all over like a hundred and sixty pounds of boil. My right arm was numb and my left thigh was aching. Breathing felt like being stabbed with rapiers and the skin of my face felt stretched tight. There was a bandage over my eyes and the place was as quiet as the grave. But I knew that I was not in any grave because my nose was working just barely well enough to register the unmistakable pungent odor that only goes with hospitals.

I tried my sense of perception, but like any delicate and critical sense, perception was one of the first to go. I could not dig out beyond a few inches. I could sense the bed and the white sheets and that was all.

Some brave soul had hauled me out of that crack-up before the fuel tank went up in the fire. I hope that whoever he was, he'd had enough sense to haul Catherine out of the mess first. The thought of living without Catherine was too dark to bear, and so I just let the blackness close down over me again because it cut out all pain, both physical and mental.

The next time I awoke there was light and a pleasant male voice saying, "Steve Cornell. Steve, can you hear me?"

I tried to answer but no sound came out. Not even a hoarse croak.

The voice went on, "Don't try to talk, Steve. Just think it."

#Catherine?# I thought sharply, because most medicos are telepath, not perceptive.

"Catherine is all right," he replied.

#Can I see her?#

"Lord no!" he said quickly. "You'd scare her half to death the way you look right now."

#How bad off am I?#

"You're a mess, Steve. Broken ribs, compound fracture of the left tibia, broken humerus. Scars, mars, abrasions, some flashburn and post-accident shock. And if you're interested, not a trace of Mekstrom's Disease."

#Mekstrom's Disease—?# was my thought of horror.

"Forget it, Steve. I always check for it because it's been my specialty. Don't worry."

#Okay. So how long have I been here?#

"Eight days."

#Eight days? Couldn't you do the usual job?#

"You were pretty badly ground up, Steve. That's what took the time. Now, suppose you tell me what happened?"

#Catherine and I were eloping. Just like most other couples do since Rhine Institute made it difficult to find personal privacy. Then we cracked up.#

"What did it?" asked the doctor. "Perceptives like you usually sense danger before you can see it."

#Catherine called my attention to a peculiar road sign, and I sent my perception back to take another dig. We hit the fallen limb of a tree and went over and over. You know the rest.#

"Bad," said the doctor. "But what kind of a sign would call your interest so deep that you didn't at least see the limb, even if you were perceiving the sign?"

#Peculiar sign,# I thought. Ornamental wrought iron gizmo with curlicues and a little decorative circle that sort of looks like the Boy Scout tenderfoot badge suspended on three spokes. One of the spokes were broken away; I got involved because I was trying to guess whether it had been shot away by some vandal who missed the central design. Then—blooie!#

"It's really too bad, Steve. But you'll be all right in a while."

#Thanks, doctor. Doctor? Doctor—?#

"Sorry, Steve. I forget that everybody is not telepath like I am. I'm James Thorndyke."

Much later I began to wake up again, and with better clarity of mind, I found that I could extend my esper as far as the wall and through the door by a few inches. It was strictly hospital all right; sere white and stainless steel as far as my esper could reach.

In my room was a nurse, rustling in starched white. I tried to speak, croaked once, and then paused to form my voice.

"Can—I see—How is—? Where is?" I stopped again, because the nurse was probably as esper as I was and required a full sentence to get the thought behind it. Only a telepath like the doctor could have followed my jumbled ideas. But the nurse was good. She tried:

"Mr. Cornell? You're awake!"

ONE MAN'S NIGHTMARE QUEST...

Part of Steve Cornell's life had been snatched away from him. It started when his fiancée vanished. It got much worse, though, when everybody insisted it didn't happen the way he believed.

Soon Steve's search for his missing fiancée brought him face to face with and incredible, mind-boggling secret. And it soon became clear that some unknown foe didn't want him to discover it. A foe who would use any means to stop him. Could Steve find that foe before they made him vanish too?

If you've enjoyed this book, you will not want to miss these terrific titles...

ARMCHAIR SCI-FI & HORROR DOUBLE NOVELS, $12.95 each

D-31 **A HOAX IN TIME** by Keith Laumer
        INSIDE EARTH by Poul Anderson

D-32 **TERROR STATION** by Dwight V. Swain
        THE WEAPON FROM ETERNITY by Dwight V. Swain

D-33 **THE SHIP FROM INFINITY** by Edmond Hamilton
        TAKEOFF by C. M. Kornbluth

D-34 **THE METAL DOOM** by David H. Keller
        TWELVE TIMES ZERO by Howard Browne

D-35 **HUNTERS OUT OF SPACE** by Joseph Kelleam
        INVASION FROM THE DEEP by Paul W. Fairman,

D-36 **THE BEES OF DEATH** by Robert Moore Williams
        A PLAGUE OF PYTHONS by Frederick Pohl

D-37 **THE LORDS OF QUARMALL** by Fritz Leiber and Harry Fischer
        BEACON TO ELSEWHERE by James H. Schmitz

D-38 **BEYOND PLUTO** by John S. Campbell
        ARTERY OF FIRE by Thomas N. Scortia

D-39 **SPECIAL DELIVERY** by Kris Neville
        NO TIME FOR TOFFEE by Charles F. Meyers

D-40 **JUNGLE IN THE SKY** by Milton Lesser
        RECALLED TO LIFE by Robert Silverberg

ARMCHAIR SCIENCE FICTION CLASSICS, $12.95 each

C-10 **MARS IS MY DESTINATION**
        by Frank Belknap Long

C-11 **SPACE PLAGUE**
        by George O. Smith

C-12 **SO SHALL YE REAP**
        by Rog Phillips

ARMCHAIR SCIENCE FICTION & HORROR GEMS SERIES, $12.95 each

G-3 **SCIENCE FICTION GEMS, Vol. Two**
       James Blish and others

G-4 **HORROR GEMS, Vol. Two**
       Joseph Payne Brennan and others

"Look—nurse—"

"Take it easy. I'm Miss Farrow. I'll get the doctor."

"No—wait. I've been here eight days—?"

"But you were badly hurt, you know."

"But the doctor. He said that she was here, too."

"Don't worry about it, Mr. Cornell."

"But he said that she was not badly hurt."

"She wasn't."

"Then why was—is—she here so long?"

Miss Farrow laughed cheerfully. "Your Christine is in fine shape. She is still here because she wouldn't leave until you were well out of danger. Now stop fretting. You'll see her soon enough."

Her laugh was light but strained. It sounded off-key because it was as off-key as a ten-yard-strip of baldfaced perjury. She left in a hurry and I was able to esper as far as outside the door, where she leaned back against the wood and began to cry. She was hating herself because she had blown her lines and she knew that I knew it.

And Catherine had never been in this hospital, because if she had been brought in with me, the nurse would have known the right name.

Not that it mattered to me now, but Miss Farrow was no esper or she'd have dug my belongings and found Catherine's name on the license. Miss Farrow was a telepath; I'd not called my girl by name, only by an affectionate mental image.

CHAPTER TWO

I was fighting my body upright when Doctor Thorndyke came running. "Easy, Steve," he said with a quiet gesture. He pushed me gently back down in the bed with hands that were as soft as a mother's, but as firm as the kind that tie bow knots in half-inch bars. "Easy," he repeated soothingly.

"Catherine?" I croaked pleadingly.

Thorndyke fingered the call button in some code or other before he answered me. "Steve," he said honestly, "you can't be kept in ignorance forever. We hoped it would be a little longer, when you were stronger—"

"Stop beating around!" I yelled. At least it felt like I was yelling, but maybe it was only my mind welling.

"Easy, Steve. You've had a rough time. Shock—" The door opened and a nurse came in with a hypo all loaded, its needle buried in a fluff of cotton. Thorndyke eyed it professionally and took it; the nurse faded quietly from the room. "Take it easy, Steve. This will—"

"No! Not until I know—"

"Easy," he repeated. He held the needle up before my eyes. "Steve," he said, "I don't know whether you have enough esper training to dig the contents of this needle, but if you haven't, will you please trust me? This contains a neurohypnotic. It won't put you under. It will leave you as wide awake as you are now, but it will disconnect your running gear and keep you from blowing a fuse." Then with swift deftness that amazed me, the doctor slid the needle into my arm and let me have the full load.

I was feeling the excitement rise in me because something was wrong, but I could also feel the stuff going to work. Within half a minute I was in a chilled-off frame of mind that was capable of recognizing the facts but not caring much one way or the other.

When he saw the stuff taking hold, Thorndyke asked, "Steve, just who is Catherine?"

The shock almost cut through the drug. My mind whirled with all the things that Catherine was to me, and the doctor followed it every bit of the way.

"Steve, you've been under an accident shock. There was no Catherine with you. There was no one with you at all. Understand that and accept it. No one. You were alone. Do you understand?"

I shook my head. I sounded to myself like an actor reading the script of a play for the first time. I wanted to pound on the table and add the vigor of physical violence to my hoarse voice, but all I could do was to reply in a calm voice:

"Catherine was with me. We were—" I let it trail off because Thorndyke knew what we were doing. We were eloping in the new definition of the word. Rhine Institute and its associated studies had changed a lot of customs; a couple intending to commit matrimony today were inclined to take off quietly and disappear from their usual haunts until they'd managed to get intimately acquainted with one another. Elopement was a means of finding some personal privacy.

We should have stayed at home and faced the crude jokes that haven't changed since Pithecanthropus first discovered that sex was funny. But our mutual desire to find some privacy in this modern fish-bowl had put me in the hospital and Catherine—where—?

"Steve, listen to me!"

"Yeah?"

"I know you espers. You're sensitive, maybe more so than telepaths. More imagination—"

This was for the birds in my estimation. Among the customs that Rhine has changed was the old argument as to whether women or men were smarter. Now the big argument was whether espers or telepaths could get along better with the rest of the world.

Thorndyke laughed at my objections and went on: "You're in accident shock. You piled up your car. You begin to imagine how terrible it would have been if your Catherine had been with you. Next you carefully build up in your subconscious mind a whole and complete story, so well put together that to you it seems to be fact."

But, #—how could anyone have taken a look at the scene of the accident and not seen traces of woman? My woman.#

"We looked," he said in answer to my unspoken question. "There was not a trace, Steve."

#Fingerprints?#

"You'd been dating her."

#Naturally!#

Thorndyke nodded quietly. "There were a lot of her prints on the remains of your car. But no one could begin to put a date on them, or tell how recent was the latest, due to the fire. Then we made a door to door canvas of the neighborhood to be sure she hadn't wandered off in a daze and shock. Not even a footprint. Nary a trace." He shook his head unhappily. "I suppose you're going to ask about that travelling bag you claim to have put in the trunk beside your own. There was no trace of any travelling bag."

"Doctor," I asked pointedly, "if we weren't together, suppose you tell me first why I had a marriage license in my pocket; second, how come I made a date with the Reverend Towle in Midtown; and third, why did I bother to reserve the bridal suite in the Reignoir Hotel in Westlake? Or was I nuts a long time before this accident. Maybe," I added, "after making reservations, I had to go out and pile myself up as an excuse for not turning up with a bride."

"I—all I can say is that there was not a trace of woman in that accident."

"You've been digging in my mind. Did you dig her telephone number?"

He looked at me blankly.

"And you found what, when you tried to call her?"

"I—er—"

"Her landlady told you that Miss Lewis was not in her apartment because Miss Lewis was on her honeymoon, operating under the name of Mrs. Steve Cornell. That about it?"

"All right. So now you know."

"Then where the hell is she, Doc?" The drug was not as all-powerful as it had been and I was beginning to feel excitement again.

"We don't know, Steve."

"How about the guy that hauled me out of that wreck? What does he say?"

"He was there when we arrived. The car had been hauled off you by block and tackle. By the time we got there the tackle had been burned and the car was back down again in a crumpled mass. He is a farmer by the name of Harrison. He had one of his older sons with him, a man about twenty-four, named Phillip. They both swore later that there was no woman in that car nor a trace of one."

"Oh, he did, did he?"

Dr. Thorndyke shook his head slowly and then said very gently. "Steve, there's no predicting what a man's mind will do in a case of shock. I've seen 'em come up with a completely false identity, all the way back to childhood. Now, let's take your case once more. Among the other incredible items—"

"Incredible?" I roared.

"Easy. Hear me out. After all, am I to believe your unsubstantiated story or the evidence of a whole raft of witnesses, the police detail, the accident squad, and the guys who hauled you out of a burning car before it blew up? As I was saying, how can we credit much of your tale when you raved about one man lifting the car and the other hauling you out from underneath?"

I shrugged. "That's obviously a mistaken impression. No one could—"

"So when you admit that one hunk of your story is mistaken—"

"That doesn't prove the rest is false!"

"The police have been tracking this affair hard," said the doctor slowly. "They've gotten nowhere. Tell me, did anyone see you leave that apartment with Miss Lewis?"

"No," I said slowly. "No one that knew us."

Thorndyke shook his head unhappily. "That's why we have to assume that you are in post-accident shock."

I snorted angrily. "Then explain the license, the date with the reverend, the hotel reservation?"

Thorndyke said quietly, "Hear me out, Steve. This is not my own idea alone, but the combined ideas of a number of people who have studied the human mind—"

"In other words, I'm nuts?"

"No. Shock."

"Shock?"

He nodded very slowly. "Let's put it this way. Let's assume that you wanted this marriage with Miss Lewis. You made preparations, furnished an apartment, got a license, made a date with a preacher, reserved a honeymoon suite, and bought flowers for the bride. You take off from work, arrive at her door, only to find that Miss Lewis has taken off for parts unknown. Maybe she left you a letter—"

"Letter!"

"Hear me out, Steve. You arrive at her apartment and find her gone. You read a letter from her saying that she cannot marry you. This is a rather deep shock to you and you can't face it. Know what happens?"

"I blow my brains out along a country road at ninety miles per hour."

"Please, this is serious."

"It sounds incredibly stupid to me."

"You're rejecting it in the same way you rejected the fact that Miss Lewis ran away rather than marry you."

"Do go on, Doctor."

"You drive along the same road you'd planned to take, but the frustration and shock pile up to put you in an accident-prone frame of mind. You then pile up, not consciously, but as soon as you come upon something like that tree limb which can be used to make an accident authentic."

"Oh, sure."

11

Thorndyke eyed me soberly. "Steve," he asked me in a brittle voice, "you won't try to convince me that any esper will let physical danger of that sort get close enough to—"

"I've told you how it happened. My attention was on that busted sign!"

"Fine. More evidence to the fact that Miss Lewis was with you? Now listen to me. In accident-shock you'd not remember anything that your mind didn't want you to recall. Failure is a hard thing to take. So now you can blame your misfortune on that accident."

"So now you tell me how you justify the fact that Catherine told landladies, friends, bosses, and all the rest that she was going to marry me a good long time before I was ready to be verbal about my plans?"

"I—"

"Suppose I've succeeded in bribing everybody to perjure themselves. Maybe we all had it in for Catherine, and did her in?"

Thorndyke shrugged. "I don't know," he said. "I really don't know, Steve. I wish I did."

"That makes two of us," I grunted. "Hasn't anybody thought of arresting me for kidnapping, suspicion of murder, reckless driving and cluttering up the highway with junk?"

"Yes," he said quietly. "The police were most thorough. They had two of their top men look into you."

"What did they find?" I asked angrily. No man likes to have his mind turned inside out and laid out flat so that all the little wheels, cables and levers are open to the public gaze. On the other hand, since I was not only innocent of any crime but as baffled as the rest of them, I'd have gone to them willingly to let them dig, to see if they could dig past my conscious mind into the real truth.

"They found that your story was substantially an honest one."

"Then why all this balderdash about shock, rejection, and so on?"

He shook his head. "None of us are supermen," he said simply. "Your story was honest, you weren't lying. You believe every word of it. You saw it, you went through it. That doesn't prove your story true."

"Now see here—"

"It does prove one thing; that you, Steve Cornell, did not have any malicious, premeditated plans against Catherine Lewis. They've checked everything from hell to breakfast, and so far all we can do is make long-distance guesses as to what happened."

I snorted in my disgust. "That's a telepath for you. Everything so neatly laid out in rows of slats like a snow fence. Me—I'm going to consult a scholar and have him really dig me deep."

Thorndyke shook his head. "They had their top men, Steve. Scholar Redfern and Scholar Berks. Both of them Rhine Scholars, *magna cum laude.*"

I blinked as I always do when I am flabbergasted. I've known a lot of doctors of this and that, from medicine to languages. I've even known a scholar or two, but none of them intimately. But when a doctor of psi is invited to take his scholarte at Rhine, that's it, brother; I pass.

Thorndyke smiled. "You weren't too bad yourself, Steve. Ran twelfth in your class at Illinois, didn't you?"

I nodded glumly. "I forgot to cover the facts. They'd called all the bright boys out and collected them under one special-study roof. I majored in mechanical ingenuity not psi. Hoped to get a D. Ing. out of it, at least, but had to stop. Partly because I'm not ingenious enough and partly because I ran out of cash."

Doctor Thorndyke nodded. "I know how it is," he said. I realized that he was leading me away from the main subject gently, but I couldn't see how to lead him back without starting another verbal hassle. He had me cold. He could dig my mind and get the best way to lead me away, while I couldn't read his. I gave up. It felt better, too, getting my mind off this completely baffling puzzle even for a moment. He caught my thoughts but his face didn't twitch a bit as he picked up his narrative smoothly:

"I didn't make it either," he said unhappily. "I'm psi and good. But I'm telepath and not esper. I weasled my way through pre-med and medical by main force and awkwardness, so to speak." He grinned at me sheepishly. "I'm not much different than you or any other psi. The espers all think that perception is superior to the ability to read minds, and vice versa. I was going to show 'em that a telepath can make Scholar of Medicine. So I 'pathed my way through med by reading the minds of my fellows, who were all good espers. I got so good that I could read the mind of an esper watching me do a delicate dissecting job, and move my hands according to his perception. I could diagnose the deep ills with the best of them—so long as there was an esper in the place."

"So what tripped you up?"

"Telepaths make out best dealing with people. Espers do better with things."

"Isn't medicine a field that deals with people?"

He shook his head. "Not when a headache means spinal tumor, or indigestion, or a bad cold. 'Doctor,' says the patient, 'I've a bad ache along my left side just below the ribs,' and after you diagnose, it turns out to be acute appendicitis. You see, Steve, the patient doesn't know what's wrong with him. Only the symptoms. A telepath can follow the patient's symptoms perfectly, but it takes an esper to dig in his guts and perceive the tumor that's pressing on the spine or the striae on his liver."

"Yeah."

"So I flopped on a couple of tests that the rest of the class sailed through, just because I was not fast enough to read their minds and put my own ability to work. It made 'em suspicious and so here I am, a mere doctor instead of a scholar."

"There are fields for you, I'm sure."

He nodded. "Two. Psychiatry and psychology, neither of which I have any love for. And medical research, where the ability to grasp another doctor or scholar's plan, ideas and theories is slightly more important than the ability to dig esper into the experiments."

"Don't see that," I said with a shake of my head.

"Well, Steve, let's take Mekstrom's Disease, for instance."

"Let's take something simple. What I know about Mekstrom's Disease could be carved on the head of a pin with a blunt butter knife."

"Let's take Mekstrom's. That's my chance to make Scholar of Medicine, Steve, if I can come up with an answer to one of the minor questions. I'll be in the clinical laboratory where the only cases present are those rare cases of Mekstrom's. The other doctors, espers every one of them, and the scholars over them, will dig the man's body right down to the last cell, looking and combing—you know some of the better espers can actually dig into the constituency of a cell?—but I'll be the doctor who can collect all their information, correlate it, and maybe come up with an answer."

"You picked a dilly," I told him.

It was a real one, all right. Otto Mekstrom had been a mechanic-tech at White Sands Space Station during the first flight to Venus, Mars and Moon round-trip with landings. About two weeks after the ship came home, Otto Mekstrom's left fingertips began to grow hard. The hardening crawled up slowly until his hand was like a rock. They studied him and worked over him and took all sorts of samples and made all sorts of tests until Otto's forearm was as hard as his hand. Then they amputated at the shoulder.

But by that time, Otto Mekstrom's toes on both feet were getting solid and his other hand was beginning to show signs of the same. On one side of the creepline the flesh was soft and normal, but on the other it was all you could do to poke a sharp needle into the skin. Poor Otto ended up a basket case, just in time to have the damned stuff start all over again at the stumps of his arms and legs. He died when hardening reached his vitals.

Since that day, some twenty-odd years ago, there had been about thirty cases a year turn up. All fatal, despite amputations and everything else known to modern medical science. God alone knew how many unfortunate human beings took to suicide without contacting the big Medical Research Center at Marion, Indiana.

Well, if Thorndyke could uncover something, no one could claim that a telepath had no place in medicine. I wished him luck.

I did not see Thorndyke again in that hospital. They released me the next day and then I had nothing to do but to chew my fingernails and wonder what had happened to Catherine.

CHAPTER THREE

I'd rather not go into the next week and a half in detail. I became known as the bridegroom who lost his bride, and between the veiled accusations and the half-covered snickers, life was pretty miserable. I talked to the police a couple-three times, first as a citizen asking for information and ending up as a complainant against party or parties unknown. The latter got me nowhere. Apparently the police had more lines out than the Grand Bank fishing fleet and were getting no more nibbles than they'd get in the Dead Sea. They admitted it; the day had gone when the police gave out news reports that an arrest was expected hourly, meaning that they were baffled. The police, with their fine collection of psi boys, were willing to admit when they were really baffled. I talked to telepaths who could tell me what I'd had for breakfast on the day I'd entered pre-school classes, and espers who could sense the color of the clothing I wore yesterday. I've a poor color-esper, primitive so to speak. These guys were good, but no matter how good they were, Catherine Lewis had vanished as neatly as Ambrose Bierce.

I even read Charles Fort, although I have no belief in the supernatural, and rather faint faith in the Hereafter. And people who enter the Hereafter leave their remains behind for evidence.

Having to face Catherine's mother and father, who came East to see me, made me a complete mental wreck.

It is harder than you think to face the parents of a woman you loved, and find that all you can tell them is that somehow you fouled your drive, cracked up, and lost their daughter. Not even dead-for-sure. Death, I think, we all could have faced. But this uncertainty was something that gnawed at the soul's roots and left it rotting.

To stand there and watch the tears in the eyes of a woman as she asks you, "But can't you remember, son?" is a little too much, and I don't care to go into details.

The upshot of it was, after about ten days of lying awake nights and wondering where she was and why. Watching her eyes peer out of a metal casting at me from a position sidewise of my head. Nightmares, either the one about us turning over and over and over, or Mrs. Lewis pleading with me only to tell her the truth. Then having the police inform me that they were marking this case down as "unexplained." I gave up. I finally swore that I was going to find her and return with her, or I was going to join her in whatever strange, unknown world she had entered.

The first thing I did was to go back to the hospital in the hope that Dr. Thorndyke might be able to add something. In my unconscious ramblings there might be something that fell into a pattern if it could be pieced together.

But this was a failure, too. The hospital super was sorry, but Dr. Thorndyke had left for the Medical Research Center a couple of days before. Nor could I get in touch with him because he had a six-week interim vacation and planned a long, slow jaunt through Yellowstone, with neither schedule nor forwarding addresses.

I was standing there on the steps hoping to wave down a cruising coptercab when the door opened and a woman came out. I turned to look and she recognized me. It was Miss Farrow, my former nurse.

"Why, Mr. Cornell, what are you doing back here?"

"Mostly looking for Thorndyke. He's not here."

"I know. Isn't it wonderful, though? He'll get his chance to study for his scholarte now."

I nodded glumly. "Yeah," I said. It probably sounded resentful, but it is hard to show cheer over the good fortune of someone else when your own world has come unglued.

"Still hoping," she said. It was a statement and not a question.

I nodded slowly. "I'm hoping," I said. "Someone has the answer to this puzzle. I'll have to find it myself. Everyone else has given up."

"I wish you luck," said Miss Farrow with a smile. "You certainly have the determination."

I grunted. "It's about all I have. What I need is training. Here I am, a mechanical engineer, about to tackle the job of a professional detective and tracer of missing persons. About all I know about the job is what I have read. One gets the idea that these writers must know something of the job, the way they write about it. But once you're faced with it yourself, you realize that the writer has planted his own clues."

Miss Farrow nodded. "One thing," she suggested, "have you talked to the people who got you out from under your car yet?"

"No, I haven't. The police talked to them and claimed they knew nothing. I doubt that I can ask them anything that the police have not satisfied themselves about."

Miss Farrow looked up at me sidewise. "You won't find anything by asking people who have never heard of you."

"I suppose not."

A coptercab came along at that moment, and probably sensing my intention, he gave his horn a tap. I'd have liked to talk longer with Miss Farrow, but a cab was what I wanted, so with a wave I took it and she went on down the steps to her own business.

I had to pause long enough to buy a new car, but a few hours afterward I was rolling along that same highway with my esper extended as far as I could in all directions. I was driving slowly, this time both alert and ready.

I went past the scene of the accident slowly and shut my mind off as I saw the black-burned patch. The block was still hanging from an overhead branch, and the rope that had burned off was still dangling, about two feet of it, looped through the pulleys and ending in a tapered, burned end.

I turned left into a driveway toward the home of the Harrisons and went along a winding dirt road, growing more and more conscious of a dead area ahead of me.

It was not a real dead zone, because I could still penetrate some of the region. But as far as really digging any of the details of the rambling Harrison house, I could get more from my eyesight than from any sense of perception. But even if they couldn't find a really dead area, the Harrisons had done very well in finding one that made my sense of perception ineffective. It was sort of like looking through a light fog, and the closer I got to the house the thicker it became.

Just about the point where the dead area was first beginning to make its effect tell, I came upon a tall, browned man of about twenty-four who had been probing into the interior of a tractor up to the time he heard my car. He waved, and I stopped.

"Mr. Harrison?"

"I'm Phillip. And you are Mr. Cornell."

"Call me Steve like everybody else," I said. "How'd you guess?"

"Recognized you," he said with a grin. "I'm the guy that pulled you out."

"Thanks," I said, offering a hand.

He chuckled. "Steve, consider the hand taken and shook, because I've enough grime to muss up a regiment."

"It won't bother me," I said.

"Thanks, but it's still a gesture, and I appreciate it, but let's be sensible. I know you can wash, but let's shake later. What can I do for you?"

"I'd like a first-hand account, Phil."

"Not much to tell. Dad and I were pulling stumps over about a thousand feet from the wreck. We heard the racket. I am esper enough to dig that distance with clarity, so we knew we'd better bring along the block and tackle. The tractor wouldn't go through. So we came on the double, Dad rigged the tackle and hoisted and I took a running dive, grabbed and hauled you out before the whole thing went *Whoosh!* We were both lucky, Steve."

I grunted a bit but managed to nod with a smile.

"I suppose you know that I'm still trying to find my fiancée?"

"I'd heard tell," he said. He looked at me sharply. I'm a total blank as a telepath, like all espers, but I could tell what he was thinking.

"Everybody is convinced that Catherine was not with me," I admitted. "But I'm not. I know she was."

He shook his head slowly. "As soon as we heard the screech of brakes and rubber we esped the place," he said quietly. "We dug you, of course. But no one else. Even if she'd jumped as soon as that tree limb came into view, she could not have run far enough to be out of range. As for removing a bag, she'd have had to wait until the slambang was over to get it out, and by the time your car was finished rolling, Dad and I were on the way with help. She was not there, Steve."

#You're a damn liar!#

Phillip Harrison did not move a muscle. He was blank telepathically. I was esping the muscles in his stomach, under his loose clothing, for that first tensing sign of anger, but nothing showed. He had not been reading my mind.

I smiled thinly at Phil Harrison and shrugged.

He smiled back sympathetically, but behind it I could see that he was wishing that I'd stop harping on a dead subject. "I sincerely wish I could be of help," he said. In that he was sincere. But somewhere, someone was not, and I wanted to find out who it was.

The impasse looked as though it might go on forever unless I turned away and left. I had no desire to leave. Not that Phil could help me, but even though this was a dead end, I was loath to leave the place because it was the last place where I had been close to Catherine.

The silence between us must have been a bit strained at this point, but luckily we had an interruption. I perceived motion, turned and caught sight of a woman coming along the road toward us.

"My sister," said Phil. "Marian."

Marian Harrison was quite a girl; if I'd not been emotionally tied to Catherine Lewis, I'd have been happy to invite myself in. Marian was almost as tall as I am, a dark, brown-haired woman with eyes of a startling, electricity colored blue. She was about twenty-two, young and healthy. Her skin was tanned toast brown so that the bright blue eyes fairly sparked out at you. Her red mouth made a pleasing blend with the tan of her skin and her teeth gleamed white against the dark when she smiled.

Insultingly, I made some complimentary but impolite mental observations about her figure, but Marion did not appear to notice. She was no telepath.

"You're Mr. Cornell," she said, "I remembered you," she said quietly. "Please believe us, Mr. Cornell, when we extend our sympathy."

"Thanks," I said glumly. "Please understand me, Miss Harrison. I appreciate your sympathy, but what I need is action and information and answers. Once I get those, the sympathy won't be needed."

"Of course I understand," she replied instantly. "We are all aware that sympathy is a poor substitute. All the world grieving with you doesn't turn a stitch to help you out of your trouble. All we can do is to wish, with you, that it hadn't happened."

"That's the point," I said helplessly. "I don't even know what happened."

"That makes it even worse," she said softly. Marian had a pleasant voice, throaty and low, that sounded intimate even when talking about something pragmatic. "I wish we could help you, Steve."

"I wish someone could."

She nodded. "They asked me about it, too, even though I was not present until afterward. They asked me," she said thoughtfully, "about the mental attitude of a woman running off to get married. I told them that I couldn't speak for your woman, but that I might be able to speak for me, putting myself in the same circumstances."

She paused a moment, and her brother turned idly back to his tractor and fitted a small end wrench to a bolt-head and gave it a twist. He seemed to think that as long as Marian and I were talking, he could well afford to get along with his work. I agreed with him. I wanted information, but I did not expect the entire world to stop progress to help me. He spun the bolt and started on another, lost in his job while Marian went on:

"I told them that your story was authentic—the one about the bridal nightgown." A very slight color came under the deep tan. "I told them that I have one, too, still in its wrapper, and that someday I'd be planning marriage and packing a go-away bag with the gown shaken out and then packed neatly. I told them that I'd be doing the same thing no matter whether we were having a formal church wedding with a four-alarm reception and all the trimmings or a quiet elopement such as you were. I told them that it was the essentials that count, not the trimmings and the tinsel. My questioner's remark was to the effect that either you were telling the truth, or that you had esped a woman about to marry and identified her actions with your own wishes."

"I know which," I said with a sour smile. "It was both."

Marian nodded. "Then they asked me if it were probable that a woman would take this step completely unprepared and I laughed at them. I told them that long before Rhine, women were putting their nuptial affairs in order about the time the gentleman was beginning to view marriage with an attitude slightly less than loathing, and that by the time he popped the question, she'd been practicing writing her name as 'Mrs.' and picking out the china-ware and prospective names for the children, and that if any woman had ever been so stunned by a proposal of marriage that she'd take off without so much as a toothbrush, no one in history had ever heard of her."

"Then you begin to agree with me?"

She shrugged. "Please," she said in that low voice, "don't ask me my opinion of your veracity. You believe it, but all the evidence lies against you. There was not a shred of woman-trace anywhere along your course, from the point along the road where you first caught sight of the limb that threw you to the place where you piled up. Nor was there a trace anywhere in a vast circle—almost a half mile they searched—from the crack-up. They had doctors of psi digging for footprints, shreds of clothing, everything. Not a trace."

"But where did she go?" I cried, and when I say 'cried' I mean just that.

Marian shook her head very slowly. "Steve," she said in a voice so low that I could hardly hear her over the faint shrill of bolts being unscrewed by her brother, "so far as we know, she was never here. Why don't you forget her—"

I looked at her. She stood there, poised and a bit tensed as though she were trying to force some feeling of affectionate kinhood across the gap that separated us, as though she wanted to give me both physical and mental comfort despite the fact that we were strangers on a ten-minute first-meeting. There was distress in her face.

"Forget her—?" I ground out. "I'd rather die!"

"Oh Steve—no!" One hand went to her throat and the other came out to fasten around my forearm. Her grip was hard.

I stood there wondering what to do next. Marian's grip on my arm relaxed and she stepped back.

I pulled myself together. "I'm sorry," I told her honestly. "I'm putting you through a set of emotional hurdles by bringing my problems here. I'd better take them away."

She nodded very slowly. "Please go. But please come back once you get yourself squared away, no matter how. We'd all like to see you when you aren't all tied up inside."

Phil looked up from the guts of the tractor. "Take it easy, Steve," he said. "And remember that you do have friends here."

Blindly I turned from them and stumbled back to my car. They were a pair of very fine people, firm, upright. Marian's grip on my arm had been no weaker than her sympathy, and Phil's less-emotional approach to my trouble was no less deep, actually. It was as strong as his good right arm, loosening the head bolts of a tractor engine with a small adjustable wrench.

I'd be back. I wanted to see them again. I wanted to go back there with Catherine and introduce them to her. But I was definitely going to go back.

I was quite a way toward home before I realized that I had not met the old man. I bet myself that Father Harrison was quite the firm, active patriarch.

CHAPTER FOUR

The days dragged slowly. I faced each morning hopefully at first, but as the days dragged on and on, I began to feel that each morning was opening another day of futility, to be barely borne until it was time to flop down in weariness. I faced the night in loneliness and in anger at my own inability to do something productive.

I pestered the police until they escorted me to the door and told me that if I came again, they'd take me to another kind of door and loose thereafter the key. I shrugged and left disconsolately, because by that time I had been able to esp, page by page, the entire file that dealt with the case of "Missing Person: Lewis, Catherine," stamped "Inactive, but not Closed."

I hated the words.

But as the days dragged out, one after another, with no respite and no hope, my raw nervous system began to heal. It was probably a case of numbness; you maul your thumb with a hammer and it will hurt just so long before it stops.

I was numb for a long time. I remember night after night, lying awake and staring into the darkness at the wall I knew was beside me, and I hated my esper because I wanted to project my mind out across some unknown space to reach for Catherine's mind. If we'd both been telepaths we could cross the universe to touch each other with that affectionate tenderness that mated telepaths always claim they have.

Instead I found myself more aware of a clouded-veil perception of Marian Harrison as she took my arm and looked into my face on that day when I admitted that I found little worth living for.

I knew what that meant—nothing. It was a case of my subconscious mind pointing out that the available present was more desirable than the unavailable not-present. At first I resented my apparent inconstancy in forming an esper projection of Marian Harrison when I was trying to project my blank telepathic inadequacy to Catherine. But as the weeks faded into the past, the shock and the frustration began to pale and I found Marian's projective image less and less an unwanted intrusion and more and more pleasant.

I had two deeply depressed spells in those six weeks. At the end of the fourth week I received a small carton containing some of my personal junk that had been in Catherine's apartment. A man can't date his girl for weeks without dropping a few things like a cigarette lighter, a tie clip, one odd cuff-link, some papers, a few letters, some books, and stuff both valuable and worthless that had turned up as gifts for one reason or another. It was a shock to get this box and its arrival bounced me deep into a doldrum-period of three or four days.

Then at the end of the sixth week I received a card from Dr. Thorndyke. It contained a lithograph in stereo of some scene in Yellowstone other than Old Faithful blowing its stack.

On the message side was a cryptic note:

Steve: I just drove along that road in the right side of the picture. It reminded me of yours, so I'm writing because I want to know how you are making out. I'll be at the Med-Center in a couple of weeks, you can write me there.

Jim Thorndyke.

I turned the postcard over and eyed it critically. Then I got it. Along the roadside was a tall ornamental standard of wrought iron. The same design as the road signs along that fatal highway of mine.

I sat there with a magnifying glass on the roadsign; its stereo image standing up alongside the road in full color and solidity. It took me back to that moment when Catherine had wriggled against my side, thrilling me with her warmth and eagerness.

That put me down a few days, too.

Another month passed. I'd come out of my shell quite a bit in the meantime. I now felt that I could walk in a bar and have a drink without wondering whether all the other people in the place were pointing at me. I'd cut myself off from all my previous friends, and I'd made no new friends in the weeks gone by. But I was getting more and more lonely and consequently more and more inclined to speak to people and want friends.

The accident had paled from its original horror; the vital scene returned only infrequently. Catherine was assuming the position of a lost love rather than a sweetheart expected to return soon. I remembered the warmth of her arms and the eagerness of her kiss in a nostalgic way and my mind, especially when in a doze, would play me tricks. I would recall Catherine, but when she came into my arms, I'd be holding Marian, brown and tawny, with her electric blue eyes and her vibrant nature.

But I did nothing about it. I knew that once I had asked Marian Harrison for a date I would be emotionally involved. And then if— no, when—Catherine turned up I would be torn between desires.

I would wake up and call myself all sorts of a fool. I had seen Marian for a total of perhaps fifteen minutes—in the company of her brother.

But eventually dreaming loses its sting just as futile waiting and searching does, and I awoke one morning in a long and involved debate between my id and my conscience. I decided at that moment that I would take that highway out and pay a visit to the Harrison farm. I was salving my slightly rusty conscience by telling myself that it was because I had never paid my respects to Father Harrison, but not too deep inside I knew that if Father were missing and Daughter were present I'd enjoy my visit to the farm with more relish.

But my id took a licking because the doorbell rang about nine o'clock that morning and when I dug the doorstep I came up with two gentlemen wearing gold badges in leather folders in their jacket pockets.

I opened the door because I couldn't have played absent to a team consisting of one esper and one telepath. They both knew I was home.

"Mr. Cornell, we'll waste no time. We want to know how well you know Doctor James Thorndyke."

I didn't blink at the bluntness of it. It is standard technique when an esper-telepath team go investigating. The telepath knew all about me, including the fact that I'd dug their wallets and identification cards, badges and the serial numbers of the nasty little automatics they carried. The idea was to drive the important question hard and first; it being impossible to not-think the several quick answers that pop through your mind. What I knew about Thorndyke was sketchy enough but they got it all because I didn't have any reason for covering up. I let them know that, too.

Finally, #That's about all,# I thought. #Now—why?#

The telepath half of the team answered. "Normally we wouldn't answer, Mr. Cornell, unless you said it aloud. But we don't mind letting you know which of us is the telepath this time. To answer, you are the last person to have received any message from Thorndyke."

"I—what?"

"That postcard. It was the last contact Thorndyke made with anyone. He has disappeared."

"But—"

"Thorndyke was due to arrive at The Medical Research Center in Marion, Indiana, three weeks ago. We've been tracking him ever since he failed to turn up. We've been able to retrace his meanderings very well up to a certain point in Yellowstone. There the trail stops. He had a telephoned reservation to a small hotel; there he dropped out of sight. Now, Mr. Cornell, may I see that postcard?"

"Certainly." I got it for them. The esper took it over to the window and eyed it in the light, and as he did that I went over to stand beside him and together we espered that postcard until I thought the edges would start to curl. But if there were any codes, concealed writings or any other form of hidden meaning or message in or on that card, I didn't dig any.

I gave up. I'm no trained investigator. But I knew that Thorndyke was fairly well acquainted with the depth of my perceptive sense, and he would not have concealed anything too deep for me.

Then the esper shook his head. He handed me the card. "Not a trace."

The telepath nodded. He looked at me and smiled sort of thin and strained. "We're naturally interested in you, Mr. Cornell. This seems to be the second disappearance. And you know nothing about either."

"I know," I said slowly. The puzzle began to go around and around in my head again, all the way back to that gleaming road and the crack-up.

"We'll probably be back, Mr. Cornell. You don't mind?"

"Look," I told them rather firmly, "if this puzzle can be unwound, I'll be one of the happiest men on the planet. If I can do anything to help, just say the word."

They left after that and so did I. I was still going to pay my visit to the Harrison farm. Another wild goose chase, but somewhere along this cockeyed row there was an angle. Honest people who are healthy and fairly happy with good prospects ahead of them do not just drop out of sight without a trace.

A couple of hours later I was making a good pace along the highway again. It was getting familiar to me.

I could not avoid letting my perceptive sense rest on the sign as I drove past. Not long enough to put me in danger, but long enough to discover to my surprise that someone had taken the trouble to repair the broken spoke. Someone must have been a perfectionist. The break was so slight that it seemed like calling in a mechanic because the ashtray in the car is full.

Then I noticed other changes that time had caused.

The burned scar was fading in a growth of tall weeds. The limb of the tree that hung out over the scene, from which block and tackle had hung, was beginning to lose its smoke-blackened appearance. The block was gone from the limb.

Give us a year, I thought, *and the only remaining scar will be the one on my mind, and even that will be fading.*

I turned into the drive, wound around the homestead road, and pulled up in front of the big, rambling house.

It looked bleak. The front lawn was a bit shaggy and there were some wisps of paper on the front porch. The venetian blinds were down and slatted shut behind closed windows. Since it was summer by now, the closed windows and the tight door, neither of which had flyscreens installed, quickly gave the fact away. The Harrisons were gone.

Another disappearance?

I turned quickly and drove to the nearest town and went to the post office.

"I'm looking for the Harrison family," I told the man behind the wicket.

"Why, they moved several weeks ago."

"Moved?" I asked with a blank-sounding voice.

The clerk nodded. Then he leaned forward and said in a confidential whisper, "Heard a rumor that the girl got a touch of that spacemen's disease."

"Mekstrom's?" I blurted.

The clerk looked at me as if I'd shouted a dirty word. "She was a fine girl," he said softly. "It's a shame."

I nodded and he went into the back files. I tried to dig alone behind him, but the files were in a small dead area in the rear of the building. I swore under my breath although I'd expected to find files in dead areas. Just as Rhine Institute was opened, the Government combed the countryside for dead or cloudy areas for their secret and confidential files. There had been one mad claim-staking rush with the Government about six feet ahead of the rest of the general public, business and the underworld.

He came back with a sorrowful look. "They left a concealed address," he said.

I felt like flashing a twenty at him like a private eye did in the old tough-books, but I knew it wouldn't work. Rhine also made it impossible for a public official to take a bribe. So instead, I tried to look distressed.

"This is extremely important. I'd say it was a matter of life and death."

"I'm sorry. A concealed forwarding address is still concealed. If you must get in touch with them, you might drop them a letter to be forwarded. Then if they care to answer, they'll reply to your home."

"Later," I told him. "I'll probably be back to mail it direct from here."

He waved at the writing desk. I nodded and left.

I drove back to the ex-Harrison Farm slowly, thinking it over. Wondering. People did not just go around catching Mekstrom's Disease, from what little I knew of it. And somehow the idea of Marian Harrison withering away or becoming a basket case, or maybe taking the painless way out was a thought that my mind kept avoiding except for occasional flashes of horror.

I drove in toward the farmhouse again and parked in front of the verandah. I was not sure of why I was there except that I wanted to wander through it to see what I could find before I went back to the post-office to write that card or letter.

The back of the house was locked with an old-fashioned slide bolt that was turned with what they used to call an "E" key. I shrugged, oiled my conscience and found a bit of bent wire. Probing a lock like that would have been easy for a total blank; with esper I lifted the simple keepers and slid back the bolt almost as swiftly as if I had used a proper key.

This was no case of disappearance. In every one of the fourteen rooms were the unmistakable signs of a deliberate removal. Discarded stuff was mixed with the odds and ends of packing case materials, a scattered collection of temporary nails, a half-finished but never used box filled with old clothing.

I pawed through this but found nothing, even though I separated it from the rest to help my esper dig it without interference.

I roamed the house slowly letting my perception wander from point to point. I tried to time-dig the place but that was futile. I didn't have enough perception.

I caught only one response. It was in one of the upper bedrooms. But then as I stopped in the room where Marian had slept, I began again to doubt my senses. It could have been esper, but it was more likely that I'd caught the dying traces of perfume.

Then I suddenly realized that the entire premises were clear to me!

An esper map of the world looked sort of like a mottled sky, with bright places and cloudy patches strewn in disorder across it. A mottled sky, except that the psi-pattern usually does not change. But this house had been in a murky area, if not dead. Now it was clear.

I left the house and went to the big combination barn and garage. It was as unsatisfying as the house had been. Phillip Harrison, or someone, had had a workshop out there. I found the bench and a small table where bolt-holes, oil marks, and other traces said that there had been one of those big combination woodworking machines there, the kind that combines circular saw, drill, lathe, planer, router, dado, and does everything. There had been some metal-working stuff there, too, but nothing as elaborate as the woodshop. Mostly things like hacksaws and an electric drill, and a circular scar where a blowtorch had been sitting.

I don't know why I kept on standing there esping the abandoned set-up. Maybe it was because my esper dug the fact that there was something there that I should know about, but which was so minute or remote that the impression did not come through. I stood there puzzled at my own reluctance to leave until something satisfied that almost imperceptible impression.

Idly I leaned down and picked up a bit of metal from the floor and fumbled it in my hand nervously. I looked around the place with my eyes and saw nothing. I gave the whole garage a thorough scanning with my esper and got zero for my trouble.

Finally I snarled at myself for being an imbecile, and left.

Everyone has done what I did, time and time again. I do not recall anything of my walk back to the car, lost in a whirl of thoughts, ideas, plans and questions. I would probably have driven all the way back to my apartment with my mind in that whirligig, driving by habit and training, but I was shaken out of it because I could not start my car by poking that bit of metal in the lock. It did not fit.

I laughed, a bit ashamed of my preoccupation, and flung the bit of metal into the grass, poked my key in the lock—

And then I was out pawing the grass for that piece of metal.

For the small piece of metal I had found on the floor of the abandoned workshop was the spoke of that road sign that had been missing when Catherine and I cracked up!

I drove out along the highway and stopped near one of the standards. I esped the sign, compared my impression against my eyesight. I made sure.

That bit of metal, a half inch long and a bit under a quarter inch in diameter, with both ends faintly broken-ragged, was identical in size and shape to the unbroken spokes in the sign!

Then I noticed something else. The trefoil ornament in the middle did not look the same as I recalled them. I took Thorndyke's card out of my pocket and looked at the stereo. I compared the picture against the real thing before me and I knew that I was right.

The trefoil gizmo was a take-off on the fleur-de-lis or the Boy Scout Tenderfoot badge, or the design they use to signify North on a compass. But the lower flare of the leaves was wider than any of the more familiar emblems; almost as wide as the top. It took a comparison to tell the difference between one of them right-side-up and another one upside-down. One assumes for this design that the larger foils are supposed to be up. If that were so, then the ones along that road out there in or near Yellowstone were right-side-up, while the ones along my familiar highway were upside-down.

I goaded myself. #Memory, have these things been turned or were they always upside-down?#

The last thing I did as I turned off the highway was to stop and let my esper dig that design once more. I covered the design itself, let my perception roam along the spokes, and then around the circlet that supported the spokes that held the trefoil emblem.

Oh, it was not obvious. It was designed in, so to speak. If I were asked even today for my professional opinion I would have to admit that the way the circlet snapped into the rest of the ornamental scrollwork was a matter of good assembly design, and not a design deliberately created so that the emblem could be turned upside down.

In fact, if it had not been for that tiny, broken spoke I found on the floor of the Harrison garage, never in a million years would I have considered these road signs significant.

At the post office I wrote a letter to Phillip Harrison:

Dear Phil:

I was by your old place today and was sorry to find that you had moved. I'd like to get in touch with you again. If I may ask, please send me your forwarding address. I'll keep it concealed if you like, or I'll reply through the post office, concealed forward.

As an item of interest, did you know that your house has lost its deadness? A medium-equipped esper can dig it with ease. Have you ever heard of the psi-pattern changing before?

Ah, and another item, that road sign with the busted spoke has been replaced. You must be a bum shot, not to hit that curlicue in the middle. I found the spoke you hit on the floor of your garage, if you'd like it for a souvenir of one close miss.

Please write and let me know how things are going. Rumor has it that Marian contracted Mekstrom's and if you will pardon my mentioning a delicate subject, I am doing so because I really want to help if I am able. After all, no matter how lightly you hold it, I still owe you my life. This is a debt I do not intend to forget.

Sincerely,

Steve Cornell.

CHAPTER FIVE

I did not go to the police.

They were sick of my face and already considering me a candidate for the paranoid ward. All I would have to do is go roaring into the station to tell them that I had uncovered some deep plot where the underground was using ornamental road signs to conceal their own network of roads and directions, and that the disappearance of Catherine Lewis, Dr. Thorndyke and the removal of the Harrisons were all tied together.

Instead, I closed my apartment and told everyone that I was going to take a long, rambling tourist jaunt to settle my nerves; that I thought getting away from the scene might finish the job that time and rest had started.

Then I started to drive. I drove for several days, not attempting to pace off miles, but covering a lot of aimless-direction territory. I was just as likely to spend four hours going North on one highway, and then take the next four coming back South on a parallel highway, and sometimes I even came back to the original starting place. After a week I had come no farther West than across that sliver of West Virginia into Eastern Ohio. And in Eastern Ohio I saw some more of the now familiar and suspicious road signs.

The emblem was right side up, and the signs looked as though they had not been up long.

I followed that road for seventy-five miles, and as I went the signs kept getting newer and newer until I finally came to a truck loaded with pipe, hardware, and ornamental ironwork. Leading the truck was one of those iron mole things.

I watched the automatic gear hoist one of the old pipe and white and black enamel roadsigns up by its roots, and place it on a truck full of discards. I watched the mole drive a corkscrew blade into the ground with a roaring of engine and bucking of the truck. It paused, pulled upward to bring out the screw and its load of dirt, stones and gravel. The crew placed one of the new signs in the cradle and I watched the machine set the sign upright, pour the concrete, tamp down the earth, and then move along down the road.

There was little point in asking questions of the crew, so I just took off and drove to Columbus as hard as I could make it.

31

Shined, cleaned, polished, and very conservatively dressed, I presented myself to the State Commissioner of Roads and Highways. I toyed briefly with the idea of representing myself as a minor official from some distant state like Alaska or the Virgin Islands, inquiring about these signs for official reasons. But then I knew that if I bumped into a hot telepath I'd be in the soup. On the other hand, mere curiosity on the part of a citizen, well oiled with compliments, would get me at the very least a polite answer.

The Commissioner's fifth-under-secretary bucked me down the hall; another office bucked me upstairs. A third buck-around brought me to the Department of Highways Marking and Road Maps.

A sub-secretary finally admitted that he might be able to help me. His name was Houghton. But whether he was telepath or esper did not matter because the Commission building was constructed right in the middle of a dead area.

I still played it straight. I told him I was a citizen of New York, interested in the new road signs, Ohio was to be commended, et cetera.

"I'm glad you feel that way," he said beaming.

"I presume these signs cost quite a bit more than the stark, black and white enamel jobs?"

"On the contrary," he said with pride. "They might, but mass-production methods brought the cost down. You see, the enamel jobs, while we buy several thousand of the plates for any highway, must be set up, stamped out, enamelled, and so on. The new signs are all made in one plant as they are needed; I don't suppose you know, but the highway number and any other information is put on the plate from loose, snap-in letters. That means we can buy so many thousand of this or that letter or number, and the necessary base plates and put them together as needed. They admitted that they were still running at a loss, but if they could get enough states interested, they'd eventually come out even, and maybe they could reduce the cost. Why, they even have a contingent-clause in the contract stating that if the cost were lowered, they would make a rebate to cover it. That's so the first users will not bide their time instead of buying now."

He went on and on and on like any bureaucrat. I was glad we were in a dead area because he'd have thrown me out of his office for what I was thinking.

Eventually Mr. Houghton ran down and I left.

I toyed around with the idea of barging in on the main office of the company but I figured that might be too much like poking my head into a hornet's nest.

I pocketed the card he gave me from the company, and I studied the ink-fresh road map, which he had proudly supplied. It pointed out in a replica panel of the fancy signs, that the State of Ohio was beautifying their highways with these new signs at no increased cost to the taxpayer, and that the dates in green on the various highways here and there gave the dates when the new signs would be installed. The bottom of the panel gave the Road Commissioner's name in boldface with Houghton's name below in slightly smaller print.

I smiled. Usually I get mad at signs that proclaim that such and such a tunnel is being created by Mayor So-and-so, as if the good mayor were out there with a shovel and hoe digging the tunnel. But this sort of thing would have been a worthy cause if it hadn't been for the sinister side.

I selected a highway that had been completed toward Cincinnati and made my way there with no waste of time.

The road was new and it was another beaut. The signs led me on, mile after mile and sign after sign.

I did not know what I was following, and I was not sure I knew what I was looking for. But I was on the trail of something and a bit of activity, both mental and physical, after weeks of blank-wall frustration made my spirits rise and my mental equipment sharper. The radio in the car was yangling with hillbilly songs, the only thing you can pick up in Ohio, but I didn't care. I was looking for something significant.

I found it late in the afternoon about half-way between Dayton and Cincinnati. One of the spokes was missing.

Fifty yards ahead was a crossroad.

I hauled in with a whine of rubber and brakes, and sat there trying to reason out my next move by logic. Do I turn with the missing spoke, or do I turn with the one that is not missing?

Memory came to my aid. The "ten o'clock" spoke had been missing back there near the Harrison farm. The Harrisons had lived on the left side of the highway. One follows the missing spoke. Here the "two o'clock" spoke was missing, so I turned to the right along the crossroad until I came to another sign that was complete.

Then, wondering, I U-turned and drove back across the main highway and drove for about five miles watching the signs as I went. The ones on my right had that trefoil emblem upside down. The ones on my left were right side up. The difference was so small that only someone who knew the significance would distinguish one from the other. So far as I could reason out, it meant that what I sought was in the other direction. When the emblem was upside down I was going away from, and when right side up, I was going toward.

Away from or toward what?

I U-turned again and started following the signs.

Twenty miles beyond the main highway where I'd seen the sign that announced the turn, I came upon another missing spoke. This indicated a turn to the left, and so I slowed down until I came upon a homestead road leading off toward a farmhouse.

I turned, determined to make like a man lost and hoping that I'd not bump into a telepath.

A few hundred yards in from the main road I came upon a girl who was walking briskly toward me. I stopped. She looked at me with a quizzical smile and asked me if she could be of any help.

Brashly, I nodded. "I'm looking for some old friends of mine," I said. "Haven't seen them for years. Named Harrison."

She smiled up at me. "I don't know of any Harrison around here." Her voice had the Ohio twang.

"No?"

"Just where do they live?"

I eyed her carefully, hoping my glance did not look like a wolf eyeing a lamb. "Well, they gave me some crude directions. Said I was to turn at the main highway onto this road and come about twenty miles and stop on the left side when I came upon one of those new road signs where someone had shot one of the spokes out."

"Spokes? Left side—" She mumbled the words and was apparently mulling the idea around in her mind. She was not more than about seventeen, sun-tanned and animal-alive from living in the open. I wondered about her. As far as I was concerned, she was part and parcel of this whole mysterious affair. No matter what she said or did, it was an obvious fact that the hidden road sign directions pointed to this farm. And since no one at seventeen can be kept in complete ignorance of the business of the parents, she must be aware of some of the ramifications.

After some thought she said, "No, I don't know of any Harrisons."

I grunted. I was really making the least of this, now that I'd arrived.

"Your folks at home?" I asked.

"Yes," she replied.

"I think I'll drop in and ask them, too."

She shrugged. "Go ahead," she said with the noncommittal attitude of youth. "You didn't happen to notice whether the mailbox flag was up, did you?"

I hadn't, but I espied back quickly and said, "No, it isn't."

"Then the mailman hasn't been to deliver," she said. "Mind if I ride back to the house with you, mister?"

"Hop in."

She smiled brightly and got in quickly. I took off down the road toward the house at an easy pace. She seemed interested in the car, and finally said, "I've never been in a car like this before. New?"

"Few weeks," I responded.

"Fast?"

"If you want to make it go fast. She'll take this rocky road at fifty, if anyone wants to be so foolish."

"Let's see."

I laughed. "Nobody but an idiot would tackle a road like this at fifty."

"I like to go fast. My brother takes it at sixty."

That, so far as I was concerned, was youthful exaggeration. I was busy telling her all the perils of fast driving when a rabbit came barrelling out of the bushes along one side and streaked across in front of me.

I twitched the wheel. The car went out of the narrow road and up on the shoulder, tilting quite a bit. Beyond the rabbit I swung back into the road, but not before the youngster had grabbed my arm to keep from being tossed all over the front seat.

Her grip was like a hydraulic vise. My arm went numb and my fingers went limp on the wheel. I struggled with my left hand to spin the wheel to keep on the narrow, winding road and my foot hit the brake to bring the car down, but fast.

Taking a deep breath as we stopped, I shook my right hand by holding it in my left at the wrist. I was a mass of tingling pins and needles because she had grabbed me just above the elbow. It felt as though it would have taken only a trifle more to pinch my arm off and leave me with a bloody stump.

"Sorry, mister," she said breathlessly, her eyes wide open. Her face was white around the corners of the mouth and at the edges of her nose. The whiteness of the flesh under the deep tan gave her a completely frightened look, far more than the shake-up could have produced.

I reached over and took her hand. "That's a mighty powerful grip you—"

The flesh of her hand was hard and solid. Not the meaty solidity of good tone, fine training and excellent health. It was the solidity of a—all I could think of at the time was a green cucumber. I squeezed a bit and the flesh gave way only a trifle. I rubbed my thumb over her palm and found it solid-hard instead of soft and yielding.

I wondered.

I had never seen a case of Mekstrom's Disease—before.

I looked down at the hand and said, "Young lady, do you realize that you have an advanced case of Mekstrom's Disease?"

She eyed me coldly. "Now," she said in a hard voice. "I know you'll come in."

Something in my make-up objects violently to being ordered around by a slip of a girl. I balance off at about one-sixty. I guessed her at about two-thirds of that, say one-ten or thereabouts—

"One-eight," she said levelly.

#A telepath!#

"Yes," she replied calmly. "And I don't mind letting you know it, so you'll not try anything stupid."

#I'm getting the heck out of here!#

"No, you're not. You are coming in with me."

"Like heck!" I exploded.

"Don't be silly. You'll come in. Or shall I lay one along your jaw and carry you?"

I had to try something, anything, to get free. Yet—

"Now you're being un-bright," she told me insolently. "You should know that you can't plan any surprise move with a telepath. And if you try a frontal attack I'll belt you so cold they'll have to put you in the oven for a week."

I just let her ramble for a few seconds because when she was rattling this way she couldn't put her entire mental attention on my thoughts. So while she was yaking it off, I had an idea that felt as though it might work.

She shut up like a clam when she realized that her mouthing had given me a chance to think, and I went into high gear with my perception:

#Not bad—for a kid. Growing up fast. Been playing hookey from momma, leaving off your panties like the big girls do. I can tell by the elastic cord marks you had 'em on not long ago.#

Seventeeners have a lot more modesty than they like to admit. She was stunned by my cold-blooded catalog of her body just long enough for me to make a quick lunge across her lap to the door handle on her side.

I flipped it over and gave her a shove at the same time. She went bottom over appetite in a sprawl that would have jarred the teeth loose in a normal body and might have cracked a few bones. But she landed on the back of her neck, rolled and came to her feet like a cat.

I didn't wait to close the door. I just tromped on the go-pedal and the car leaped forward with a jerk that slammed the door for me. I roared forward and left her just as she was making another grab.

How I hoped to get out of there I did not know. All I wanted was momentary freedom to think. I turned this way and that to follow the road until I came to the house. I left the road, circled the house with the turbine screaming like a banshee and the car taking the corners on the outside wheels. I skidded into a turn like a racing driver and ironed my wheels out flat on the takeaway, rounded another corner and turned back into the road again going the other way.

She was standing there waiting for me as I pelted past at a good sixty, and she reached out one girder-strong arm, latched onto the frame of the open window on my side, and swung onto the half-inch trim along the bottom of the car-body like a switchman hooking a freight car.

She reached for the steering wheel with her free hand.

I knew what was to happen next. She'd casually haul and I'd go off the road into a tree or pile up in a ditch, and while the smoke was clearing out of my mind, she'd be untangling me from the wreck and carting me over her shoulder, without a scratch to show for her adventure.

I yanked the wheel—whip! whap!—cutting an arc. I slammed past a tree, missing it by half an inch. I wiped her off the side of the car like a mailbag is clipped from the fast express by the catch-hook.

I heard a cry of "Whoof!" as her body hit the trunk of the tree. But as I regained the road and went racing on to safety, I saw in the rear view mirror that she had bounced off the tree, sprawled a bit, caught her balance, and was standing in the middle of the road, shaking her small but very dangerous fist at my tail license plate.

I didn't stop driving at one-ten until I was above Dayton again. Then I paused along the road to take stock.

Stock? What the hell did I know, really?

I'd uncovered and confirmed the fact that there was some secret organization that had a program that included their own highway system, concealed within the confines of the United States. I was almost certain by this time that they had been the prime movers in the disappearance of Catherine and Dr. Thorndyke. They—

I suddenly re-lived the big crack-up.

Willingly now, no longer rejecting the memory, I followed my recollection as Catherine and I went along that highway at a happy pace. With care I recalled every detail of Catherine, watching the road through my mind and eyes, how she'd mentioned the case of the missing spoke, and how I'd projected back to perceive that which I had not been conscious of.

Reminding myself that it was past, I went through it again, deliberately. The fallen limb that blocked the road, my own horror as the wheels hit it. The struggle to regain control of the careening car.

As a man watching a motion picture, I watched the sky and the earth turn over and over, and I heard my voice mouthing wordless shouts of fear. Catherine's cry of pain and fright came, and I listened as my mind reconstructed it this time without wincing. Then the final crash, the horrid wave of pain and the sear of the flash-fire. I went through my own horror and self condemnation, and my concern over Catherine. I didn't shut if off. I waded through it.

Now I remembered something else.

Something that any normal, sensible mind would reject as an hallucination. Beyond any shadow of a doubt there had been no time for a man to rig a block and tackle on a tree above a burning automobile in time to get the trapped victims out alive. And even more certain it was that no normal man of fifty would have had enough strength to lift a car by its front bumper while his son made a rush into the flames.

That tackle had been rigged and burned afterward. But who would reject a block and tackle in favor of an impossibly strong man? No, with the tackle in sight, the recollection of a man lifting that overturned automobile like a weight lifter pressing up a bar bell would be buried in any mind as a rank hallucination. Then one more item came driving home hard. So hard that I almost jumped when the idea crossed my mind.

Both Catherine and Dr. Thorndyke had been telepaths.

A telepath close to any member of his underground outfit would divine their purpose, come to know their organization, and begin to grasp the fundamentals of their program. Such a person would be dangerous.

On the other hand, an esper such as myself could be turned aside with bland remarks and a convincing attitude. I knew that I had no way of telling lie from truth and that made my problem a lot more difficult.

From the facts that I did have, something smelled of overripe seafood. Government and charities were pouring scads of dough into a joint called the Medical Research Center. To hear the scholars of medicine tell it, Mekstrom's Disease was about the last human frailty that hadn't been licked to a standstill. They boasted that if a victim of practically anything had enough life left in him to crawl to a telephone and use it, his life could be saved. They grafted well. I'd heard tales of things like fingers, and I know they were experimenting on hands, arms and legs with some success. But when it came to Mekstrom's they were stopped cold. Therefore the Medical Research Center received a walloping batch of money for that alone; all the money that used to go to the various heart, lung, spine and cancer funds. It added up well.

But the Medical Research Center seemed unaware that some group had solved their basic problem.

From the books I've read I am well aware of one of the fundamental principles of running an underground: *Keep it underground!* The Commie menace in these United States might have won out in the middle of the century if they'd been able to stay a secret organization. So the Highways in Hiding could stay underground and be an efficient organization only until someone smoked them out.

That one was going to be me.

But I needed an aide-de-camp. Especially and specifically I needed a trained telepath, one who would listen to my tale and not instantly howl for the nut-hatch attendants. The F.B.I. were all trained investigators and they used esper-telepath teams all the time. One dug the joint while the other dug the inhabitant, which covered the situation to a faretheewell.

It would take time to come up with a possible helper. So I spent the next hour driving toward Chicago, and by the time I'd crossed the Ohio-Indiana line and hit Richmond, I had a plan laid out. I placed a call to New York and within a few minutes I was talking to Nurse Farrow.

I'll not go into detail because there was a lot of mish-mash that is not particularly interesting and a lot more that covered my tracks since I'd parted company with her on the steps of the hospital. I did not, of course, mention my real purpose over the telephone and Miss Farrow could not read my mind from New York.

The upshot of the deal was that I felt that I needed a nurse for a while, not that I was ill, but that I felt a bit woozy now and then because I hadn't learned to slow down. I worked too fast and too long and my condition was not up to it yet. This Miss Farrow allowed as being quite possible. I repeated my offer to pay her at the going prices for registered nurses with a one-month guarantee, paid in advance. That softened her quite a bit. Then I added that I'd videograph her a check large enough to cover the works plus a round trip ticket. She should come out and have a look, and if she weren't satisfied, she could return without digging into her own pocket. All she'd lose was one day, and it might be a bit of a vacation if she enjoyed flying in a jetliner at sixty thousand feet.

The accumulation of offers finally sold her and she agreed to arrange a leave of absence. She'd meet me in the morning of the day-after-tomorrow, at Central Airport in Chicago.

I videographed the check and then took off again, confident that I'd be able to sell her on the idea of being the telepath half of my amateur investigation team.

Then because I needed some direct information, I turned west and crossed the line into Indiana, heading to Marion. So far I had a lot of logical suspicions, but until I was certain, I could do no more than postulate ideas. I had to know definitely how to identify Mekstrom's

Disease, or at least the infected flesh. I have a fairly good recall; all I needed now was to have someone point to a Case and say flatly that this was a case of Mekstrom's Disease. Then I'd know whether what I'd seen in Ohio was actually one hundred percent Mekstrom.

CHAPTER SIX

I walked into the front office with a lot of self-assurance. The Medical Center was a big, rambling place with a lot of spread-out one- and two-story buildings that looked so much like "Hospital" that no one in the world would have mistaken them for anything else. The main building was by the road, the rest spread out behind as far as I could see; beyond my esper range even though the whole business was set in one of the clearest psi areas that I'd even been in.

I was only mildly worried about telepaths. In the first place, the only thing I had to hide was my conviction about a secret organization and how part of it functioned. In the second place, the chances were good that few, if any, telepaths were working there, if the case of Dr. Thorndyke carried any weight. That there were some telepaths, I did not doubt, but these would not be among the high-powered help.

So I sailed in and faced the receptionist, who was a good-looking chemical-type blonde with a pale skin, lovely complexion and figure to match. She greeted me with a glacial calm and asked my business.

Brazenly I lied. "I'm a freelance writer looking for material."

"Have you an assignment?" she asked without a trace of interest in the answer.

"Not this time. I'm strictly freelance. I like it better this way because I can write whatever I like."

Her glacial air melted a bit at the inference that my writing had not been in vain. "Where have you been published?" she asked.

I made a fast stab in the dark, aimed at a direction that looked safe. "Last article was one on the latest archeological findings in Assyria. Got my source material direct from the Oriental Institute in Chicago."

"Too bad I missed it," she said, looking regretful. I'd avoided giving the name of the publication and the supposed date. She went on, "I suppose you wouldn't be happy with the usual press release?"

"Handouts contain material, all right, but they're so confounded trite and impersonal. People prefer to read anecdotes about the people rather than a listing of facts and figures."

She nodded at that. "Just a moment," she said. Then she addressed her telephone in a voice that I couldn't hear. When she finished, she smiled in a warmish-type manner as if to indicate that she'd gone all out in my behalf and that I'd be a heel to forget it. I nodded back and tried to match the tooth-paste-ad smile. Then the door opened and a man came in briskly.

He was a tall man, as straight as a ramrod, with a firm jaw and a close-clipped moustache. He had an air like a thin-man's Captain Bligh. When he spoke, his voice was as clipped and precise as his moustache; in fact it was so precise that it seemed almost mechanical.

"I am Dr. Lyon Sprague," he clipped. "What may I do for you?"

"I'm Steve Cornell," I said. "I'm here after source material for a magazine article about Mekstrom's Disease. I'd prefer not to take my material from a handout."

"Do you hope to get more?" he demanded.

"I usually do. I've seen your handouts; I could get as much by taking last year's medical encyclopedia. Far too dry, too uninteresting, too impersonal."

"Just exactly what do you have in mind?"

I eyed him tentatively. Here was not a man who would take kindly to imaginative conjecture. So Dr. Lyon Sprague was not the man I'd like to talk to. With an inward smile, I said, "I have a rather new idea about Mekstrom's that I'd like to discuss with the right party."

He looked down at me, although our eyes were on the same level. "I doubt that any layman could possibly come up with an idea that has not been most thoroughly discussed here among the research staff."

"In cold words you feel that no untrained lunk has a right to have an idea."

He froze. "I did not say that."

"You implied, at least, that suggestions from outsiders were not welcome. I begin to understand why the Medical Center has failed to get anywhere with Mekstrom's in the past twenty years."

"What do you mean?" he snapped.

"Merely that it is the duty of all scientists to listen to every suggestion and to discard it only after it has been shown wrong."

"Such as—?" he said coldly, with a curl of his eyebrows.

"Well, just for instance, suppose some way were found to keep a victim alive during the vital period, so that he would end up a complete Mekstrom Human."

"The idea is utterly fantastic. We have no time for such idle speculation. There is too much foggy thinking in the world already. Why, only last week we had a Velikovsky Adherent tell us that Mekstrom's had been predicted in the Bible. There are still people reporting flying saucers, you know. We have no time for foolish notions or utter nonsense."

"May I quote you?"

"Of course not," he snapped stiffly. "I'm merely pointing out that non-medical persons cannot have the grasp—"

The door opened again and another man entered. The new arrival had pleasant blue eyes, a van dyke beard, and a good-natured air of self-confidence. "May I cut in?" he said to Dr. Sprague.

"Certainly. Mr. Cornell, this is Scholar Phelps, Director of the Center. Scholar Phelps, this is Mr. Steve Cornell, a gentleman of the press," he added in a tone of voice that made the identification a sort of nasty name. "Mr. Cornell has an odd theory about Mekstrom's Disease that he intends to publish unless we can convince him that it is not possible."

"Odd theory?" asked Scholar Phelps with some interest. "Well, if Mr. Cornell can come up with something new, I'll be most happy to hear him out."

Dr. Lyon Sprague decamped with alacrity. Scholar Phelps smiled after him, then turned to me and said, "Dr. Sprague is a diligent worker, businesslike and well-informed, but he lacks the imagination and the sense of humor that makes a man brilliant in research. Unfortunately, Dr. Sprague cannot abide anything that is not laid out as neat as an interlocking tile floor. Now, Mr. Cornell, how about this theory of yours?"

"First," I replied, "I'd like to know how come you turn up in the nick of time."

He laughed good-naturedly. "We always send Dr. Sprague out to interview visitors. If the visitor can be turned away easily, all is well and quiet. Dr. Sprague can do the job with ease. But if the visitor, like yourself, proposes something that distresses the good Dr. Sprague and will not be loftily dismissed, Dr. Sprague's blood pressure goes up. We all keep a bit of esper on his nervous system and when the fuse begins to blow, we come out and effect a double rescue."

I laughed with him. Apparently the Medical Center staff enjoyed needling Dr. Sprague. "Scholar Phelps, before I get into my theory,

I'd like to know more about Mekstrom's Disease. I may not be able to use it in my article, but any background material works well with writers of fact articles."

"You're quite right. What would you like to know?"

"I've heard, too many times, that no one knows anything at all about Mekstrom's. This is unbelievable, considering that you folks have been working on it for some twenty years."

He nodded. "We have some, but it's precious little."

"It seems to me that you could analyze the flesh—"

He smiled. "We have. The state of analytical chemistry is well advanced. We could, I think, take a dry scraping out of the cauldron used by MacBeth's witches, and determine whether Shakespeare had reported the formula correctly. Now, young man, if you think that something is added to the human flesh to make it Mekstrom's Flesh, you are wrong. Standard analysis shows that the flesh is composed of exactly the same chemicals that normal flesh contains, in the same proportion. Nothing is added, as, for instance, in the case of calcification."

"Then what is the difference?"

"The difference lies in the structure. By X-ray crystallographic method, we have determined that Mekstrom's Flesh is a micro-crystalline formation, interlocked tightly." Scholar Phelps looked at me thoughtfully. "Do you know much about crystallography?"

As a mechanical engineer I did, but as a writer of magazine articles I felt I should profess some ignorance, so I merely said that I knew a little about the subject.

"Well, Mr. Cornell, you may know that in the field of solid geometry there are only five possible regular polyhedrons. Like the laws of topology that state that no more than four colors need be used to print a map on a flat surface, or that no more than seven colors are required to print separate patches on a toroid, the laws of solid geometry prove that no more than five regular polyhedrons are possible. Now in crystallography there are only thirty-two possible classes of crystal lattice construction. Of these only thirty have ever been discovered in nature. Yet we know how the other two would appear if they did emerge in natural formation."

I knew it all right but I made scribblings in my notebooks as if the idea were of interest. Scholar Phelps waited patiently until I'd made the notation.

"Now, Mr. Cornell, here comes the shock. Mekstrom's Flesh is one of the other two classes."

This was news to me and I blinked.

Then his face faded into a solemn expression. "Unfortunately," he said in a low voice, "knowing how a crystal should form does not help us much in forming one to that class. We have no real control over the arrangement of atoms in a crystal lattice. We can prevent the crystal formation, we can control the size of the crystal as it forms. But we cannot change the crystal into some other class."

"I suppose it's sort of like baking a cake. Once the ingredients are mixed, the cake can be big or small or shaped to fit the pan, or you can spoil it complete. But if you mix devil's food, it either comes out devil's food or nothing."

"An amusing analogy and rather correct. However I prefer the one used years ago by Dr. Willy Ley, who observed that analysis is fine, but you can't learn how a locomotive is built by melting it down and analyzing the mess."

Then he went on again. "To get back to Mekstrom's Disease and what we know about it. We know that the crawl goes at about a sixty-fourth of an inch per hour. If, for instance, you turned up here with a trace on your right middle finger, the entire first joint would be Mekstrom's Flesh in approximately three days. Within two weeks your entire middle finger would be solid. Without anesthesia we could take a saw and cut off a bit for our research."

"No feeling?"

"None whatever. The joints knit together, the arteries become as hard as steel tubing and the heart cannot function properly—not that the heart cares about minor conditions such as the arteries in the extremities, but as the Mekstrom infection crawls up the arm toward the shoulder the larger arteries become solid and then the heart cannot drive the blood through them in its accustomed fashion. It gets like an advanced case of arteriosclerosis. Eventually the infection reaches and immobilizes the shoulder; this takes about ninety days. By this time, the other extremities have also become infected and the crawl is coming up all four limbs."

He looked at me very solemnly at that. "The rest is not pretty. Death comes shortly after that. I can almost say that he is blessed who catches Mekstrom's in the left hand for them the infection reaches the heart before it reaches other parts. Those whose initial infection is in the toes are particularly cursed, because the infection reaches the lower parts of the body. I believe you can imagine the result, elimination is prevented because of the stoppage of peristalsis. Death comes of autointoxication, which is slow and painful."

I shuddered at the idea. The thought of death has always bothered me. The idea of looking at a hand and knowing that I was going to die by the calendar seemed particularly horrible.

Taking the bit between my teeth, I said, "Scholar Phelps, I've been wondering whether you and your Center have ever considered treating Mekstrom's by helping it?"

"Helping it?" he asked.

"Sure. Consider what a man might be if he were Mekstrom's all the way through."

He nodded. "You would have a physical superman," he said. "Steel-strong muscles driving steel-hard flesh covered by a near impenetrable skin. Perhaps such a man would be free of all minor pains and ills. Imagine a normal bacterium trying to bore into flesh as hard as concrete. Mekstrom Flesh tends to be acid-resistant as well as tough physically. It is not beyond the imagination to believe that your Mekstrom Superman might live three times our frail four-score and ten. But—"

Here he paused.

"Not to pull down your house of cards, this idea is not a new one. Some years ago we invited a brilliant young doctor here to study for his scholarate. The unfortunate fellow arrived with the first traces of Mekstrom's in his right middle toe. We placed about a hundred of our most brilliant researchers under his guidance, and he decided to take this particular angle of study. He failed; for all his efforts, he did not stay his death by a single hour. From that time to the present we have maintained one group on this part of the problem."

It occurred to me at that moment that if I turned up with a trace of Mekstrom's I'd be seeking out the Highways in Hiding rather than the Medical Center. That fast thought brought a second: Suppose that Dr. Thorndyke learned that he had a trace, or rather, the Highways found it out. What better way to augment their medical staff than to approach the victim with a proposition: You help us, work with us, and we will save your life.

That, of course, led to the next idea: That if the Highways in Hiding had any honest motive, they'd not be hidden in the first place and they'd have taken their cure to the Medical Center in the second. Well, I had a bit of something listed against them, so I decided to let my bombshell drop.

"Scholar Phelps," I said quietly, "one of the reasons I am here is that I have fairly good evidence that the cure for Mekstrom's Disease does exist, and that it produces people of ultrahard bodies and superhuman strength."

He smiled at me with the same tolerant air that father uses on the offspring who comes up with one of the standard juvenile plans for perpetual motion.

"What do you consider good evidence?"

"Suppose I claimed to have seen it myself."

"Then I would say that you had misinterpreted your evidence," he replied calmly. "The flying saucer enthusiasts still insist that the things they see are piloted by little green men from Venus, even though we have been there and found Venus to be absolutely uninhabited by anything higher than slugs, grubs, and little globby animals like Tellurian leeches."

"But—"

"This, too, is an old story," he told me with a whimsical smile. "It goes with the standard routine about a secret organization that is intending to take over the Earth. The outline has been popular ever since Charles Fort. Now—er—just tell me what you saw."

I concocted a tale that was about thirty-three percent true and the rest partly distorted. It covered my hitting a girl in Ohio with my car, hard enough to clobber her. But when I stopped to help her, she got up and ran away unhurt. She hadn't left a trace of blood although the front fender of the car was badly smashed.

He nodded solemnly. "Such things happen," he said. "The human body is really quite durable; now and then comes the lucky happenstance when the fearful accident does no more than raise a slight bruise. I've read the story of the man whose parachute did not open and who lived to return it to the factory in person, according to the old joke. But now, Mr. Cornell, have you ever considered the utter impossibility of running any sort of secret organization in this world of today. Even before Rhine it was difficult. You'll be adding to your tale next—some sort of secret sign, maybe a form of fraternity grip, or perhaps even a world-wide system of local clubs and hangouts, all aimed at some dire purpose."

I squirmed nervously for a bit. Scholar Phelps was too close to the truth to make me like it, because he was scoffing. He went right on making me nervous.

"Now before we get too deep, I only want to ask about the probable motives of such an organization. You grant them superhuman strength, perhaps extreme longevity. If they wanted to take over the Earth, couldn't they do it by a show of force? Or are they mild-mannered supermen, only quietly interested in overrunning the human race and waiting out the inevitable decline of normal homo sapiens? You're not endowing them with extraterrestrial origin, are you?"

I shook my head unhappily.

"Good. That shows some logic, Mr. Cornell. After all, we know now that while we could live on Mars or Venus with a lot of home-sent aid, we'd be most uncomfortable there. We could not live a minute on any planet of our solar system without artificial help."

"I might point out that our hypothetical superman might be able to stand a lot of rough treatment," I blurted.

"Oh, this I'll grant if your tale held any water at all. But let's forget this fruitless conjecture and take a look at the utter impossibility of running such an organization. Even planting all of their secret hangouts in dead areas and never going into urban centers, they'd still find some telepath or esper on their trail. Perhaps a team. Let's go back a step and consider, even without psi training, how long such an outfit could function. It would run until the first specimen had an automobile accident on, say Times Square; or until one of them walked—or ran—out of the fire following a jetliner crash."

He then spared me with a cold eye. "Write it as fiction, Mr. Cornell. But leave my name out of it. I thought you were after facts."

"I am. But the better fact articles always use a bit of speculation to liven it up."

"Well," he grunted, "one such fanciful suggestion is the possibility of such an underground outfit being able to develop a 'cure' while we cannot. We, who have had the best of brains and money for twenty years."

I nodded, and while I did not agree with Phelps, I knew that to insist was to insult him to his face, and get myself tossed out.

"You do seem to have quite a set-up here," I said, off-hand.

At this point Phelps offered to show me around the place, and I accepted. Medical Center was far larger than I had believed at first; it spread beyond my esper range into the hills beyond the main plant. The buildings were arranged in a haphazard-looking pattern out in the back section; I say "looking" because only a psi-trained person can dig a pattern. The wide-open psi area did not extend for miles. Behind the main buildings it closed down into the usual mottled pattern and the medical buildings had been placed in the open areas. Dwellings and dormitories were in the dark places. A nice set-up.

I did not meet any of the patients, but Phelps let me stand in the corridor outside a couple of rooms and use my esper on the flesh. It was both distressing and instructive.

He explained, "The usual thing after someone visits this way, is that the visitor goes out itching. In medical circles this is a form of what we call 'Sophomore's Syndrome.' Ever heard of it?"

I nodded. "That's during the first years at pre-med. Knowing all too little of medicine, every disease they study produces the same symptoms that the student finds in himself. Until tomorrow, when they study the next. Then the symptoms in the student change."

"Right. So in order to prevent 'Sophomore's Syndrome' among visitors we usually let them study the real thing. Also," he added seriously, "we'd like to have as many people as possible recognize the real thing as early as possible. Even though we can't do anything for them at the present time, someday we will."

He stopped before a closed door. "In here is a girl of eighteen, doomed to die in a month." His voice trailed off as he tapped on the door of the room.

I froze. A few beads of cold sweat ran down my spine, and I fought myself into a state of nervous calmness. I put the observation away, buried it as deep as I could, tried to think around it, and so far as I knew, succeeded.

The tap of Scholar Phelps' finger against the door panel was the rap-rap-rap sound characteristic of hard-tanned leather tapping wood.

Scholar Phelps was a Mekstrom!

I paid only surface attention to the rest of my visit. I thanked my personal gods that esper training had also given me the ability to dissemble. It was impossible to not think of something but it is possible to keep the mind so busy with surface thoughts that the underlying idea does not come through the interference.

Eventually I managed to leave the Medical Center without exciting anyone, and when I left I took off like a skyrocket for Chicago.

CHAPTER SEVEN

Nurse Gloria Farrow waved at me from the ramp of the jetliner, and I ran forward to collect her baggage. She eyed me curiously but said no more than the usual greetings and indication of which bag was hers.

I knew that she was reading my mind like a psychologist all the time, and I let her know that I wanted her to. I let my mind merely ramble on with the usual pile of irrelevancies that the mind uses to fill in blank spaces. It came up with a couple of notions here and there but nothing definite. Miss Farrow followed me to my car without saying a word, and let me install her luggage in the trunk.

Then, for the first time, she spoke: "Steve Cornell, you're as healthy as I am."

"I admit it."

"Then what is this all about? You don't need a nurse!"

"I need a competent witness, Miss Farrow."

"For what?" She looked puzzled. "Suppose you stay right here and start explaining."

"You'll listen to the bitter end?"

"I've two hours before the next plane goes back. You'll have that time to convince me—or else. Okay?"

"That's a deal." I fumbled for a beginning, and then I decided to start right at the beginning, whether it sounded phony or not.

Giving information to a telepath is the easiest thing in the world. While I started at the beginning, I fumbled and finally ended up by going back and forth in a haphazard manner, but Miss Farrow managed to insert the trivia in the right chronological order so that when I finished, she nodded with interest.

I posed the question: #Am I nuts?#

"No, Steve," she replied solemnly. "I don't think so. You've managed to accept data which is obviously mingled truth and falsehood, and you've managed to question the validity of all of it."

I grunted. "How about the crazy man who questions his own sanity, using this personal question as proof of his sanity since real nuts *know* they're sane?"

"No nut can think that deep into complication. What I mean is that they cannot even question their own sanity in the first premise of postulated argument. But forget that, what I wanted to know is where you intend to go from here."

I shook my head unhappily. "When I called you I had it all laid out like a roadmap. I was going to show you proof and use you as an impartial observer to convince someone else. Then we'd go to the Medical Center and hand it to them on a platter. Since then I've had a shock that I can't get over, or plan beyond. Scholar Phelps is a Mekstrom. That means that the guy knows what gives with Mekstrom's Disease and yet he is running an outfit that professes to be helpless in the face of this disease. For all we know Phelps may be the head of the Highways in Hiding, an organization strictly for profit of some sort at the expense of the public welfare."

"You're certain that Phelps is a Mekstrom?"

"Not absolutely positive. I had to close my mind because there might be a telepath on tap. But I can tell you that nobody with normal flesh-type fingers ever made that solid rap."

"A fingernail?"

I shook my head at her. "That's a click. With an ear at all you'd note the difference."

"I'll accept it for the moment. But lacking your original plan, what are you going to do now?"

"I'm not sure beyond showing you the facts. Maybe I should call up that F.B.I. team that called on me after Thorndyke's disappearance and put it in their laps."

"Good idea. But why would Scholar Phelps be lying? And beyond your basic suspicions, what can you prove?"

"Very little. I admit that my evidence is extremely thin. I saw Phillip Harrison turning head bolts on a tractor engine with a small end wrench. It should require a crossbar socket and a lot of muscle. Next is the girl in Ohio who should be a bloody mess from the way she was treated. Instead she got up and tried to chase me. Then answer me a puzzler: Did the Harrisons move because Marian caught Mekstrom's, or did they move because they felt that I was too close to discovering their secret? The Highway was relocated after that, you'll recall."

"It sounds frightfully complicated, Steve."

"You bet it does," I grunted. "So next I meet a guy who is supposed to know all the answers; a man dedicated to the public welfare, medicine, and the ideal of Service. A man sworn to the Hippocratic Oath. Or," I went on bitterly, "is it the Hypocritic Oath?"

"Steve, please—"

"Please, Hell!" I stormed. "Why is he quietly sitting there in Mekstrom hide while he is overtly grieving over the painful death of his fellow man?"

"I wouldn't know."

"Well, I'm tired of being pushed around," I growled.

"Pushed around?" she asked quietly.

With a trace of scorn, I said, "Miss Farrow, I can see two possible answers. Either I am being pushed around for some deliberate reason, or I'm too smart, too cagey and too dangerous for them to handle directly. It takes only about eight weeks for me to reluctantly abandon the second in favor of the first."

"But what makes you think you are being pushed?" she wanted to know.

"You can't tell me that I am so important that they couldn't erase me as easily as they did Catherine and Dr. Thorndyke. And now that his name comes up, let's ask why any doctor who once met a casual patient would go to the bother of sending a postcard with a message on it that is certain to cause me unhappiness. He's also the guy who nudged me by calling my attention to my so-called 'shock hallucination' about Father Harrison lifting my car while Phillip Harrison raced into the fire to make the rescue. Add it up," I told her sharply. "Next he is invited to Medical Center to study Mekstrom's. Only instead of landing there, he sends me a postcard with one of the Highways in the picture, after which he disappears."

Miss Farrow nodded thoughtfully. "It is all tied up with your Highways and your Mekstrom People."

"That isn't all," I said. "How come the Harrisons moved so abruptly?"

"You're posing questions that I can't answer," complained Miss Farrow. "And I'm not one hundred percent convinced that you are right."

"You are here, and if you take a look at what I'll show you, you'll be convinced. We'll put it this way, to start: Something cockeyed is going on. Now, one more thing I can add, and this is the part that confuses me: Everything that has been done seems to point to me. So far as I can see they are operating just as though they want me to start a big hassle that will end up by getting the Highways out of their Hiding."

"Why on earth would they be doing that?" she wanted to know.

"I don't have the foggiest notion. But I do have that feeling and there is evidence pointing that way. They've let me in on things that normally they'd be able to conceal from a highly trained telepath. So I intend to go along with them, because somewhere at the bottom of it all we'll find the answer."

She nodded agreement.

Now I started up the car, saying, "I'm going to find us one of the Highways in Hiding, and we'll follow it to one of the way stations. Then you'll see for yourself that there is something definitely fishy going on."

"This I'd like to see," she replied quietly. Almost too quietly. I took a dig at her as I turned the car out through a tight corner of the lot onto the road. She was sitting there with a noncommittal expression on her face and I wondered why. She replied to my thought: "Steve, you must face one thing. Anything you firmly believe will necessarily pass across your mind as fact. So forgive me if I hold a few small doubts until I have a chance to survey some of the evidence at first hand."

"Sure," I told her. "The first bit won't be hard."

I drove eagerly across Illinois into Iowa watching for road signs. I knew that once I convinced someone else, it would be easier to convince a third, and a fourth, and a fiftieth until the entire world was out on the warpath. We drove all day, stopping for chow now and then, behaving like a couple out on a vacation tour. We stopped in a small town along about midnight and found a hotel without having come upon any of the hidden highways.

We met at breakfast, talked our ideas over mildly, and took off again. We crossed into Nebraska about noon and continued to meander until late in the afternoon when we came upon our first giveaway road sign.

"There," I told her triumphantly.

She nodded. "I see the sign, Steve. That much I knew. Now all you have to do is to show me the trial-blazes up in that emblem."

"Unless they've changed their method," I told her, "this one leads West, slightly south of." I stopped the car not many yards from the sign and went over it with my sense of perception. #You'll note the ease with which the emblem could be turned upside down,# I interjected. #Note the similar width of the top and bottom trefoil, so that only a trained and interested observer can tell the difference.#

I drove along until we saw one on the other side of the road and we stopped again, giving the sign a thorough going over. #Note that the signs leading away from the direction are upside down,# I went on. I didn't say a word, I was using every ounce of energy in running my perception over the sign and commenting on its various odds and ends.

#Now,# I finished, #we'll drive along this Highway in Hiding until we come to some intersection or hideout. Then you'll be convinced.#

She was silent.

We took off along that road rather fast and we followed it for miles, passing sign after sign with its emblem turned up along the right side of the road and turned upside-down when the sign was on the left.

Eventually we came to a crossing highway, and at that I pointed triumphantly. "Note the missing spoke!" I said with considerable enthusiasm. "Now, Miss Farrow, we shall first turn against it for a few miles and then we shall U-turn and come back along the cross highway with it."

"I'm beginning to be convinced, Steve."

We turned North against the sign and went forty or fifty miles, just to be sure. The signs were all against us. Eventually I turned into a gas station and filled the carte up to the scuppers. As we turned back South, I asked her, "Any more comment?"

She shook her head. "Not yet."

I nodded. "If you want, we'll take a jaunt along our original course."

"By all means."

"In other words you are more than willing to be convinced?"

"Yes," she said simply. She went silent then and I wondered what she was thinking about, but she didn't bother to tell me.

Eventually we came back to the crossroad, and with a feeling of having been successful, I continued South with a confidence that I had not felt before. We stopped for dinner in a small town, ate hastily but well, and then had a very mild debate.

"Shall we have a drink and relax for a moment?"

"I'd like it," she replied honestly. "But somehow I doubt that I could relax."

"I know. But it does seem like a good idea to take it easy for a half hour. It might even be better if we stopped over and took off again in the morning."

"Steve," she told me, "the only way I could relax or go to sleep would be to take on a roaring load so that I'd pass out cold. I'd rather not because I'd get up tomorrow with a most colossal hangover. Frankly, I'm excited and I'd prefer to follow this thing to a finish."

"It's a deal," I said. "We'll go until we have to stop."

It was about eight o'clock when we hit the road again.

By nine-forty-five we'd covered something better than two hundred miles, followed another intersection turn according to the missing spoke, and were heading well toward the upper right-hand corner of Colorado on the road map.

At ten o'clock plus a few minutes we came upon the roadsign that pointed the way to a ranch-type house set prettily on the top of a small knoll several hundred yards back from the main road. I stopped briefly a few hundred feet from the lead-in road and asked Miss Farrow:

"What's your telepath range? You've never told me."

She replied instantly, "Intense concentration directed at me is about a half mile. Superficial thinking that might include me or my personality as a by-thought about five hundred yards. To pick up a thought that has nothing to do with me or my interests, not much more than a couple of hundred feet. Things that are definitely none of my business close down to forty or fifty feet."

That was about the average for a person with a bit of psi training either in telepathy or in esper; it matched mine fairly well, excepting that part about things that were none of my business. She meant *thoughts* and not *things*. I had always had a hard time differentiating between things that were none of my damned business, although I do find it more difficult to dig the contents of a letter between two unknown parties at a given distance than it is to dig a letter written or addressed to a person I know. *Things* are, by and large, a lot less personal than thoughts, if I'm saying anything new.

"Well," I told her, "this is it. We're going to go in close enough for you to take a 'pathic look-around. Keep your mind sensitive. If you dig any danger, yell out. I'm going to extend my esper as far as I can and if I suddenly take off it's because I've uncovered something disagreeable. But keep your mind on them and not me, because I'm relying on you to keep posted on their mental angle."

Miss Farrow nodded. "It's hard to remember that other people haven't the ability to make contact mentally. It's like a normal man talking to a blind man and referring constantly to visible things because he doesn't understand. I'll try to remember."

"I'm going to back in," I said. "Then if trouble turns up, I'll have an advantage. As soon as they feel our minds coming in at them, they'll know that we're not in there for their health. So here we go!"

"I'm a good actor," she said. "No matter what I say, I'm with you all the way!"

I yanked the car forward, and angled back. I hit the road easily and started backing along the driveway at a rather fast speed with my eyes half-closed to give my esper sense the full benefit of my concentration along the road. When I was not concentrating on how I was going to turn the wheel at the next curve I thought, #I hope these folks know the best way to get to Colorado Springs from here. Dammit, we're lost!#

Miss Farrow squeezed my arm gently, letting me know that she was thinking the same general thoughts.

Suddenly she said, "It's a dead area, Steve."

It was a dead area, all right. My perception came to a barrier that made it fade from full perception to not being able to perceive anything in a matter of yards. It always gives me an eerie feeling when I approach a dead area and find that I can see a building clearly and not be able to cast my perception beyond a few feet.

I kept on backing up into the fringe of that dead area until I was deep within the edge and it took all my concentration to perceive the road a few feet ahead of my rear wheels so that I could steer. I was inching now, coming back like a blind man feeling his way. We were within about forty feet of the ranch house when Miss Farrow yelped:

"They're surrounding us, Steve!"

My hands whipped into action and my heavy right foot came down on the gas-pedal. The car shuddered, howled like a wounded banshee, and then leaped forward with a roar.

A man sprang out of the bushes and stood in front of the car like a statue with his hand held up. Miss Farrow screamed something unintelligible and clutched at my arm frantically. I threw her hand off with a snarl, kept my foot rammed down hard and hit the man dead center. The car bucked and I heard metal crumple angrily. We lurched, bounced viciously twice as my wheels passed over his floundering body, and then we were racing like complete idiots along a road that should not have been covered at more than twenty. The main road came into sight and I sliced the car around with a screech of the rear tires, controlled the deliberate skid with some fancy wheelwork and some fast digging of the surrounding dangers.

Then we were tearing along the broad, beautifully clear concrete with the speedometer needle running into the one-fifteen region.

"Steve," said Miss Farrow breathlessly, "That man you hit—"

In a hard voice I said, "He was getting to his feet when I drove out of range."

"I know," she said in a whimper. "I was in his mind. He was not hurt! God! Steve—what are we up against?" Her voice rose to a wail.

"I don't know, exactly," I said. "But I know what we're going to do."

"But Steve—what can we do?"

"Alone or together, very little. But we can bring one person more out along these Highways and then convince a fourth and a fifth and a fiftieth and a thousandth. By then we'll be shoved back off the stage while the big wheels grind painfully slow but exceedingly meticulous."

"That'll take time."

"Certainly. But we've got a start. Look how long it took getting a start in the first place."

"But what is their purpose?" she asked.

"That I can't say. I can't say a lot of things, like how, and why and wherefore. But I know that now we have a front tooth in this affair we're not going to let go." I thought for a moment. "I could use Thorndyke; he'd be the next guy to convince if we could find him. Or maybe Catherine, if we could find her. The next best thing is to get hold of that F.B.I. Team that called on me. There's a pair of cold-blooded characters that seem willing to sift through a million tons of ash to find one valuable cinder. They'll listen. I—"

Miss Farrow looked at her watch; I dug it as she made the gesture. #Eleven o'clock.#

57

"Going to call?" she asked.

"No," I said. "It's too late. It's one in New York now and the F.B.I. Team wouldn't be ready for a fast job at this hour."

"So?"

"I have no intention of placing a 'When you are ready' call to a number identified with the FBI. Not when a full eight hours must elapse between the call and a reply. Too much can happen to us in the meantime. But if I call in the morning, we can probably take care of ourselves well enough until they arrive if we stay in some place that is positively teeming with citizens. Sensible?"

"Sounds reasonable, Steve."

I let the matter drop at that; I put the go-pedal down to the floor and fractured a lot of speed laws until we came to Denver.

We made Denver just before midnight and drove around until we located a hotel that filled our needs. It was large, which would prevent overt operations on the part of the 'enemy' and it was a dead area, which would prevent one of them from reading our minds while we slept, and so enable them to lay counterplans against us.

The bellhop gave us a knowing leer as we registered separately, but I was content to let him think that way. Better that he get the wrong idea about us than the right one. He fiddled around in Miss Farrow's room on the ninth, bucking for a tip—not for service, but for leaving us alone, which he did by showing how big a nuisance he could be if not properly rewarded. But finally he got tired of his drawer-opening and lamp-testing and towel-stacking, and escorted me to the twelfth. I led him out with a five clutched in his fist and the leer even stronger.

If he expected me to race downstairs as soon as he was out of earshot, he was mistaken, for I hit the sack like the proverbial ton of crushed mortar. It had been literally weeks since I'd had a pleasant, restful sleep that was not broken by fitful dreams and worry-insomnia. Now that we had something solid to work on, I could look forward to some concrete action instead of merely feeling pushed around.

CHAPTER EIGHT

I'd put in for an eight o'clock call, but my sleep had been so sound and perfect that I was all slept out by seven-thirty. I was anxious to get going so I dressed and shaved in a hurry and cancelled the eight o'clock call. Then I asked the operator to connect me with 913.

A gruff, angry male voice snarled out of the earpiece at me. I began to apologize profusely but the other guy slammed the phone down on the hook hard enough to make my ear ring.

I jiggled my hook angrily and when the operator answered I told her that she'd miscued. She listened to my complaint and then replied in a pettish tone, "But I did ring 913, sir. I'll try again."

I wanted to tell her to just try, that there was no 'again' about it, but I didn't. I tried to dig through the murk to her switchboard but I couldn't dig a foot through this area. I waited impatiently until she re-made the connections at her switchboard and I heard the burring of the phone as the other end rang. Then the same mad-bull-rage voice delivered a number of pointed comments about people who ring up honest citizens in the middle of the night; and he hung up again in the middle of my apology. I got irked again and demanded that the operator connect me with the registration clerk. To him I told my troubles.

"One moment, sir," he said. A half minute later he returned with, "Sorry, sir. There is no Farrow registered. Could I have mis-heard you?"

"No, dammit," I snarled. "It's Farrow. F as in Frank; A as in Arthur; Double R as in Robert Robert; O as in Oliver; and W as in Washington. I saw her register, I went with her and the bellhop to her room, Number 913, and saw her installed. Then the same 'hop took me up to my room in 1224 on the Twelfth."

There was another moment of silence. Then he said, "You're Mr. Cornell. Registered in Room 1224 last night approximately four minutes after midnight."

"I know all about me. I was there and did it myself. And if I registered at four after midnight, Miss Farrow must have registered about two after midnight because the ink was still wet on her card when I wrote my name. We came in together, we were travelling together. Now, what gives?"

"I wouldn't know, sir. We have no guest named Farrow."

"See here," I snapped, "did you ever have a guest named Farrow?"

"Not in the records I have available at this desk. Perhaps in the past there may have been—"

"Forget the past. What about the character in 913?"

The registration clerk returned and informed me coldly, "Room 913 has been occupied by a Mr. Horace Westfield for over three months, Mr. Cornell. There is no mistake." His voice sounded professionally sympathetic, and I knew that he would forget my troubles as soon as his telephone was put back on its hook.

"Forget it," I snapped and hung up angrily. Then I went to the elevators, walking in a daze. There was a cold lump of something concrete-hard forming in the pit of my stomach. Wetness ran down my spine and a drop of sweat dropped from my armpit and hit my body a few inches above my belt like a pellet of icy hail. My face felt cold but when I wiped it with the palm of a shaking hand I found it beaded with an oily sweat. Everything seemed unreally horrifying.

"Nine," I told the elevator operator in a voice that sounded far away and hoarse.

I wondered whether this might not be a very vivid dream, and maybe if I went all the way back to my room, took a short nap, and got up to start all over again, I would awaken to honest reality.

The elevator stopped at Nine and I walked the corridor that was familiar from last night. I rapped on the door of Room 913.

The door opened and a big stubble-faced gorilla gazed out and snarled at me: "Are you the persistent character?"

"Look," I said patiently, "last night a woman friend of mine registered at this hotel and I accompanied her to this door. Number 913. Now—"

A long apelike arm came out and caught me by the coat lapels. He hauled and I went in fast. His breath was sour and his eyes were bloodshot and he was angry all the way through. His other hand caught me by the seat of the pants and he danced me into the room like a jumping jack.

"Friend," he ground out, "Take a look. There ain't no woman in this room, see?"

He whirled, carrying me off my feet. He took a lunging step forward and hurled me onto the bed, where I carried the springs deep down, to bounce up and off and forward to come up flat against the far wall. I landed sort of spread-eagle flat and seemed to hang there before I slid down the wall to the floor with a meaty-sounding Whump! Then before I could collect my wits or myself, he came over the bed in one long leap and had me hauled upright by the coat lapels again. The other hand was cocked back level with his shoulder it looked the size of a twenty-five pound sack of flour and was probably as hard as set cement.

Steve, I told myself, *this time you're in for it!*

"All right," I said as apologetically as I knew how, "so I've made a bad mistake. I apologize. I'll also admit that you could wipe up the hotel with me. But do you have to prove it?"

Mr. Horace Westfield's mental processes were not slow, cumbersome, and crude. He was as fast and hard on his mental feet as he was on his physical feet. He made some remarks about my intelligence, my upbringing, my parentage and its legal status, and my unwillingness to face a superior enemy. During this catalog of my virtueless existence, he gandy-walked me to the door and opened it. He concluded his lecture by suggesting that in the future I accept anything that any registration clerk said as God-Stated Truth, and if I then held any doubts I should take them to the police. Then he hurled me out of the room by just sort of shoving me away. I sailed across the hall on my toes, backward, and slapped my frame flat again, and once more I hung against the wall until the kinetic energy had spent itself. Then I landed on wobbly ankles as the door to Room 913 came closed with a violent slam.

I cursed the habit of building hotels in dead areas, although I admitted that I'd steer clear of any hotel in a clear area myself. But I didn't need a clear area nor a sense of perception to inform me that Room 913 was absolutely and totally devoid of any remote sign of female habitation. In fact, I gathered the impression that for all of his brute strength and virile masculinity, Mr. Horace Westfield hadn't entertained a woman in that room since he'd been there.

There was one other certainty: It was impossible for any agency short of sheer fairyland magic to have produced overnight a room that displayed its long-term occupancy by a not-too-immaculate character. That distinctive sour smell takes a long time to permeate the furnishings of any decent hotel; I wondered why a joint as well kept as this one would put up with a bird as careless of his person as Mr. Horace Westfield.

So I came to the reluctant conclusion that Room 913 was not occupied by Nurse Farrow, but I was not yet convinced that she was totally missing from the premises.

Instead of taking the elevator, I took to the stairs and tried the eighth. My perception was not too good for much in this murk, but I was mentally sensitive to Nurse Farrow and if I could get close enough to her, I might be able to perceive some trace of her even through the deadness. I put my forehead against the door of Room 813 and drew a blank. I could dig no farther than the inside of the door. If Farrow were in 813, I couldn't dig a trace of her. So I went to 713 and tried there.

I was determined to try every -13th room on every floor, but as I was standing with my forehead against the door to Room 413, someone came up behind me quietly and asked in a rough voice: "Just what do you think you're doing, Mister?"

His dress indicated housedick, but of course I couldn't dig the license in his wallet any more than he could read my mental, #None of your business, flatfoot!# I said, "I'm looking for a friend."

"You'd better come with me," he said flatly. "There's been complaints."

"Yeah?" I growled. "Maybe I made one of them myself."

"Want to start something?" he snapped.

I shrugged and he smiled. It was a stony smile, humorless as a crevasse in a rock-face. He kept that professional-type smile on his face until we reached the manager's office. The manager was out, but one of the assistant managers was in his desk. The little sign on the desk said "Henry Walton. Assistant Manager."

Mr. Walton said, coldly, "What's the trouble, Mr. Cornell?"

I decided to play it just as though I were back at the beginning again. "Last night," I explained very carefully, "I checked into this hotel. I was accompanied by a woman companion. A registered nurse. Miss Gloria Farrow. She registered first, and we were taken by one of your bellboys to Rooms 913 and 1224 respectively. I went with Miss Farrow to 913 and saw her enter. Then the bellhop escorted me to 1224 and left me for the night. This morning I can find no trace of Miss Farrow anywhere in this fleabag."

He bristled at the derogatory title but he covered it quickly. "Please be assured that no one connected with this hotel has any intention of confusing you, Mr. Cornell."

"I'm tired of playing games," I snapped. "I'll accept your statement so far as the management goes, but someone is guilty of fouling up your registration lists."

"That's rather harsh," he replied coldly. "Falsifying or tampering with hotel registration lists is illegal. What you've just said amounts to libel or slander, you know."

"Not if it's true."

I half expected Henry Walton to backwater fast, but instead, he merely eyed me with the same expression of distaste that he might have used upon finding half of a fuzzy caterpillar in his green salad. As cold as a cake of carbon dioxide snow, he said, "Can you prove this, Mr. Cornell?"

"Your night crew—"

"You've given us a bit of trouble this morning," he informed me. "So I've taken the liberty of calling in the night crew for you." He pressed a button and a bunch came in and lined up as if for formal inspection. "Boys," said Walton quietly, "suppose you tell us what you know about Mr. Cornell's arrival here last night."

They nodded their heads in unison.

"Wait a minute," I snapped. "I want a reliable witness to listen to this. In fact, if I could, I'd like to have their stories made under oath."

"You'd like to register a formal charge? Perhaps of kidnapping, or maybe illegal restraint?"

"Just get me an impartial witness," I told him sourly.

"Very well." He picked up his telephone and spoke into it. We waited a few minutes, and finally a very prim young woman came in. She was followed by a uniformed policeman. She was carrying one of those sub-miniature silent typewriters which she set up on its little stand with a few efficient motions.

"Miss Mason is our certified public stenographer," he said. "Officer, I'll want your signature on her copy when we're finished. This is a simple routine matter, but it must be legal to the satisfaction of Mr. Cornell. Now, boys, go ahead and explain. Give your name and position first for Miss Mason's record."

It was then that I noticed that the night crew had arranged themselves in chronological order. The elderly gent spoke first. He'd been the night doorman but now he was stripped of his admiral's gold braid and he looked just like any other sleepy man of middle age.

"George Comstock," he announced. "Doorman. As soon as I saw the car angling out of traffic, I pressed the call-button for a bell boy. Peter Wright came out and was standing in readiness by the time Mr. Cornell's car came to a stop by the curb. Johnny Olson was out next, and after Peter had taken Mr. Cornell's bag, Johnny got into Mr. Cornell's car and took off for the hotel garage—"

Walton interrupted. "Let each man tell what he did himself. No prompting, please."

"Well, then, you've heard my part in it. Johnny Olson took off in Mr. Cornell's car and Peter Wright took off with Mr. Cornell's bag, and Mr. Cornell followed Peter."

The next man in line, at a nod from the assistant manager, stepped forward about a half a pace and said, "I'm Johnny Olson. I followed Peter Wright out of the door and after Peter had collected Mr. Cornell's bag, I got in Mr. Cornell's car and took it to the hotel garage."

The third was Peter Wright, the bellhop. "I carried his bag to the desk and waited until he registered. Then we went up to Room 1224. I opened the door, lit the lights, opened the window, and stuff. Mr. Cornell tipped me five bucks and I left him there. Alone."

"I'm Thomas Boothe, the elevator operator. I took Mr. Cornell and Peter Wright to the Twelfth. Peter said I should wait because he wouldn't be long, and so I waited on the Twelfth until Peter got back. That's all."

"I'm Doris Caspary, the night telephone operator. Mr. Cornell called me about fifteen minutes after twelve and asked me to put him down for a call at eight o'clock this morning. Then he called at about seven thirty and said that he was already awake and not to bother."

Henry Walton said, "That's about it, Mr. Cornell."

"But—"

The policeman looked puzzled. "What is the meaning of all this? If I'm to witness any statements like these, I'll have to know what for."

Walton looked at me. I couldn't afford not to answer. Wearily I said, "Last night I came in here with a woman companion and we registered in separate rooms. She went into 913 and I waited until she was installed and then went to my own room on the Twelfth. This morning there is no trace of her."

I went on to tell him a few details, but the more I told him the more he lifted his eyebrows.

"Done any drinking?" he asked me curtly.

"No."

"Certain?"

"Absolutely."

Walton looked at his crew. They burst into a chorus of, "Well, he *was* steady on his feet," and "He didn't *seem* under the influence," and a lot of other statements, all generally indicating that for all they knew I could have been gassed to the ears, but one of those rare guys who don't show it.

The policeman smiled thinly. "Just why was this registered nurse travelling with you?"

I gave them the excuse-type statement; the one about the accident and that I felt I was still a bit on the rocky side and so forth. About all I did for that was to convince the policeman that I was not a stable character. His attitude seemed to indicate that any man travelling with a nurse must either be physically sick or maybe mentally out of tune.

Then with a sudden thought, I whirled on Johnny Olson. "Will you get my car?" I asked him. He nodded after a nod from Walton. I said, "There's plenty of evidence in my car. In the meantime, let's face one thing, officer. I've been accused of spinning a yarn. I'd hardly be demanding witnesses if I weren't telling the truth. I was standing beside Miss Farrow when she signed the register, complete with the R.N. title. It's too bad that hotels have taken to using card files instead of the old registration book. Cards are so easy to misplace—"

Walton cut in angrily. "If that's an accusation, I'm inclined to see that you make it in a court of law."

The policeman looked calm. "I'd take it easy, Mr. Cornell. Your story is not corroborated. But the employees of the hotel bear one another out. And from the record, it would appear that you were under the eyes of at least two of them from the moment your car slowed down in front of the main entrance up to the time that you were escorted to your room."

"I object to being accused of complicity in a kidnapping," put in the assistant manager.

"I object to being accused of mental incompetence," I snapped. "Why do we stand around accusing people back and forth when there's evidence if you'll only uncover it."

We stood glaring at one another. The air grew tense. The only ones in the place who didn't have chips on their shoulders were the policeman and the certified stenographer, who clicked her silent keys in lightning manner, taking down every comment as it was uttered.

Eventually Olson returned, to put an end to the thick silence. "Y'car's outside," he told me angrily.

"Fine," I said. "Now we'll go outside and take a look. You'll find plenty of traces of Miss Farrow's having been there. Officer—are you telepath or perceptive?"

"Perceptive," he said. "But not in here."

"How far out does this damn dead area extend?" I asked Walton.

"About half way across the sidewalk."

"Okay. So let's all go."

We traipsed out to the curb. Miss Mason brought her little silent along, slipping the stand high up so that she could type from an erect position. We lined up along the curb and I looked into my car with a triumphant feeling.

And then that cold chill congealed my spine again. My car was clean and shining. It had been washed and buffed and polished until it looked as new as the day I picked it out on the salesroom floor.

Walton looked blank, and I whipped a thought at him: #Damned telepath!#

He nodded perceptibly and said smoothly, "I'm sorry we couldn't find any fingerprints. Because now, you see," and here he turned to the policeman and went on, "Mr. Cornell will now accuse us of having washed his car to destroy the evidence. However, you'll find that as a policy of the hotel, the car-washing is performed as a standard service. In fact, if any guest parks his car in our garage and his car is not rendered spick and span, someone's going to get fired for negligence."

So that was that. I took a fast look around, because I knew that I had to get out of there fast. If I remained to carry on any more argument, I'd be tapped for being a nuisance and jugged.

I had no doubt at all that the whole hotel staff were all involved in Nurse Farrow's disappearance. But they'd done their job in such a way that if the question were pushed hard, I would end up answering formal charges, the topmost of which might be murder and concealment of the body.

I could do nothing by sitting in jail. This was the time to get out first and worry about Farrow later.

So I opened the car door and slipped in. I fiddled with the so-called glove compartment and opened it; the maps were all neatly stacked and all the flub had been cleaned out. I fumbled inside and dropped a couple of road maps to the floor, and while I was down picking them up I turned the ignition key which Olson had left plugged in the lock.

I took off with a jerk and howl of tires.

There was the sudden shrill of a police whistle but it was stopped after one brief blast. As I turned the corner, I caught a fast backwards dig at them. They were filing back into the hotel. I did not believe that the policeman was part of the conspiracy, but I was willing to bet that Walton was going to slip the policeman a box of fine cigars as a reward for having helped them to get rid of a very embarrassing screwball.

CHAPTER NINE

I put a lot of miles between me and my recent adventure before I stopped to take stock. The answer to the mess was still obscure, but the elimination of Nurse Farrow fell into the pattern very neatly.

Alone, I was no problem. So long as my actions were restricted to meandering along the highways, peering into nooks and crannies and crying, "Catherine," in a plaintive voice, no one cared. But when I teamed up with a telepath, they moved in with the efficiency of a well-run machine and extracted the disturbing element. In fact, their machinations had been so smooth that I was beginning to believe that my 'Discoveries' were really an assortment of unimportant facts shown to me deliberately for some reason of their own.

The only snag in the latter theory was the fact of our accident. Assuming that I had to get involved in the mess, there were easier ways to introduce me than by planning a bad crack-up that could have been fatal, even granting the close proximity of the Harrison tribe to come to the rescue. The accident had to be an accident in the dictionary definition of the word itself. Under the circumstances, a planned accident could only be accepted under an entirely different set of conditions. For instance, let's assume that Catherine was a Mekstrom and I was about to disclose the fact. Then she or they could plan such an accident, knowing that she could walk out of the wreck with her hair barely mussed, leaving me dead for sure.

But Catherine was not a Mekstrom. I'd been close enough to that satin skin to know that the body beneath it was soft and yielding.

Yet the facts as they stood did not throw out my theory. It merely had to be revised. Catherine was no Mekstrom, but if the Harrisons had detected the faintest traces of an incipient Mekstrom infection, they could very well have taken her in. I fumed at the idea. I could almost visualize them pointing out her infection and then informing her bluntly that she could either swear in with them and be cured or she could die alone and miserably.

This could easily explain her disappearance. Naturally, being what they were, they cared nothing for me or any other non-Mekstrom. I was no menace. Not until I teamed up with a telepath, and they knew what to do about that.

Completely angry, I decided that it was time that I made a noise like an erupting volcano. With plans forming, I took off again towards Yellowstone, pausing only long enough at Fort Collins to buy some armament.

Colorado is still a part of the United States where a man can go into a store and buy a gun over the counter just like any tool. I picked out a Bonanza .375 because it is small enough to fit the hip pocket, light because of the new alloys so it wouldn't unballast me, and mostly because it packs enough wallop to stop a charging hippo. I did not know whether it would drill all the way through a Mekstrom hide, but the impact would at least set any target back on the seat of his pants.

Then I drove into Wyoming and made my way to Yellowstone, and one day I was driving along the same road that had been pictured in Dr. Thorndyke's postcard. I drove along it boldly, loaded for bear, and watching the Highway signs that led me nicely toward my goal.

Eventually I came to the inevitable missing spoke. It pointed to a ranch-type establishment that lay sprawled out in a billow of dead area. I eyed it warily and kept on driving because my plans did not include marching up to the front door like a rug peddler.

Instead, I went on to the next town, some twenty miles away, which I reached about dark. I stopped for a leisurely dinner, saw a moving picture at the drive-in, killed a few at the bar, and started back to the way station about midnight.

The name, dug from the mailbox, was Macklin.

Again I did not turn in. I parked the car down the highway by about three miles, figuring that only a psi of doctor's degree would be able to dig anything at that distance. I counted on there being no such mental giant in this out of the way place.

I made my way back toward the ranch house across the fields and among the rolling rock. I extended my perception as far as I could; I made myself sensitive to danger and covered the ground foot by foot, digging for traps, alarm lines, photocell trips, and parties who might be lying in wait for me.

I encountered no sign of any trip or trap all the way to the fringe of the dead zone.

The chance that they knew of my presence and were comfortably awaiting me deep within the zone occurred to me. So I was cautious as I cased the layout and decided to make my entry at the point where the irregular boundary of the dead area was closest to the house itself.

I entered and became completely psi-blind. Starlight cast just enough light so that I could see to walk without falling into a chuck hole or stumbling over something, but beyond a few yards everything lost shape and became a murky blob. The night was dead silent except for an occasional hiss of wind through the brush.

Esperwise I was not covering much more than my eyes could see. I stepped deeper into the zone and lost another yard of perception. I kept probing at the murk, like poking a finger at a hanging blanket. It moved if I dug hard enough in any direction, but as soon as I released the pressure, the murk moved right back where it was before.

I crouched and took a few more steps into the zone, got to a place where I could begin to see the outlines of the house itself.

Dark, silent, it looked uninhabited. I wished that there had been a college course in housebreaking, prowling and second-story operations. I went at it very slowly. I took my sweet time crossing the boards of the back verandah, even though the short hair on the back of my neck was beginning to prickle from nervousness. I was also scared. At any given moment, they had the legal right to open a window, poke out a field-piece, and blow me into bloody ribbons where I stood.

The zone was really a dead one. My esper range was no more than about six inches from my forehead; a motion picture of Steve Cornell sounding out the border of a window with his forehead would have looked funny, it was not funny at the time. But I found that the sash was not locked and that the flyscreen could be unshipped from the outside.

I entered a dining room. Inside, it was blacker than pitch.

I crossed the dining room by sheer feel and instinct and managed to get to the hallway without making any racket. At this point I stopped and asked myself what the heck I thought I was trying to do. I had to admit that I had no plan in definite form. I was just prowling the joint to see what information I might be able to pick up.

Down the hall I found a library. I'd been told that you tell what kind of people folks are by inspecting their library, and so I conned the book titles by running my head along a row of books.

The books in the library indicated to me that this was a family of some size with rather broad tastes. There was everything from science fiction to Shakespeare, everything from philosophy to adventure. A short row of kid's books. A bible. Encyclopedia Brittanica (Published in Chicago), in fifty-four volumes, but there were no places that were worn that might give me an idea as to any special interest.

The living room was also blank of any evidence of anything out or the ordinary. I turned away and stood in the hallway, blocked by indecision. I was a fool, I kept telling myself, because I did not have any experience in casing a joint, and what I knew had been studied out of old-time detective tales. Even if the inhabitants of the place were to let me go at it in broad daylight, I'm not too sure that I'd do a good job of finding something of interest except for sheer luck.

But on the other hand, I'd gotten nowhere by dodging and ducking. I was in no mood to run quivering in fear. I was more inclined to emit a bellow just to see what would happen next.

So instead of sneaking quietly away, I found the stairs and started to go up very slowly.

It occurred to me at about the third step that I must be right. Anybody with any sense wouldn't keep anything dangerous in their downstairs library. It would be too much like a safe-cracker storing his nitro in the liquor cabinet or the murderer who hangs his weapon over the mantelpiece.

Yet everybody kept some sort of records, or had things in their homes that were not shown to visiting firemen. And if it weren't on the second floor, then it might be in the cellar. If I weren't caught first, I'd prowl the whole damned place, inch by inch—avoiding if possible those rooms in which people slept.

The fifth step squeaked just faintly, but it sounded like someone pulling a spike out of a packing case made of green wood. I froze, half aching for some perceptive range so that I could dig any sign of danger, and half remembering that if it weren't for the dead area, I'd not be this far. I'd have been frightened to try it in a clear zone.

Eventually I went on up, and as my head came above the level of the floor, everything became psi-clear once more.

Here was as neat a bit of home planning as I have ever seen. Just below the level of the second floor, their dead area faded out, so that the top floor was clean, bright, and clear as day. I paused, startled at it, and spent a few moments digging outside. The dead area billowed above the rooftop out of my range; from what little I could survey of the dark psi area, it must have been shaped sort of like an angel-food cake, except that the central hole did not go all the way down. Only to the first-floor level. It was a wonderful set-up for a home; privacy was granted on the first floor and from the road and all the surrounding territory, but on the second floor there was plenty of pleasant esperclear space for the close-knit family and friends. Their dead area was shaped in the ideal form for any ideal home.

Then I stopped complimenting the architect and went on about my business, because there, directly in front of my nose, I could dig the familiar impression of a medical office.

I went the rest of the way up the stairs and into the medical office. There was no mistake. The usual cabinets full of instruments, a laboratory examination table, shelves of little bottles, and along one wall was a library of medical books. All it needed was a sign on the door: 'S. P. Macklin, MSch' to make it standard.

At the end of the library was a set of looseleaf notebooks, and I pulled the more recent of them out and held it up to my face. I did not dare snap on a light, so I had to go it esper.

Even in the clear area, this told me very little. Esper is not like eyesight, any more than you can hear printed words or perhaps carry on a conversation by watching the wiggly green line on an oscilloscope. I wished it was. Instead, esper gives you a grasp of materials and shapes and things in position with regard to other things. It is sort of like seeing something simultaneously from all sides, if you can imagine such a sensation. So instead of being able to esper-read the journal, I had to take it letter by letter by digging the shape of the ink on the page with respect to the paper and the other letters, and since the guy's handwriting was atrocious, I could get no more than if the thing were written in Latin. If it had been typewritten, or with a stylized hand, it would have been far less difficult; or if it had been any of my damned business I could have dug it easily. But as it was——

"Looking for something, Mr. Cornell?" asked a cool voice that dripped with acid sarcasm. At the same instant, the lights went on.

I whirled, clutched at my hip pocket, and dropped to my knees at the same time. The sights of my .375 centered in the middle of a silk-covered midriff.

She stood there indolently, disdainful of the cannon that was aimed at her. She was not armed; I'd have caught the esper warning of danger if she'd come at me with a weapon of some sort, even though I was preoccupied with the bookful of evidence.

I stood up and faced her and let my esper run lightly over her body. She was another Mekstrom, which did not surprise me a bit.

"I seem to have found what I was looking for," I said.

Her laugh was scornful but not loud. "You're welcome, Mr. Cornell."

#Telepath?#

"Yes, and a good one."

#Who else is awake?#

"Just me, so far," she murmered. "But I'll be glad to call out—"

#Keep it quiet, Sister Macklin.#

"Stop thinking like an idiot, Mr. Cornell. Quiet or not, you'll not leave this house until I permit you to go."

I let my esper roam quickly through the house. An elderly couple slept in the front bedroom. A man slept alone in the room beside them; a pair of young boys slept in an over-and-under bunk in the room across the hall. The next room must have been hers, the bed was tumbled but empty. The room next to the medical office contained a man trussed in traction splints, white bandages, and literally festooned with those little hanging bottles that contain everything from blood plasma to food and water, right on down to lubrication for the joints. I tried to dig his face under the swath of bandage but I couldn't make out much more than the fact that it was a face and that the face was half Mekstrom Flesh.

"He is a Mekstrom Patient," said Miss Macklin quietly. "At this stage, he is unconscious."

I sort of sneered at her. "Good friend of yours, no doubt."

"Not particularly," she said. "Let's say that he is a poor victim that would die if we hadn't found his infection early." The tone and expression of her voice made me seethe; she sounded as though she felt herself to be a real benefactor to the human race, and that she and her outfit would do the same for any other poor guy that caught Mekstrom's—providing they learned about this unfortunate occurrence in time.

"We would, Mr. Cornell."

"Bah-loney," I grunted.

"Why dispute my word?" she asked in the same tone of innocent honesty.

I eyed her angrily and I felt my hand tighten on the revolver. "I've a reason to become suspicious," I told her in a voice that I hoped was as mild-mannered as her own. "Because three people have disappeared in the past half-year without a trace, but under circumstances that put me in the middle. All of them, somehow, seem to be involved with your hidden road sign system and Mekstrom's Disease."

"That's unfortunate," she said quietly.

I had to grab myself to keep from yelling, "Unfortunate?" and managed to muffle it down to a mere voice-volume sound. "People dying of Mekstrom's because you're keeping this cure a secret and I'm batted from pillar to post because—" I gave up on that because I really did not know why.

"It's unfortunate that you had to become involved," she said firmly. "Because you—"

"It's unfortunate for everybody," I snapped, "because I'm going to bust you all wide open!"

"I'm afraid not. You see, in order to do that you'll have to get out of here and that I will not permit."

I grunted. "Miss Macklin, you Mekstroms have hard bodies, but do you think your hide will stop a slug from this?"

"You'll never know. You see, Mr. Cornell, you do not have the cold, brittle, determined guts that you'd need to pull that trigger."

"No?"

"Pull it," she said. "Or do you agree, now that you're of age, that you can't bluff a telepath."

I eyed her sourly because she was right. She held that strength that lies in weakness; I could not pull that trigger and fire a .375 inch slug into that slender, silk-covered midriff. And opposite that, Miss Macklin also had a strength that was strength itself. She could hold me aloft with one hand kicking and squirming while she was twisting my arms and legs off with her other hand.

She held all the big cards of her sex, too. I couldn't slug her with my fist, even though I knew that I'd only break my hand without even bruising her. I was in an awkward situation and I knew it. If she'd been a normal woman I could have shrugged my way past her and left, but she was determined not to let me leave without a lot of physical violence. Violence committed on a woman gets the man in dutch no matter how justified he is.

Yet in my own weakness there was a strength; there was another way out and I took it. Abruptly and without forethought.

CHAPTER TEN

Shifting my aim slightly, I pulled the trigger. The .375 Bonanza went off with a sound like an atom bomb in a telephone booth, and the slug whiffed between her arm and her body and drilled a crater in the plaster behind her.

The roar stunned her stiff. The color drained from her face and she swayed uncertainly. I found time enough to observe that while her body was as hard as chromium, her nervous system was still human and sensitive enough to make her faint from a sudden shock. She caught herself, and stood there stiff and white with one delicate (but steel-hard) hand up against her throat.

Then I dug the household. They were piling out of the hay like a bunch of trained firemen answering a still alarm. They arrived in all stages of nightdress in the following order:

The man, about twenty-two or three, who skidded into the room on dead gallop and put on brakes with a screech as he caught sight of the .375 with its thin wisp of blue vapor still trailing out of the muzzle.

The twins, aged about fourteen, who might have turned to run if they'd not been frightened stiff at the sight of the cannon in my fist.

Father and then Mother Macklin, who came in briskly but without panic.

Mr. Macklin said, crisply, "May I have an explanation, Mr. Cornell?"

"I'm a cornered rat," I said thickly. "And so I'm scared. I want out of here in one piece. I'm so scared that if I'm intercepted, I may get panicky, and if I do someone is likely to get hurt. Understand?"

"Perfectly," said Mr. Macklin calmly.

"Are you going to let him get away with this?" snapped the eldest son.

"Fred, a nervous man with a revolver is very dangerous. Especially one who lacks the rudimentary training in the simpler forms of burglary."

I couldn't help but admire the older gentleman's bland self-confidence. "Young man," he said to me, "You've made a bad mistake."

"No I haven't," I snapped. "I've been on the trail of something concrete for a long time, and now that I've found it I'm not going to let it go easily." I waved the .375 and they all cringed but Mr. Macklin.

He said, "Please put that weapon down, Mr. Cornell. Let's not add attempted murder to your other crimes."

"Don't force me to it, then. Get out of my way and let me go."

He smiled. "I don't have to be telepath to tell you that you won't pull that trigger until you're sorely driven," he replied calmly. He was so right that it made me mad. He added, "also, you've got four shells left since you carry the firearm on an empty chamber. Not used to guns, are you, Mr. Cornell?"

Well, I wasn't used to wearing a gun. Now that he mentioned it, I remembered that it was impossible to fire the shell under the hammer by any means except by pulling the trigger.

What he was telling me meant that even if I made a careful but bloody sweep of it with my four shells, there would be two of them left, and even the twins were more than capable of taking me apart inch by inch once my revolver was empty.

"Seems to be an impasse, Mr. Cornell," he said with an amused smile.

"You bland-mannered bunch of—"

"Ah now, please," he said abruptly. "My wife is not accustomed to such language, nor is my daughter, although my son and the twins probably know enough definitions to make them angry. This is an impasse, Mr. Cornell, and it behooves all of us to be extremely polite to one another. For one wrong move and you'll fire; this will mean complete chaos for all of us. One wrong word from you and someone of us will take offense, which will be equally fatal. Now, let's all stand quietly and talk this over."

"What's to talk over?" I demanded.

"A truce. Or call it an armistice."

"Do go on."

He looked at his family, and I followed his gaze. Miss Macklin was leaning against the wall with a look of concentrated interest. Her elder brother Fred was standing alert and ready but not quite poised for a leap. Mrs. Macklin had a motherly-looking smile on her face which for some unknown reason she was aiming at me in a disarming manner. The twins were standing close together, both of them puzzled-looking. I wondered whether they were esper or telepath (twins are always the same when they're identical, and opposite when fraternal). The thing that really bothered me was their attitude They all seemed to look at me as though I were a poor misguided individual who had unwittingly tromped on their toes after having fallen in among bad company. They reminded me of the Harrisons, who looked and sounded so sympathetic when I'd gone out there seeking Catherine.

A fine bunch to trust! First they swipe my girl and erase all traces of her; then when I go looking they offer me help and sympathy for my distress. The right hand giveth and the left hand taketh away, yeah!

I hated them all, yet I am not a hero-type. I wanted the whole Highways in Hiding rolled up like an old discarded corridor carpet, with every Mekstrom on Earth rolled up in it. But even if I'd been filled to the scuppers with self-abnegation in favor of my fellow man, I could not have pulled the trigger and started the shambles. For instead of blowing the whole thing wide open because of a batch of bodies, the survivors would have enough savvy to clean up the mess before our bodies got cold, and the old Highways crowd would be doing business at the same old stand. Without, I might add, without the minor nuisance that people call Steve Cornell.

What I really wanted was to find Catherine.

And then it came to me that what I really wanted second of all was to possess a body of Mekstrom Flesh, to be a physical superman.

"Suppose," said Miss Macklin unexpectedly, "that it is impossible?"

"Impossible?" I roared. "What have you got that I haven't got?"

"Mekstrom's Disease," replied Miss Macklin quietly.

"Fine," I sneered. "So how do I go out and get it?"

"You'll get it naturally—or not at all," she said.

"Now see here—" I started off, but Mr. Macklin stopped me with an upraised hand.

"Mr. Cornell," he said, "we are in the very awkward position of trying to convince a man that his preconceived notion is incorrect. We can produce no direct evidence to support our statement. All we can do is to tell you that so far as we know, and as much as we know about Mekstrom's Disease, no one has ever contracted the infection artificially."

"And how can I believe you?"

"That's our awkward position. We cannot show you anything that will support our statement. We can profess the attitudes of honesty, truth, honor, good-will, altruism, and every other word that means the same thing. We can talk until doomsday and nothing will be said."

"So where is all this getting us?" I asked.

"I hope it is beginning to cause your mind to doubt the preconceived notion," he said. "Ask yourself why any outfit such as ours would deliberately show you evidence."

"I have it and it does not make sense."

He smiled. "Precisely. It does not."

Fred Macklin cut in, "Dad, why are we bothering with all this"

"Because I have hopes that Mr. Cornell can be made to see our point, to join, as it were, our side."

"Fat chance," I snapped.

"Please, I'm your elder and not at all inclined to waste my time. You came here seeking information and you shall have it. You will not believe it, but it will, I hope, fill in some blank spots after you have had a chance to compare, sort, and use your own logic on the problem. As a mechanical engineer, you are familiar with the line of reasoning that we non-engineering people call Occam's Razor?"

"The law of least reaction," I said automatically.

"The what?" asked Mrs. Macklin.

Miss Macklin said, "I'll read it from Mr. Cornell's mind, mother. The law of least reaction can be demonstrated by the following: If a bucket of mixed wood-shavings and gasoline are heated, there is a calculable probability that the gasoline will catch fire first because the gasoline is easier—least reaction—to set on fire."

"Right," I said. "But how does this apply to me?"

Mr. Macklin took up the podium again: "For one thing, your assumption regarding Catherine is correct. At the time of the accident she was found to have Mekstrom's Disease in its earliest form. The Harrisons did take her in to save her life. Now, dropping that side of the long story, we must follow your troubles. The accident, to a certain group of persons, was a fortunate one. It placed under their medical care a man—you—in whose mind could be planted a certain mild curiosity about a peculiar road sign and other evidences. The upshot of this was that you took off on a tour of investigation."

That sounded logical, but there were a lot of questions that had open, ragged ends flying loose.

Mr. Macklin went on: "Let's diverge for the moment. Mr. Cornell, what is your reaction to Mekstrom's Disease at this point?"

That was easy. It was a curse to the human race, excepting that some outfit knew how to cure it. Once cured, it made a physical superman of the so-called victim. What stuck in my craw was the number of unfortunate people who caught it and died painfully—or by their own hand in horror—without the sign of aid or assistance.

He nodded when I'd gone about half-way through my conclusions and before I got mentally violent about them.

"Mr. Cornell, you've expressed your own doom at certain hands. You feel that the human race could benefit by exploitation of Mekstrom's Disease."

"It could, if everybody helped out and worked together."

"Everybody?" he asked with a sly look. I yearned again for the ability of a telepath, and I knew that the reason why I was running around loose was because I was only an esper and therefore incapable of learning the truth directly. I stood there like a totem pole and tried to think.

Eventually it occurred to me. Just as there are people who cannot stand dictatorships, there are others who cannot abide democracy; in any aggregation like the human race there will be the warped souls who feel superior to the rest of humanity. They welcome dictatorships providing they can be among the dictators and if they are not included, they fight until the other dictatorship is deposed so they can take over.

"True," said Mr. Macklin, "And yet, if they declared their intentions, how long would they last?"

"Not very long. Not until they had enough power to make it stick," I said.

"And above all, not until they have the power to grant this blessing to those whose minds agree with theirs. So now, Mr. Cornell, I'll make a statement that you can accept as a mere collection of words, to be used in your arguments with yourself: We'll assume two groups, one working to set up a hierarchy of Mekstroms in which the rest of the human race will become hewers of wood and drawers of water. Contrasting that group is another group who feels that no man or even a congress of men are capable of choosing the individual who is to be granted the body of the physical superman. We cannot hope to watch the watchers, Mr. Cornell, and we will not have on our conscience the weight of having to select A over B as being more desirable. Enough of this! You'll have to argue it out by yourself later."

"Later?" grunted Fred Macklin. "You're not going to—"

"I certainly am," said his father firmly. "Mr. Cornell may yet be the agency whereby we succeed in winning out." He spoke to me again. "Neither group dares to come into the open, Mr. Cornell. We cannot accuse the other group of anything nefarious, any more than they dare to accuse us. Their mode of attack is to coerce you into exposing us for a group of undercover operators who are making supermen."

"Look," I asked him, "why not admit it? You've got nothing sinister in mind."

"Think of all the millions of people who have not had schooling beyond the preparatory grades," he said. "People of latent psi ability instead of trained practice, or those poor souls who have no psi ability worth mentioning. Do you know the history of the Rhine Institute, Mr. Cornell?"

"Only vaguely."

"In the early days of Rhine's work at Duke University, there were many scoffers. The scoffers and detractors, naturally enough, were those people who had the least amount of psi ability. Admitting that at the time all psi ability was latent, they still had less of it. But after Rhine's death, his associates managed to prove his theories and eventually worked out a system of training that would develop the psi ability. Then, Mr. Cornell, those who are blessed with a high ability in telepathy or perception—the common term of esper is a misnomer, you know, because there's nothing extra-sensory about perception— found themselves being suspected and hated by those who had not this delicate sense. It took forty of fifty years before common public acceptance got around to looking at telepathy and perception in the same light as they saw a musician with a trained ear or an artist with a trained eye. Psi is a talent that everybody has to some degree, and today this is accepted with very little angry jealousy.

"But now," he went on thoughtfully, "consider what would happen if we made a public statement that we could cure Mekstrom's Disease by making a physical superman out of the victim. Our main enemy would then stand up and howl that we are concealing the secret; he would be believed. We'd be tracked down and persecuted, eventually wiped out, while he sat behind his position and went on picking and choosing victims whose attitude parallel his own."

"And who is the character?" I demanded. I knew. But I wanted him to say it aloud.

He shook his head. "I'll not say it," he said. "Because I will not accuse him aloud, any more than he dares to tell you flatly that we are an underground organization that must be rooted out. He knows about our highways and our way stations and our cure, because he uses the same cure. He can hide behind his position so long as he makes no direct accusation. You know the law, Mr. Cornell."

Yes, I knew the law. So long as the accuser came into court with a completely clean mind, he was safe. But Scholar Phelps could hardly make the accusation, nor could he supply the tiniest smidgin of direct evidence to me. For in my accusation I'd implicate him as an accessory-accuser and then he would be called upon to supply not only evidence but a clear, clean, and open mind. In shorter words, the old stunt of pointing loudly to someone else as a dodge for covering up your own crime was a lost art in this present-day world of telepathic competence. The law, of course, insisted that no man could be convicted for what he was thinking, but only upon direct evidence of action. But a crooked-thinking witness found himself in deep trouble anyway, even though crooked thinking was in itself no crime.

"Now for one more time," said Mr. Macklin. "Consider a medical person who cannot qualify because he is a telepath and not a perceptive. His very soul was devoted to being a scholar of medicine like his father and his grandfather, but his telepath ability does not allow him to be the full scholar. A doctor he can be. But he can never achieve the final training, again the ultimate degree. Such a man overcompensates and becomes the frustrate; a ripe disciple for the superman theory."

"Dr. Thorndyke!" I blurted.

His face was as blank, as noncommittal as a bronze bust; I could neither detect affirmation nor negation in it. He was playing it flat; I'd never get any evidence from him, either.

"So now, Mr. Cornell, I have given you food for thought. I've made no direct statements; nothing that you could point to. I've defended myself as any man will do, but only by protestations of innocence. Therefore I suggest that you take your artillery and vacate the premises."

I remembered the Bonanza .375 that was hanging in my hand. Shamefacedly I slipped it back in my hip pocket. "But look, sir—"

"Please leave, Mr. Cornell. Any more I cannot say without laying us wide open for trouble. I am sorry for you, it is no joy being a pawn. But I hope that your pawn-ship will work for our side, and I hope that you will come through it safely. Now, please leave us quietly."

I shrugged. I left. And as I was leaving, Miss Macklin touched my arm and said in a soft voice: "I hope you find your Catherine, Steve. And I hope that someday you'll be able to join her."

I nodded dumbly. It was not until I was back to my car that I remembered that her last statement was something similar to wishing me a case of measles so that I'd be afterward immune from them.

CHAPTER ELEVEN

As the miles separated me from the Macklins, my mind kept whirling around in a tight circle. I had a lot of the bits, but none of them seemed to lock together very tight. And unhappily, too many of the bits that fit together were hunks that I did not like.

I knew the futility of being non-telepath. Had Mr. Macklin given me the truth or was I being sold another shoddy bill of goods? Or had he spun me a yarn just to get me out of his house without a riot? Of course, there had been a riot, and he'd been expecting it. If nothing else, it proved that I was a valuable bit of material, for some undisclosed reason.

I had to grin. I didn't know the reason, but whatever reason they had, it must gripe the devil out of them to be unable to erase me.

Then the grin faded. No one had told me about Catherine. They'd neatly avoided the subject. Well, since I'd taken off on this still hunt to find Catherine, I'd continue looking, even though every corner I looked into turned out to be the hiding place for another bunch of mad spooks.

My mind took another tack: Admitting that neither side could rub me out without losing, why in heck didn't they just collect me and put me in a cage? Dammit, if I had an organization as well oiled as either of them, I could collect the President right out of the New White House and put him in a cage along with the King of England, the Shah of Persia, and the Dali Lama to make a fourth for bridge.

This was one of those questions that cannot be answered by the application of logic, reasoning, or by applying either experience or knowledge. I did not know, nor understand. And the only way I would ever find out was to locate someone who was willing to tell.

Then it occurred to me that—aside from my one experience in housebreaking—that I'd been playing according to the rules. I'm pretty much a law-abiding citizen. Yet it did seem to me that I learned more during those times when the rules, if not broken, at least were bent rather sharply. So I decided to try my hand at busting a couple of rather high-level rules.

There was a way to track down Catherine.

So I gassed up the buggy, turned the nose East, and took off like a man with a purpose in mind. En route, I laid out my course. Along that course there turned out to be seven Way Stations, according to the Highway signs. Three of them were along U.S. 12 on the way from Yellowstone to Chicago. One of them was between Chicago and Hammond, Indiana. There was another to the south of Sandusky, Ohio, one was somewhere south of Erie, Pa., and the last was in the vicinity of Newark. There were a lot of the Highways themselves, leading into and out of my main route—as well as along it.

But I ignored them all, and nobody gave me a rough time.

Eventually I walked into my apartment. It was musty, dusty, and lonesome. Some of Catherine's things were still on the table where I'd dropped them; they looked up at me mutely until I covered them with the walloping pile of mail that had arrived in my long absence. I got a bottle of beer and began to go through the mail, wastebasketing the advertisements, piling the magazines neatly, and filing some offers of jobs (Which reminded me that I was still an engineer and that my funds wouldn't last indefinitely) and went on through the mail until I came to a letter—The Letter.

Dear Mr. Cornell:

We're glad to hear from you. We moved, not because Marian caught Mekstrom's, but because the dead area shifted and left us sort of living in a fish-bowl, psi-wise.

Everybody is hale and hearty here and we all wish you the best.

Please do not think for a moment that you owe us anything. We'd rather be free of your so-called debt. We regret that Catherine was not with you, maybe the accident might not have happened. But we do all think that we stand as an association with a very unhappy period in your life, and that it will be better for you if you try to forget that we exist. This is a hard thing to say, Steve, but really, all we can do for you is to remind you of your troubles.

Therefore with love from all of us, we'd like to make this a sincerely sympathetic and final—

Farewell, Philip Harrison.

I grunted unhappily. It was a nice-sounding letter, but it did not ring true, somehow. I sat there digging it for hidden meanings, but none came. I didn't care. In fact, I didn't really expect any more than this. If they'd not written me at all, I'd still have done what I did. I sat down and wrote Phillip Harrison another letter:

Dear Philip:

I received your letter today, as I returned from an extended trip through the west. I'm glad to hear that Marian is not suffering from Mekstrom's Disease. I am told that it is fatal to the—uninitiated.

However, I hope to see you soon.

Regards, Steve Cornell.

That, I thought, *should do it!*

Then to help me and my esper, I located a tiny silk handkerchief of Catherine's, one she'd left after one of her visits. I slipped it into the envelope and slapped a stamp and a notation on the envelope that this letter was to be forwarded to Phillip Harrison. I dropped it in the box about eleven that night, but I didn't bother trying to follow it until the morning.

Ultimately it was picked up and taken to the local post office, and from there it went to the clearing station at Pennsylvania Station at 34th St., where I hung around the mail-baggage section until I attracted the attention of a policeman.

"Looking for something, Mr. Cornell?"

"Not particularly," I told the telepath cop. "Why?"

"You've been digging every mailbag that comes out of there."

"Am I?" I asked ingeniously.

"Can it Buster, or we'll let you dig your way out of a jail."

"You can't arrest a man for thinking."

"I'll be happy to make it loitering," he said sharply.

"I've a train ticket."

"Use it, then."

"Sure. At train time I'll use it."

"Which train?" he asked me sourly. "You've missed three already."

"I'm waiting for a special train, officer."

"Then please go and wait in the bar, Mr. Cornell."

"Okay. I'm sorry I caused you any trouble, but I've a bit of a personal problem. It isn't illegal."

"Anything that involves taking a perceptive dig at the U.S. Mail is illegal," said the policeman. "Personal or not, it's out. So either you stop digging or else."

I left. There was no sense in arguing with the cop. I'd just end up short. So I went to the bar and I found out why he'd recommended it. It was in a faintly-dead area, hazy enough to prevent me from taking a squint at the baggage section. I had a couple of fast ones, but I couldn't stand the suspense of not knowing when my letter might take off without me.

Since I'd also pushed my loitering-luck I gave up. The only thing I could hope for was that the sealed forwarding address had been made out at that little town near the Harrisons and hadn't been moved. So I went and took a train that carried no mail.

It made my life hard. I had to wander around that tank town for hours, keeping a blanket-watch on the post office for either the income or the outgo of my precious hunk of mail. I caught some hard eyes from the local yokels but eventually I discovered that my luck was with me.

A fast train whiffled through the town and they baggage-hooked a mailbag off the car at about a hundred and fifty per. I found out that the next stop of that train was Albany. I'd have been out of luck if I'd hoped to ride with the bag.

Then came another period of haunting that dinky post office (I've mentioned before that it was in a dead area, so I couldn't watch the insides, only the exits) until at long last I perceived my favorite bit of mail emerging in another bag. It was carted to the railroad station and hung up on another pick-up hook. I bought a ticket back to New York and sat on a bench near the hook, probing into the bag as hard as my sense of perception could dig.

I cursed the whole world. The bag was merely labelled "Forwarding Mail" in letters that could be seen at ninety feet. My own letter, of course, I could read very well, to every dotted 'i' and crossed 't' and the stitching in Catherine's little kerchief. But I could not make out the address printed on the form that was pasted across the front of the letter itself.

As I sat there trying to probe that sealed address, a fast train came along and scooped the bag off the hook.

I caught the next train. I swore and I squirmed and I groaned because that train stopped at every wide spot in the road, paused to take on milk, swap cars, and generally tried to see how long it could take to make a run of some forty miles. This was Fate. Naturally, any train that stopped at my rattle burg would also stop at every other point along the road where some pioneer had stopped to toss a beer bottle off of his covered wagon.

At long last I returned to Pennsylvania Station just in time to perceive my letter being loaded on a conveyor for LaGuardia.

Then the same damned policeman collared me.

"This is it," he said.

"Now see here, officer. I—"

"Will you come quietly, Mr. Cornell? Or shall I put the big arm on you?"

"For what?"

"You've been violating the 'Disclosure' section of the Federal Communications Act, and I know it."

"Now look, officer, I said this was not illegal."

"I'm not an idiot, Cornell!" I noted uncomfortably that he had dropped the formal address. "You have been trailing a specific piece of mail with the express purpose of finding out where it is going. Since its destination is a sealed forwarding address, your attempt to determine this destination is a violation of the act." He eyed me coldly as if to dare me to deny it. "Now," he finished, "Shall I read you chapter and verse?"

He had me cold. The 'Disclosure' Act was an old ruling that any transmission must not be used for the benefit of any handler. When Rhine came along, 'Disclosure' Act was extended to everything.

"Look officer, it's my girl," hoping that would make a difference.

"I know that," he told me flatly. "Which is why I'm not running you in. I'm just telling you to lay off. Your girl went away and left you a sealed forwarding address. Maybe she doesn't want to see you again."

"She's sick," I said.

"Maybe her family thinks you made her sick. Now stop it and go away. And if I ever find you trying to dig the mail again, you'll dig iron bars. Now scat!"

He urged me towards the outside of the station like a sheep-dog hazing his flock. I took a cab to LaGuardia, even though it was not as fast as the subway. I was glad to be out of his presence.

I connected with my letter again at LaGuardia. It was being loaded aboard a DC-16 headed for Chicago, Denver, Los Angeles, Hawaii, and Manila. I didn't know how far it was going so I bought a ticket for the route with my travel card and I got aboard just ahead of the closing door.

My bit of mail was in the compartment below me, and in the hour travel time to Chicago, I found out that Chicago was the destination for the mailbag, although the superscript on the letter was still hazy.

I followed the bag off the plane at Chicago and stopped long enough to cancel the rest of my ticket. There was no use wasting the money for the unused fare from Chicago to Manila. I rode into the city in a combination bus-truck less than six feet from my little point-of-interest. During the ride I managed to dig the superscript.

It forwarded the letter to Ladysmith, Wisconsin, and from there to a rural route that I couldn't understand although I got the number.

Then I went back to Midway Airport and found to my disgust that the Chicago Airport did not have a bar. I dug into this oddity for a moment until I found out that the Chicago Airport was built on Public School Property and that according to law, they couldn't sell anything harder than soda pop within three hundred feet of public school property, no matter who rented it. So I dawdled in the bar across Cicero Avenue until plane time, and took an old propeller-driven Convair to Eau Claire on a daisy-clipping ride that stopped at every wide spot on the course. From Eau Claire the mail bag took off in the antediluvian Convair but I took off by train because the bag was scheduled to be dropped by guided glider into Ladysmith.

At Ladysmith I rented a car, checked the rural routes, and took off about the same time as my significant hunk of mail.

Nine miles from Ladysmith is a flagstop called Bruce, and not far from Bruce there is a body of water slightly larger than a duck pond called Caley Lake.

A backroad, decorated with ornamental metal signs, led me from Bruce, Wisconsin, to Caley Lake, where the road signs showed a missing spoke.

I turned in, feeling like Ferdinand Magellan must have felt when he finally made his passage through the Strait to discover the open sea that lay beyond the New World. I had done a fine job of tailing and I wanted someone to pin a leather medal on me. The side road wound in and out for a few hundred yards, and then I saw Phillip Harrison.

He was poking a long tool into the guts of an automatic pump, built to lift water from a deep well into a water tower about forty feet tall. He did not notice my arrival until I stopped my rented car beside him and said:

"Being a mechanical engineer and an esper, Phil, I can tell you that you have a—"

"A worn gasket seal," he said. "It doesn't take an esper engineer to figure it out. How the heck did you find us?"

"Out in your mailbox there is a letter," I told him. "I came with it."

He eyed me humorously. "How much postage did you cost? Or did you come second class mail?"

I was not sure that I cared for the inference, but Phillip was kidding me by the half-smile on his face. I asked, "Phil, please tell me—what is going on?"

His half-smile faded. He shook his head unhappily as he said, "Why can't you leave well-enough alone?"

My feelings welled up and I blew my scalp. "Let well enough alone?" I roared. "I'm pushed from pillar to post by everybody. You steal my girl. I'm in hokus with the cops, and then you tell me that I'm to stay—"

"Up the proverbial estuary lacking the customary means of locomotion," he finished with a smile.

I couldn't see the humor in it. "Yeah," I drawled humorlessly.

"You realize that you're probably as big a liability with us as you were trying to find us?"

I grunted. "I could always blow my brains out."

"That's no solution and you know it."

"Then give me an alternative."

Phillip shrugged. "Now that you're here, you're here. It's obvious that you know too much, Steve. You should have left well enough alone."

"I didn't know well enough. Besides, I couldn't have been pushed better if someone had slipped me—" I stopped, stunned at the idea and then I went on in a falter, "—a post-hypnotic suggestion."

"Steve, you'd better come in and meet Marian. Maybe that's what happened."

"Marian?" I said hollowly.

"She's a high-grade telepath. Master of psi, no less."

My mind went red as I remembered how I'd catalogued her physical charms on our first meeting in an effort to find out whether she were esper or telepath. Marian had fine control; her mind must have positively seethed at my invasion of her privacy. I didn't want to meet Marian face to face right now but there wasn't a thing I could do.

Phillip left his pump and waved for me to follow. He took off in his jeep and I trailed him to the farmhouse. We went through a dim area that was almost the ideal shape for a home. The ring was not complete, but the open part faced the fields behind the house so that good privacy was ensured for all practical purposes.

On the steps of the verandah stood Marian.

Sight of her was enough to make me forget my self-accusation of a few moments ago. She stood tall and lissome, the picture of slender, robust health.

"Come in, Steve," she said, holding out her hand. I took it. Her grip was firm and hard, but it was gentle. I knew that she could have pulped my hand if she squeezed hard.

"I'm very happy to see that rumor is wrong and that you're not—suffering—from Mekstrom's Disease," I told her.

"So now you know, Steve. Too bad."

"Why?"

"Because it adds a load to all of us. Even you." She looked at me thoughtfully for a moment, then said, "Well, come on in and relax, Steve. We'll talk it out."

We all went inside.

On a divan in the living room, covered by a light blanket, resting in a very light snooze, was a woman. Her face was turned away from me, but the hair and the line of the figure and the—

#Catherine!#

She turned and sat up at once, alive and shocked awake. She rubbed the sleep from her eyes with swift knuckles and then looked over her hands at me.

"Steve!" she cried, and all the world and the soul of her was in the throb of her voice.

CHAPTER TWELVE

Catherine took one unsteady step towards me and then came forward with a rush. She hurled herself into my arms, pressed herself against me, held me tight.

It was like being attacked by a bulldozer.

Phillip stayed my back against her headlong rush or I would have been thrown back out through the door, across the verandah, and into the middle of the yard. The strength of her crushed my chest and wrenched my spine. Her lips crushed mine. I began to black out from the physical hunger of a woman who did not know the extent of her new-found body. All that Catherine remembered was that once she held me to the end of her strength and yearned for more. To hold me that way now meant—death.

Her body was the same slenderness, but the warm softness was gone. It was a flesh-warm waist of flexible steel. I was being held by a statue of bronze, animated by some monster servo-mechanism. This was no woman.

Phillip and Marian pried her away from me before she broke my back. Phillip led her away, whispering softly in her ear. Marian carried me to the divan and let me down on my face gently. Her hands were gentle as she pressed the air back into my lungs and soothed away the awful wrench in my spine. Gradually I came alive again, but there was pain left that made me gasp at every breath.

Then the physical hurt went away, leaving only the mental pain; the horror of knowing that the girl that I loved could never hold me in her arms. I shuddered. All that I wanted out of this life was marriage with Catherine, and now that I had found her again, I had to face the fact that the first embrace would kill me.

I cursed my fate just as any invalid has cursed the malady that makes him a responsibility and a burden to his partner instead of a joy and helpmeet. Like the helpless, I didn't want it; I hadn't asked for it; nor had I earned it. Yet all I could do was to rail against the unfairness of the unwarranted punishment.

Without knowing that I was asking, I cried out, "But why?" in a plaintive voice.

In a gentle tone, Marian replied: "Steve, you cannot blame yourself. Catherine was lost to you before you met her at her apartment that evening. What she thought to be a callous on her small toe was really the initial infection of Mekstrom's Disease. We're all psi-sensitive to Mekstrom's Disease, Steve. So when you cracked up and Dad and Phil went on the dead run to help, they caught a perception of it. Naturally we had to help her."

I must have looked bitter.

"Look, Steve," said Phillip slowly. "You wouldn't have wanted us not to help? After all, would you want Catherine to stay with you? So that you could watch her die at the rate of a sixty-fourth of an inch each hour?"

"Hell," I snarled, "Someone might have let me know."

Phillip shook his head. "We couldn't Steve. You've got to understand our viewpoint."

"To heck with your viewpoint!" I roared angrily. "Has anybody ever stopped to consider mine?" I did not give a hoot that they could wind me around a doorknob and tuck my feet in the keyhole. Sure, I was grateful for their aid to Catherine. But why didn't someone stop to think of the poor benighted case who was in the accident ward? The bird that had been traipsing all over hell's footstool trying to get a line on his lost sweetheart. I'd been through the grinder; questioned by the F.B.I., suspected by the police; and I'd been the guy who'd been asked by a grieving, elderly couple, "But can't you remember, son?" Them and their stinking point of view!

"Easy, Steve," warned Phillip Harrison.

"Easy nothing! What possible justification have you for putting me through my jumps?"

"Look, Steve. We're in a precarious position. We're fighting a battle against an unscrupulous enemy, an undercover battle, Steve. If we could get something on Phelps, we'd expose him and his Medical Center like that. Conversely, if we slip a millimeter, Phelps will clip us so hard that the sky will ring. He—damn him—has the Government on his side. We can't afford to look suspicious."

"Couldn't you have taken me in too?"

He shook his head sadly. "No," he said. "There was a bad accident, you know. The authorities have every right to insist that each and every automobile on the highway be occupied by a minimum of one driver. They also believe that for every accident there must be a victim, even though the damage is no more than a bad case of fright."

I could hardly argue with that. Changing the subject, I asked, "but what about the others who just drop out of sight?"

"We see to it that plausible letters of explanation are written."

"So who wrote me?" I demanded hotly.

He looked at me pointedly. "If we'd known about Catherine before, she'd have—disappeared—leaving you a trite letter. But no one could think of a letter to explain her disappearance from an accident, Steve."

"Oh fine."

"Well, you'd still prefer to find her alive, wouldn't you?"

"Couldn't someone tell me?"

"And have you radiating the fact like a broadcasting station?"

"Why couldn't I have joined her—you—?"

He shook his head in the same way that a man shakes it when he is trying to explain *why* two plus two are four and not maybe five or three and a half. "Steve," he said, "You haven't got Mekstroms' Disease."

"How do I get it?" I demanded hotly.

"Nobody knows," he said unhappily. "If we did, we'd be providing the rest of the human race with indestructible bodies as fast as we could spread it and take care of them."

"But couldn't I have been told *something*?" I pleaded. I must have sounded like a hurt kitten.

Marian put her hand on my arm. "Steve," she said, "You'd have been smoothed over, maybe brought in to work for us in some dead area. But then you turned up acting dangerously for all of us."

"Who—me?"

"By the time you came for your visit, you were dangerous to us."

"What do you mean?"

"Let me find out. Relax, will you Steve? I'd like to read you deep. Catherine, you come in with me."

"What are we looking for?"

"Traces of post-hypnotic suggestion. It'll be hard to find because there will be only traces of a plan, all put in so that it looks like natural, logical reasoning."

Catherine doubtfully said, "When would they have the chance?" .

"Thorndyke. In the hospital."

Catherine nodded and I relaxed. At the beginning I was very reluctant. I didn't mind Catherine digging into the dark and dusty corners of my mind, but Marian Harrison bothered me.

"Think of the accident, Steve," she said.

Then I managed to lull my reluctant mind by remembering that she was trying to help me. I relaxed mentally and physically and regressed back to the day of the accident. I found it hard even then to go through the love-play and sweet seriousness that went on between Catherine and me, knowing that Marian Harrison was a sort of mental spectator. But I fought down my reticence and went on with it.

I practically re-lived the accident. It was easier now that I'd found Catherine again. It was like a cleansing bath. I began to enjoy it. So I went on with my life and adventures right up to the present. Having come to the end, I stopped.

Marian looked at Catherine. "Did you get it?"

Silence. More silence. Then, "It seems dim. Almost incredulous—that it could be—" with a trail-off into thought again.

Phillip snorted. "Make with the chin-music, you two. The rest of us aren't telepaths, you know."

"Sorry," said Marian. "It's complicated and hard to figure, you know. What seems to be the case is sort of like this," she went on in an uncertain tone, "We can't find any direct evidence of anything like hypnotic suggestion. The urge to follow what you call the Highways in Hiding is rather high for mere curiosity, but nothing definite. I think you were probably urged very gently. Catherine objects, saying that it would take a top psycho-telepath to do a job delicate enough to produce the urge without showing the traces of the operation."

"Someone of scholar grade in both psychology and telepathy," said Catherine.

I thought it over. "It seems that whoever did it—if it was done—was well aware that a good part of this urge would be generated by Catherine's total and unexplicable disappearance. You'd have saved yourselves a lot of trouble—and saved me a lot of heartache if you'd let me know something. God! Haven't you any feelings?"

Catherine looked at me from hurt eyes. "Steve," she said quietly, "A billion girls have sworn that they'd rather die than live without their one and only. I swore it too. But when your life's end is shown to you on a microscope slide, love becomes less important. What should I do? Just die? Painfully?"

That was handing it to me on a platter. It hurt but I am not chuckleheaded enough to insist that she come with me to die instead of leaving me and living. What really hurt was not knowing.

"Steve," said Marian. "You know that we couldn't have told you the truth."

"Yeah," I agreed disconsolately.

"Let's suppose that Catherine wrote you a letter telling you that she was alive and safe, but that she'd reconsidered the marriage. You were to forget her and all that. What happens next?"

Unhappily I told him. "I'd not have believed it."

Phillip nodded. "Next would have been a telepath-esper team. Maybe a perceptive with a temporal sense who could retrace that letter back to the point of origin, teamed up with a telepath strong enough to drill a hole through the dead area that surrounds New Washington. Why, even before Rhine Institute, it was sheer folly for a runaway to write a letter. What would it be now?"

I nodded. What he said was true, but it did not ease the hurt.

"Then on the other hand," he went on in a more cheerful vein, "Let's take another look at us and you, Steve. Tell me, fellow, where are you now?"

I looked up at him. Phillip was smiling in a knowing-superior sort of manner. I looked at Marian. She was half-smiling. Catherine looked satisfied. I got it.

"Yeah. I'm here."

"You're here without having any letters, without leaving any broad trail of suspicion upon yourself. You've not disappeared, Steve. You've been a-running up and down the country all on your own decision. Where you go and what you do is your own business and nobody is going to set up a hue and cry after you. Sure, it took a lot longer this way. But it was a lot safer." He grinned wide then as he went on, "And if you'd like to take some comfort out of it, just remember that you've shown yourself to be quite capable, filled with dogged determination, and ultimately successful."

He was right. In fact, if I'd tried the letter-following stunt long earlier, I'd have been here a lot sooner.

"All right," I said. "So what do we do now?"

"We go on and on and on, Steve, until we're successful."

"Successful?"

He nodded soberly. "Until we can make every man, woman, and child on the face of this Earth as much physical superman as we are, our job is not finished."

I nodded. "I learned a few of the answers at the Macklin Place."

"Then this does not come as a complete shock."

"No. Not a complete shock. But there are a lot of loose ends still. So the basic theme I'll buy. Scholar Phelps and his Medical Center are busy using their public position to create the nucleus of a totalitarian state, or a physical hierarchy. You and the Highways in Hiding are busy tearing Phelps down because you don't want to see any more rule by the Divine Right of Kings, Dictators, or Family Lines."

"Go on, Steve."

"Well, why in the devil don't you announce yourselves?"

"No good, old man. Look, you yourself want to be a Mekstrom. Even with your grasp of the situation, you resent the fact that you cannot."

"You're right."

Phillip nodded slowly. "Let's hypothesize for a moment, taking a subject that has nothing to do with Mekstrom's Disease. Let's take one of the old standby science-fiction plots. Some cataclysm is threatening the solar system. The future of the Earth is threatened, and we have only one spacecraft capable of carrying a hundred people to safety—somewhere else. How would you select them?"

I shrugged. "Since we're hypothecating, I suppose that I'd select the more healthy, the more intelligent, the more virile, the more—" I struggled for another category and then let it stand right there because I couldn't think of another at that instant.

Phillip agreed. "Health and intelligence and all the rest being pretty much a matter of birth and upbringing, how can you explain to Wilbur Zilch that Oscar Hossenpfeiffer has shown himself smarter and healthier and therefore better stock for survival? Maybe you can, but the end-result is that Wilbur Zilch slaughters Oscar Hossenpfeiffer. This either provides an opening for Zilch, or if he is caught at it, it provides Zilch with the satisfaction of knowing that he's stopped the other guy from getting what he could not come by honestly."

"So what has this to do with Mekstrom's Disease and supermen?"

"The day that we—and I mean either of us—announces that we can 'cure' Mekstrom's Disease and make physical supermen of the former victims, there will be a large scream from everybody to give them the same treatment. No, we'll tell them, we can't cure anybody who hasn't caught it. Then some pedagogue will stand up and declare that we are suppressing information. This will be believed by enough people to do us more harm than good. Darn it, we're not absolutely indestructible, Steve. We can be killed. We could be wiped out by a mob of angry citizens who saw in us a threat to their security. Neither we of the Highways nor Phelps of The Medical Center have enough manpower to be safe."

"So that I'll accept. The next awkward question comes up: What are we going to do with me?"

"You've agreed that we cannot move until we know how to inoculate healthy flesh. We need normal humans, to be our guinea pigs. Will you help bring to the Earth's People the blessing that is now denied them?"

"If you are successful, Steve," said Marian, "You'll go down in History along with Otto Mekstrom. You could be the turning point of the human race, you know."

"And if I fail?"

Phillip Harrison's face took on a hard and determined look. "Steve, there can be no failure. We shall go on and on until we have success."

That was a fine prospect. Old guinea-pig Cornell, celebrating his seventieth birthday as the medical experimentation went on and on.

Catherine was leaning forward, her eyes bright. "Steve," she cried, "You've just *got* to!"

"Just call me the unwilling hero," I said in a drab voice. "And put it down that the condemned specimen drank a hearty dinner. I trust that there is a drink in the house."

There was enough whiskey in the place to provide the new specimen with a near-total anesthesia. The evening was spent in forced badinage, shallow laughter, and a pointed avoidance of the main subject. The whiskey was good; I took it undiluted and succeeded in getting blasted before they carted me off to bed.

I did not sleep well despite my anesthesia. There was too much on my mind and very little of it was the fault of the Harrisons. One of the things that I had to face was the cold fact that part of Catherine's lack of communication with me was caused by logic and good sense. Both History and Fiction are filled with cases where love was set aside because consummation was impossible for any number of good reasons.

So I slept fitfully, and my dreams were as unhappy as the thoughts I had during my waking moments. Somehow I realized that I'd have been far better off if I'd been able to forget Catherine after the accident, if I'd been able to resist the urge to follow the Highways in Hiding, if I'd never known that those ornamental road signs were something more than the desire of some road commissioner to beautify the countryside. But no, I had to go and poke my big bump of curiosity into the problem. So here I was, resentful as all hell because I was denied the pleasure of living in the strong body of a Mekstrom.

It was not fair. Although Life itself is seldom fair, it seemed to me that Life was less fair to me than to others.

And then to compound my feelings of persecution, I woke up once about three in the morning with a strong urge to take a perceptive dig down below. I should have resisted it, but of course, no one has ever been able to resist the urge of his sense of perception.

Down in the living room, Catherine was crying on Phillip Harrison's shoulder. He held her gently with one arm around her slender waist and he was stroking her hair softly with his other hand. I couldn't begin to dig what was being said, but the tableau was unmistakable.

She leaned back and looked at him as he said something. Her head moved in a 'No' motion as she took a deep breath for another bawl. She buried her face in his neck and sobbed. Phillip held her close for a moment and then loosed one hand to find a handkerchief for her. He wiped her eyes gently and talked to her until she shook her head in a visible effort to shake away both the tears and the unhappy thoughts.

Eventually he lit two cigarettes and handed one to her. Side by side they walked to the divan and sat down close together. Catherine leaned against him gently and he put his arm over her shoulders and hugged her to him. She relaxed, looking unhappy, but obviously taking comfort in the strength and physical presence of him.

It was a hell of a thing to dig in my mental condition. I drifted off to a sleep filled with unhappy dreams while they were still downstairs. Frankly, I forced myself into fitful sleep because I did not want to stay awake to follow them.

As bad as the nightmare quality of my dreams were, they were better for me than the probable reality.

Oh, I'd been infernally brilliant when I uncovered the first secret of the Highways in Hiding. I found out that I did not know one-tenth of the truth. They had a network of Highways that would make the

Department of Roads and Highways look like a backwood, second-rate, political organization.

I'd believed, for instance, that the Highways were spotted only along main arteries to and from their Way Stations. The truth was that they had a complete system from one end of the country to the other. Lanes led from Maine and from Florida into a central main Highway that laid across the breadth of the United States. Then from Washington and from Southern California another branching network met this main Highway. Lesser lines served Canada and Mexico. The big Main Trunk ran from New York to San Francisco with only one large major division: A heavy line that led down to a place in Texas called *Homestead*. Homestead, Texas, was a big center that made Scholar Phelps' Medical Center look like a Teeny Weeny Village by comparison.

We drove in Marian's car. My rented car was returned to the agency and my own bus would be ferried out as soon as it could be arranged so that I'd not be without personal transportation in Texas. Catherine stayed in Wisconsin because she was too new at being a Mekstrom to know how to conduct herself so that the fact of her super-powerful body did not cause a lot of slack jaws and suspicion.

We drove along the Highways to Homestead, carrying a bag of the Mekstrom Mail.

The trip was uneventful.

CHAPTER THIRTEEN

Since this account of my life and adventures is not being written without some plan, it is no mere coincidence that this particular section comes under Chapter Thirteen. Old Unlucky Thirteen covers ninety days which I consider the most dismal ninety days of my life. Things, which had been going along smoothly had, suddenly got worse.

We started with enthusiasm. They cut and they dug and they poked needles into me and trimmed out bits of my hide for slides. I helped them by digging my own flesh and letting their better telepaths read my results for their records.

They were nice to me. I got the best of everything. But being nice to me was not enough; it sort of made me feel like Gulliver in Brobdingnag. They were so over-strong that they did not know their own strength. This was especially true of the youngsters of Mekstrom parents. I tried to re-diaper a baby one night and got my ring finger gummed for my efforts. It was like wrestling Bad Cyril in a one-fall match, winner take all.

As the days added up into weeks, their hope and enthusiasm began to fade. The long list of proposed experiments dwindled and it became obvious that they were starting to work on brand new ideas. But brand new ideas are neither fast in arriving nor high in quantity, and time began to hang dismally heavy.

They began to avoid my eyes. They stopped discussing their attempts on me; I no longer found out what they were doing and how they hoped to accomplish the act. They showed the helplessness that comes of failure, and this feeling of utter futility was transmitted to me.

At first I was mentally frantic at the idea of failure, but as the futile days wore on and the fact was practically shoved down my throat, I was forced to admit that there was no future for Steve Cornell.

I began at that time to look forward to my visit to reorientation.

Reorientation is a form of mental suicide. Once reoriented, the problems that make life intolerable are forgotten, your personality is changed, your grasp of everything is revised, your appreciation of all things comes from an entirely new angle. You are a new person.

Then one morning I faced my image in the mirror and came to the conclusion that if I couldn't be Me, I didn't want to be Somebody Else. It is no good to be alive if I am not me, I told my image, who obediently agreed with me.

I didn't even wait to argue with Me. I just went out and got into my car and sloped. It was not hard; everybody in Homestead trusted me.

CHAPTER FOURTEEN

I left homestead with a half-formed idea that I was going to visit Bruce, Wisconsin, long enough to say goodbye to Catherine and to release her from any matrimonial involvement she may have felt binding. I did not relish this idea, but I felt that getting it out, done, and agreed was only a duty.

But as I hit the road and had time to think, I knew that my half-formed intention was a sort of martyrdom; I was going to renounce myself in a fine welter of tears and then go staggering off into the setting sun to die of my mental wounds. I took careful stock of myself and faced the fact that my half-baked idea was a sort of suicide-wish; walking into any Mekstrom way station now was just asking for capture and a fast trip to their reorientation rooms. The facts of my failure and my taking-of-leave would be indication enough for Catherine that I was bowing out. It would be better for Catherine, too, to avoid a fine, high-strung, emotional scene. I remembered the little bawling session in the Harrison living room that night; Catherine would not die for want of a sympathetic hand on her shoulder. In fact, as she'd said pragmatically, well balanced people never die of broken hearts.

Having finally convinced myself of the validity of this piece of obvious logic, I suddenly felt a lot better. My morose feeling faded away; my conviction of utter uselessness died; and my half-formed desire to investigate a highly hypothetical Hereafter took an abrupt about-face. And in place of this collection of undesirable self-pities came a much nicer emotion. It was a fine feeling, that royal anger that boiled up inside of me. I couldn't lick 'em and I couldn't join 'em, so I was going out to pull something down, even if it all came down around my own ears.

I stopped long enough to check the Bonanza .375 both visually and perceptively and then loaded it full. I consulted a road map to chart a course. Then I took off with the coal wide open and the damper rods all the way out and made the wheels roll towards the East.

I especially gave all the Highways a very wide berth. I went down several, but always in the wrong direction. And in the meantime, I kept my sense of perception on the alert for any pursuit. I drove with my eyes alone. I could have made it across the Mississippi by nightfall if I'd not taken the time to duck Highway signs. But when I got good, and sick, and tired of driving, I was not very far from the River. I found a motel in a rather untravelled spot and sacked in for the night.

I awoke at the crack of dawn with a feeling of impending *something*. It was not doom, because any close-danger would have nudged me on the bump of perception. Nor was it good, because I'd have awakened looking forward to it. Something odd was up and doing. I dressed hastily, and as I pulled my clothing on I took a slow dig at the other cabins in the motel.

Number One contained a salesman type, I decided, after digging through his baggage. Number Two was occupied by an elderly couple who were loaded with tourist-type junk and four or five cameras. Number Three harbored a stopover truck driver and Number Four was almost overflowing with a gang of schoolgirls packed sardine-wise in the single bed. Number Five was mine. Number Six was vacant. Number Seven was also vacant but the bed was tumbled and the water in the washbowl was still running out, and the door was still slamming, and the little front steps were still clicking to the fast clip of high heels, and——

I hauled myself out of my cabin on a dead gallop and made a fast line for my car. I hit the car, clawed myself inside, wound up the turbine and let the old heap in gear in one unbroken series of motions. The wheels spun and sent back a hail of gravel, then they took a bite out of the parking lot and the take-off snapped my head back.

Both esper and eyesight were very busy cross-stitching a crooked course through the parking lot between the parked cars and the trees that were intended to lend the outfit a rustic atmosphere. So I was too busy to take more than a vague notice of a hand that clamped onto the doorframe until the door opened and closed again. By then I was out on the highway and I could relax a bit.

"Steve," she said, "why do you do these things?"

Yeah, it was Marian Harrison. "I didn't ask to get shoved into this mess," I growled.

"You didn't ask to be born, either," she said.

I didn't think the argument was very logical, and I said so. "Life wasn't too hard to bear until I met you people," I told her sourly. "Life would be very pleasant if you'd go away. On the other hand, life is all I've got and it's far better than the alternative. So if I'm making your life miserable, that goes double for me."

"Why not give it up?" she asked me.

I stopped the car. I eyed her dead center, eye to eye until she couldn't take it any more. "What would you like me to just give up, Marian? Shall I please everybody by taking a bite of my hip-pocket artillery sights whilst testing the trigger pull with one forefinger? Will it make anybody happy if I walk into the nearest reorientation museum blowing smoke out of my nose and claiming that I am a teakettle that's gotta be taken off the stove before I blow my lid?"

Marian's eyes dropped.

"Do you yourself really expect me to seek blessed oblivion?"

She shook her head slowly.

"Then for the love of God, what do you expect of me?" I roared. "As I am, I'm neither flesh nor fish; just foul. I'm not likely to give up, Marian. If I'm a menace to you and to your kind, it's just too tough. But if you want me out of your hair, you'll have to wrap me up in something suitable for framing and haul me kicking and screaming to your mind-refurbishing department. Because I'm not having any on my own. Understand?"

"I understand, Steve," she said softly. "I know you; we all know you and your type. You can't give up. You're unable to."

"Not when I've been hypnoed into it," I said.

Marian's head tossed disdainfully. "Thorndyke's hypnotic suggestion was very weak," she explained. "He had to plant the idea in such a way as to remain unidentified afterwards. No, Steve, your urge has always been your own personal drive. All that Thorndyke did was to point you slightly in our direction and give you a nudge. You did the rest."

"Well, you're a telepath. Maybe you're also capable of planting a post-hypnotic suggestion that I forget the whole idea."

"I'm not," she said with a sudden flare.

I looked at her. Not being a telepath I couldn't read a single thought, but it was certain that she was telling the truth, and telling it in such a manner as to be convincing. Finally I said, "Marian, if you know that I'm not to be changed by logic or argument, why do you bother?"

For a full minute she was silent, then her eyes came up and gave it back to me with their electric blue. "For the same reason that Scholar Phelps hoped to use you against us," she said. "Your fate and your future is tied up with ours whether you turn out to be friend or enemy."

I grunted. "Sounds like a soap opera, Marian," I told her bitterly. "Will Catherine find solace in Phillip's arms? Will Steve catch Mekstrom's Disease? Will the dastardly Scholar Phelps—"

"Stop it!" she cried.

"All right. I'll stop as soon as you tell me what you intend to do with me now that you've caught up with me again."

She smiled. "Steve, I'm going along with you. Partly to play the telepath-half of your team. If you'll trust me to deliver the truth. And partly to see that you don't get into trouble that you can't get out of again."

My mind curled its lip. Pappy had tanned my landing gear until I was out of the habit of using mother for protection against the slings and arrows of outrageous schoolchums. I'd not taken sanctuary behind a woman's skirts since I was eight. So the idea of running under the protection of a woman went against the grain, even though I knew that she was my physical superior by no sensible proportion. Being cared for physically by a dame of a hundred-ten—

"Eighteen."

—didn't sit well on me.

"Do you believe me, Steve?"

"I've got to. You're here to stay. I'm a sucker for a good-looking woman anyway, it seems. They tell me anything and I'm not hardhearted enough to even indicate that I don't believe them."

She took my arm impulsively; then she let me go before she pinched it off at the elbow. "Steve," she said earnestly, "Believe me and let me be your—"

#Better half?# I finished sourly.

"Please don't," she said plaintively. "Steve, you've simply *got* to trust *somebody*!"

I looked into her face coldly. "The hardest job in the world for a non-telepath is to locate someone he can trust. The next hardest is to explain that to a telepath; because telepaths can't see any difficulty in weeding out the non-trustworthy. Now—"

"You still haven't faced the facts."

"Neither have you, Marian. You intend to go along with me, ostensibly to help me in whatever I intend to do. That's fine. I'll accept it. But you know good and well that I intend to carry on and on until something cracks. Now, tell me honestly, are you going along to help me crack something wide open, or just to steer me into channels that will not result in a crack-up for your side?"

Marian Harrison looked down for a moment; I didn't need telepathy to know that I'd touched the sore spot. Then she looked up and said, "Steve, more than anything, I intend to keep you out of trouble. You should know by now that there is very little you can really do to harm either side of our own private little war."

#And if I can't harm either side, I can hardly do either side any good.#

She nodded.

#Yet I must be of some importance.#

She nodded again. At that point I almost gave up. I'd been around this circle so many times in the past half-year that I knew how the back of my head looked. Always, the same old question.

#*Cherchez le angle,*# I thought in bum French. Something I had was important enough to both sides to make them keep me on the loose instead of erasing me and my nuisance value. So far as I could see, I was as useless to either side as a coat of protective paint laid on stainless steel. I was immune to Mekstrom's Disease; the immunity of one who has had everything tried on him that scholars of the disease could devise. About the only thing that ever took place was the sudden disappearance of everybody that I came in contact with.

Marian touched my arm gently. "You mustn't think like that, Steve," she said gently. "You've done enough useless self-condemnation. Can't you stop accusing yourself of some evil factor? Something that really is not so?"

"Not until I know the truth," I replied. "I certainly can't dig it; I'm no telepath. Perhaps if I were, I'd not be in this awkward position."

Again her silence proved to me that I'd hit a touchy spot. "What am I?" I demanded sourly. "Am I a great big curse? What have I done, other than to be present just before several people turn up missing? Makes me sort of a male Typhoid Mary, doesn't it?"

"Now, Steve—"

"Well, maybe that's the way I feel. Everything I put my great big clutching hands on turns dark green and starts to rot. Regardless of which side they're on, it goes one, two, three, four; Catherine, Thorndyke, You, Nurse Farrow."

"Steve, what on Earth are you talking about?"

I smiled down at her in a crooked sort of quirk. "You, of course, have not the faintest idea of what I'm thinking."

"Oh, Steve—"

"And then again maybe you're doing your best to lead my puzzled little mind away from what you consider a dangerous subject?"

"I'd hardly do that—"

"Sure you would. I'd do it if our positions were reversed. I don't think it un-admirable to defend one's own personal stand, Marian. But you'll not divert me this time. I have a hunch that I am a sort of male Typhoid Mary. Let's call me old Mekstrom Steve. The carrier of

Mekstrom's Disease, who can innocently or maliciously go around handing it out to anybody that I contact. Is that it, Marian?"

"It's probably excellent logic, Steve. But it isn't true."

I eyed her coldly. "How can I possibly believe you?"

"That's the trouble," she said with a plaintive cry. "You can't. You've got to believe me on faith, Steve."

I smiled crookedly. "Marian," I said, "That's just the right angle to take. Since I cannot read your mind, I must accept the old appeal to the emotions. I must tell myself that Marian Harrison just simply could not lie to me for many reasons, among which is that people do not lie to blind men nor cause the cripple any hurt. Well, phooey. Whatever kind of gambit is being played here, it is bigger than any of its parts or pieces. I'm something between a queen and a pawn, Marian; a piece that can be sacrificed at any time to further the progress of the game. Slipping me a lie or two to cause me to move in some desired direction should come as a natural."

"But why would we lie to you?" she asked, and then she bit her lip; I think that she slipped, that she hadn't intended to urge me into deeper consideration of the problem lest I succeed in making a sharp analysis. After all, the way to keep people from figuring things out is to stop them from thinking about the subject. That's the first rule. Next comes the process of feeding them false information if the First Law cannot be invoked.

"Why would you lie to me?" I replied in a sort of sneer. I didn't really want to sneer but it came naturally. "In an earlier age it might not be necessary."

"What?" she asked in surprise.

"Might not be necessary," I said. "Let's assume that we are living in the mid-Fifties, before Rhine. Steve Cornell turns up being a carrier of a disease that is really a blessing instead of a curse. In such a time, Marian, either side could sign me up openly as a sort of missionary; I could go around the country inoculating the right people, those citizens who have the right kind of mind, attitude, or whatever-factor. Following me could be a clean-up corps to collect the wights who'd been inoculated by my contact. Sounds reasonable, doesn't it?" Without waiting for either protest or that downcast look of agreement, I went on: "But now we have perception and telepathy all over the place. So Steve Cornell, the carrier, must be pushed around from pillar to post, meeting people and inoculating them without ever knowing what he is doing. Because once he knows what he is doing, his usefulness is ended in this world of Rhine Institute."

"Steve—" she started, but I interrupted again.

"About all I have to do now is to walk down any main street radiating my suspicions," I said bitterly. "And it's off to Medical Center for Steve—unless the Highways catch me first."

Very quietly, Marian said, "We really dislike to use reorientation on people. It changes them so—"

"But that's what I'm headed for, isn't it?" I demanded flatly.

"I'm sorry, Steve."

Angrily I went on, not caring that I'd finally caught on and by doing so had sealed my own package. "So after I have my mind ironed out smoothly, I'll still go on and on from pillar to post providing newly inoculated Mekstroms for your follow-up squad."

She looked up at me and there were tears in her eyes. "We were all hoping—" she started.

"Were you?" I asked roughly. "Were you all working to innoculate me at Homestead, or were you really studying me to find out what made me a carrier instead of a victim?"

"Both, Steve," she said, and there was a ring of honesty in her tone. I had to believe her, it made sense.

"Dismal prospect, isn't it?" I asked. "For a guy that's done nothing wrong."

"We're all sorry."

"Look," I said with a sudden thought, "Why can't I still go on? I could start a way station of some sort, on some pretext, and go on innoculating the public as they come past. Then I could go on working for you and still keep my right mind."

She shook her head. "Scholar Phelps knows," she said. "Above all things we must keep you out of his hands. He'd use you for his own purpose."

I grunted sourly. "He has already and he will again," I told her. "Not only that, but Phelps has had plenty of chance to collect me on or off the hook. So what you fear does not make sense."

"It does now," she told me seriously. "So long as you did not suspect your own part in the picture, you could do more good for Phelps by running free. Now you know and Phelps' careful herding of your motions won't work."

"Don't get it."

"Watch," she said with a shrug. "They'll try. I don't dare experiment, Steve, or I'd leave you right now. You'd find out very shortly that you're with me because I got here first."

"And knowing the score makes me also dangerous to your Highways? Likely to bring 'em out of Hiding?"

"Yes."

"So now that I've dumped over the old apple cart, I can assume that you're here to take me in."

"What else can I do, Steve?" she said unhappily.

I couldn't answer. I sat there looking at her, trying to remember that her shapely one hundred and eighteen pounds were steel hard and monster strong and that she could probably carry me under one arm all the way to Homestead without breathing hard. I couldn't cut and run; she could outrun me. I couldn't slug her on the jaw and get away; I'd break my hand. The Bonanza .375 would probably stun her, but I have not the cold blooded viciousness to pull a gun on a woman and drill her. I grunted sourly, that weapon had been about as useful to me as a stuffed bear or an authentic Egyptian Obelisk.

"Well, I'm not going," I said stubbornly.

She looked at me in surprise. "What are you going to do?" she asked me.

I felt a glow of self-confidence. If I could not run loose with guilty knowledge of my being a Mekstrom Carrier, it was equally impossible for anybody to kidnap me and carry me across the country. I'd radiate like mad; I'd complain about the situation at every crossroad, at every filling station, before every farmer. I'd complain mentally and bitterly, and sooner or later someone would get suspicious.

"Don't think like an idiot," she told me sharply. "You drove across the country before, remember? How many people did you convince?"

"I wasn't trying, then—"

"How about the people in the hotel in Denver?" she asked me pointedly. "What good did you do there?"

#Very little, but—#

"One of the advantages of a telepath is that we can't be taken by surprise," she informed me. "Because no one can possibly work without plans of some kind."

"One of the troubles of a telepath," I told her right back, "is that they get so confounded used to knowing what is going to happen next that it takes all the pleasant element of surprise out of their lives. That makes 'em dull and—"

The element of surprise came in through the back window, passed between us and went *Splat!* against the wind-shield. There was the sound like someone chipping ice with a spike followed by the distant bark of a rifle. A second slug came through the back window about the time that the first one landed on the floor of the car. The second slug, not slowed by the shatter-proof glass in the rear, went through the shatter-proof glass in the front. A third slug passed through the same tunnel.

These were warning shots. He'd missed us intentionally. He'd proved it by firing three times through the same hole, from beyond my esper range.

I wound up the machinery and we took off. Marian cried something about not being foolish, but her words were swept out through the hole in the rear window, just above the marks on the pavement caused by my tires as we spun the wheels.

CHAPTER FIFTEEN

"Steve, stop it!" cried Marian as soon as she could get her breath.

"Nuts," I growled. I took a long curve on the outside wheels and ironed out again. "He isn't after our corpse, honey. He's after our hide. I don't care for any."

The fourth shot went singing off the pavement to one side. It whined into the distance making that noise that sets the teeth on edge and makes one want to duck. I lowered the boom on the go pedal and tried to make the meter read off the far end of the scale; I had a notion that the guy behind might shoot the tires out if we were going slow enough so that a blowout wouldn't cause a bad wreck; but he probably wouldn't do it once I got the speed up. He was not after Marian. Marian could walk out of any crack-up without a bruise, but I couldn't.

We went roaring around a curve. I fought the wheel into a nasty double 's' curve to swing out and around a truck, then back on my own side of the road again to avoid an oncoming car. I could almost count the front teeth of the guy driving the car as we straightened out with a coat of varnish to spare. I scared everybody in all three vehicles, including me.

Then I passed a couple of guys standing beside the road; one of them waved me on, the other stood there peering past me down the road. As we roared by, another group on the other side of the highway came running out hauling a big old hay wagon. They set the wagon across the road and then sloped into the ditch on either side of it.

I managed to dig the bare glimmer of firearms before I had to yank my perception away from them and slam it back on the road in front. I was none too soon, because dead ahead by a thousand feet or so, they were hauling a second road block out.

Marian, not possessed of esper, cried out as soon as she read this new menace in my mind. I rode the brakes easily and came to a stop long before we hit it. In back sounded a crackle of rifle fire; in front, three men came out waving their rifles at us.

I whipped the car back, spun it in a seesaw, and took off back towards the first road block. Half way back I whirled my car into a rough sideroad just as the left hand rear tire went out with a roar. The car sagged and dragged me to a stop with my nose in a little ditch. The heap hadn't stopped rocking yet before I was out and on the run.

"Steve!" cried Marian. "Come back!"

#To heck with it.# I kept right on running. Before me by a couple of hundred yards was a thicket of trees; I headed that way fast. I managed to sling a dig back; Marian was joining the others; pointing in my direction. One of them raised the rifle but she knocked it down.

I went on running. It looked as though I'd be all right so long as I didn't get in the way of an accidental shot. My life was once more charmed with the fact that no one wanted me dead.

The thicket of woods was not as thick as I'd have liked. From a distance they'd seemed almost impenetrable, but when I was running through them towards the center, they looked pitifully thin. I could see light from any direction and the floor of the woods was trimmed, the underbrush cleaned out, and a lot of it was tramped down.

Ahead of me I perceived a few of them coming towards the woods warily, behind me there was another gang closing in. I began to feel like the caterpillar on the blade of grass in front of the lawn mower.

I tried to hide under a deadfall, knowing that it was poor protection against rifle fire. I hauled out the Bonanza and checked the cylinder. I didn't know which side I was going to shoot at, but that didn't bother me. I was going to shoot at the first side that got close.

A couple of shots whipped by over my head, making noises like someone snapping a bullwhip. I couldn't tell which direction they came from; I was too busy trying to stuff my feet into a gopher hole under my deadfall.

I cast around the thicket with my sense of perception and caught the layout. Both sides were spread out, stalking forward like infantry advancing through disputed ground. Now and then one of them would raise his rifle and fire at some unexpected motion. This, I gathered, was more nervousness than fighting skill because no group of telepaths and/or perceptives would be so jittery on the trigger if they weren't basically nervous. They should, as I did, have the absolute position of both the enemy and their own side.

With a growing nervous sweat I dug their advances. They were avoiding my position, trying to encircle me by making long semicircular marches, hoping to get between me and the other side. This was a rough maneuver, sort of like two telepaths playing chess. Both sides knew to a minute exactly what the other had in mind, where he was, and what he was going to do about his position. But they kept shifting, feinting and counter-advancing, trying to gain the advantage of number or position so that the other would be forced to retreat. It became a war of nerves; a game of seeing who had the most guts; who could walk closer to the muzzle of an enemy rifle without getting hit.

Their rifles were mixed; there were a couple of deer guns, a nice 35-70 Express that fired a slug slightly smaller than a panetella cigar, a few shotguns, a carbine sports rifle that looked like it might have been a Garand with the barrel shortened by a couple of inches, some revolvers, one nasty-looking Colt .45 Automatic, and so on.

I shivered down in my little hideout; as soon as the shooting started in earnest, they were going to clean out this woods but good. It was going to be a fine barrage, with guns going off in all directions, because it is hard to keep your head in a melee. Esper and telepathy go by the board when shooting starts.

I still didn't know which side was which. The gang behind me were friends of Marian Harrison; but that did not endear them to me any more than knowing that the gang in front were from Scholar Phelps Medical Center or some group affiliated with him. In the midst of it, I managed to bet myself a new hat that old Scholar Phelps didn't really know what was going on. He would be cagey enough to stay ignorant of any overt strife or any other skullduggery that could be laid at his door.

Then on one edge of the woodsy section, two guys of equal damfool-factor advanced, came up standing, and faced one another across fifty feet of open woods. Their rifles came up and yelled at one another like a string of firecrackers; they wasted a lot of powder and lead by not taking careful aim. One of them emptied his rifle and started to fade back to reload, the other let him have it in the shoulder. It spun the guy around and dumped him on his spine. His outflung hand slammed his rifle against a tree, which broke it. He gave a painful moan and started to crawl back, his arm hanging limp-like but not broken. From behind me came a roar and a peltering of shotgun pellets through the trees; it was answered by the heavy bark of the 35-70 Express. I'm sure that in the entire artillery present, the only rifle heavy enough to really damage those Mekstroms was that Express, which would stop a charging rhino. When you get down to facts, my Bonanza .375 packed a terrific wallop but it did not have the shocking power of the heavy big-game rifle.

Motion caught my perception to one side; two of them had let go shotgun blasts from single-shot guns. They were standing face to face swinging their guns like a pair of axemen; swing, chop! swing, chop! and with each swing their guns were losing shape, splinters from the butts, and bits of machinery. Their clothing was in ribbons from the shotgun blasts. But neither of them seemed willing to give up. There was not a sign of blood; only a few places on each belly that looked shiny-like. On the other side of me, one guy let go with a rifle that slugged the other bird in the middle. He folded over the shot and his middle went back and down, which whipped his head over, back, and down where it hit the ground with an audible thump. The first guy leaped forward just as the victim of his attack sat up, rubbed his belly ruefully, and drew a hunting knife with his other hand. The first guy took a running dive at the supine one, who swung the hunting knife in a vicious arc. The point hit the chest of the man coming through the air but it stopped as though the man had been wearing plate armor. You could dig the return shock that stunned the knife-wielder's arm when the point turned. All it did was rip the clothing. Then the pair of them were at it in a free-for-all that made the woods ring. This deadly combat did not last long. One of them took aim with a fist and let the other have it. The rifle shot hadn't stopped him but the hard fist of another Mekstrom laid him out colder than a mackerel iced for shipment.

The deadly 35-70 Express roared again, and there started a concentration of troops heading towards the point of origin. I had a hunch that the other side did not like anybody to be playing quite as rough as a big-game gun. Someone might really get hurt.

Now they were all in close and swinging; now and then someone would stand off and gain a few moments of breathing space by letting go with a shotgun or knocking someone off of his feet with a carbine. There was some bloodshed, too; not all these shots bounced. But from what I could perceive, none of them were fatal—just painful. The guy who'd been stopped first with the rifle slug and then the other Mekstrom's fist was still out cold and bleeding lightly from the place in his stomach. A bit horrified, I perceived that the pellet was embedded about a half-inch in. The two birds who'd been hacking at one another with the remains of their shotguns had settled it bare-handed, too. The loser was groaning and trying to gather his wits. The shiny spots on his chest were shotgun pellets stuck in the skin.

It was one heck of a fight.

Mekstroms could play with guns and knives and go around taking swings at one another with hunks of tree or clubbed rifles, or they could stand off and hurl boulders. Such a battlefield was no place for a guy named Steve Cornell.

By now all good sense and fine management was gone. If I'd been spotted, they'd have taken a swing at me, forgetting that I am no Mekstrom. So I decided that it was time for Steve to leave.

I cast about me with my perception; the gang that Marian had joined had advanced until they were almost even with my central position; there were a couple of swinging matches to either side and one in front of me. I wondered about Marian; somehow I still don't like seeing a woman tangled up in a free-for-all. Marian was out of esper range, which was all right with me.

I crawled out of my hideout cautiously, stood up in a low crouch and began to run. A couple of them caught sight of me and put up a howl, but they were too busy with their personal foe to take off after me. One of them was free; I doubled him up and dropped him on his back with a slug from my Bonanza .375. Somehow it did not seem rough or vicious to shoot since there was nothing lethal in it. It was more like a game of cowboy and Indian than deadly earnest warfare.

Then I was out and free of them all, out of the woods and running like a deer. I cursed the car with its blown out tire; the old crate had been a fine bus, nicely broken in and conveniently fast. But it was as useful to me now as a pair of skids.

A couple of them behind me caught on and gave chase. I heard cries for me to stop, which I ignored like any sensible man. Someone cut loose with a roar; the big slug from the Express whipped past and went *Sprang!* off a rock somewhere ahead.

It only added a few more feet per second to my flight. If they were going to play that rough, I didn't care to stay.

I fired an unaimed shot over my shoulder, which did no good at all except for lifting my morale. I hoped that it would slow them a bit, but if it did I couldn't tell. Then I leaped over a ditch and came upon a cluster of cars. I dug at them as I approached and selected one of the faster models that still had its key dangling from the lock.

I was in and away as fast as a scared man can move. They were still yelling and fighting in the woods when I raced out of my range.

The heap I'd jumped was a Clinton Special with rock-like springs and a low slung frame that hugged the ground like a clam. I was intent upon putting as many miles as I could between me and the late engagement in as short a time as possible, and the Clinton seemed especially apt until I remembered that the figure 300 on the dial meant kilometers instead of miles per hour. Then I let her out a bit more and tried for the end of the dial. The Clinton tried with me, and I had to keep my esper carefully aimed at the road ahead because I was definitely overdriving my eyesight and reaction-time.

I was so intent upon making feet that I did not notice the jetcopter that came swooping down over my head until the howl of its vane-jets raised hell with my eardrums. Then I slowed the car and lifted my perception at the same time for a quick dig.

The jetcopter was painted Policeman Blue and it sported a large gold-leaf on its side, and inside the cabin were two hard-faced gentlemen wearing uniforms with brass buttons and that Old Bailey look in their eye. The one on the left was jingling a pair of handcuffs.

They passed over my head at about fifteen feet, swooped on past by a thousand, and dropped a road-block bomb. It flared briefly and let out with a billow of thick red smoke.

I leaned on the brakes hard enough to stand the Clinton up on its nose, because if I shoved my front bumper through that cloud of red smoke it was a signal for them to let me have it. I came to a stop about a foot this side of the bomb, and the jetcopter came down hovering. Its vanes blew the smoke away and the 'copter landed in front of my swiped Clinton Special.

The policeman was both curt and angry. "Driver's ticket, registration, and maybe your pilot's license," he snapped.

Well, that was *it*. I had a driver's ticket all right, *but* it did not permit me to drive a car that I'd selected out of a group willy nilly. The car registration was in the glove box where it was supposed to be, but what it said did not match what the driver's license claimed. No matter what I said, there would be the Devil to pay.

"I'll go quietly, officer," I told him.

"Darn' white of you, pilot," he said cynically. He was scribbling on a book of tickets and it was piling up deep. Speeding, reckless driving, violation of ordinance something-or-other by number. Driving a car without proper registration in the absence of the rightful owner (Check for stolen car records) and so on and on and on until it looked like a life term in the local jug.

"Move over, Cornell," he said curtly. "I'm taking you in."

I moved politely. The only time it pays to be arrogant with the police is long after you've proved them wrong, and then only when you're home telling yourself what you should have said.

I was driven to court; escorted in by the pair of them and seated with one on each side. The sign on the judge's table said: Magistrate Hollister.

Magistrate Hollister was an elderly gentleman with a cast iron jaw and a glance as cold as a bucket of snow. He dealt justice with a sharp-edged shovel and his attitude seemed to be that everybody was either guilty as charged or was contemplating some form of evil to be committed as soon as he was out of the sight of Justice. I sat there squirming while he piled the top on a couple whose only crime was parking overtime; I itched from top to bottom while he slapped one miscreant in gaol for turning left in violation of City Ordinance. His next attempt gave a ten dollar fine for failing to come to a full and grinding halt at the sign of the big red light, despite the fact that the criminal was esper to a fine degree and dug the fact that there was no cross-traffic for a half mile.

Then His Honor licked his chops and called my name.

He speared me with an icicle-eye and asked sarcastically: "Well, Mr. Cornell, with what form of sophistry are you going to explain your recent violations?"

I blinked.

He aimed a cold glance at the bailiff, who arose and read off the charges against me in a deep, hollow intonation.

"Speak up!" he snapped. "Are you guilty or not guilty?"

"Guilty," I admitted.

He beamed a sort of self-righteous evil. It was easy to see that never in his tenure of office had he ever encountered a criminal as hardened and as vicious as I. Nor one who admitted to his turpitude so blandly. I felt it coming, and it made me itch, and I knew that if I tried to scratch His Honor would take the act as a personal affront. I fought down the crazy desire to scratch everything I could reach and it was hard; about the time His Honor added a charge of endangering human life on the highway to the rest of my assorted crimes, the itch had localized into the ring finger of my left hand. That I could scratch by rubbing it against the seam of my trousers.

Then His Honor went on, delivering Lecture Number Seven on Crime, Delinquency, and Grand Larceny. I was going to be an example, he vowed. I was assumed to be esper since no normal— that's the word he used, which indicated that the old bird was a blank and hated everybody who wasn't—human being would be able to drive as though he had eyes mounted a half mile in front of him. Not that my useless life was in danger, or that I was actually not-in-control of my car, but that my actions made for panic among normal—again he used it!—people who were not blessed with either telepathy or perception by a mere accident of birth. The last one proved it; it was not an accident of birth so much as it was proper training, to my way of thinking. Magistrate Hollister hated psi-trained people and was out to make examples of them.

He polished off his lecture by pronouncing sentence: "—and the Law provides punishment by a fine not to exceed one thousand dollars, or a sentence of ninety days in jail—*or both*." He rolled the latter off as though he relished the sound of the words.

I waited impatiently. The itch on my finger increased; I flung a fast dig at it but there was nothing there but Sophomore's Syndrome. Good old nervous association. It was the finger that little Snoodles, the three-month baby supergirl had munched to a faretheewell.

Darned good thing the kid didn't have teeth! But I was old Steve, the immune, the carrier, the—

"Well, Mr. Cornell?"

I blinked. "Yes, your honor?"

"Which will it be? I am granting you the leniency of selecting which penalty you prefer."

I could probably rake up a thousand by selling some stock, personal possessions, and draining my already-weakened bank account. The most valuable of my possessions was parked in a ditch with a blowout and probably a bent frame and even so, I only owned about six monthly payments worth of it.

"Your Honor, I will prefer to pay the fine—if you'll grant me time in which to go and collect—"

He rapped his desk with his gavel. "Mr. Cornell," he boomed angrily. "A thief cannot be trusted. Within a matter of minutes you could remove yourself from the jurisdiction of this court unless a binding penalty is placed against your person. You may go on your search for money, but only after posting bond—to the same amount as your fine!"

Lenient—?

"However, unless you are able to pay, I have no recourse but to exact the prison sentence of ninety days. Bailiff—!"

I gave up. It even felt sort of good to give up, especially when the turn is called by someone too big to be argued with. No matter what, I was going to take ninety days off, during which I could sit and think and plan and wonder and chew my fingernails.

The itch in my finger burned again, deep this time, and not at all easy to satisfy by rubbing it against my trousers. I picked at it with the thumbnail and the nail caught something hard.

I looked down at the itching finger and sent my perception into it with as much concentration as I could.

My thumbnail had lifted a tiny circle no larger than the head of a pin. Blood was oozing from beneath the lifted rim, and I nervously picked off the tiny patch of hard, hard flesh and watched the surface blood well out into a tiny droplet. My perception told me the truth: It was Mekstrom's Disease and not a doubt. The Immune had caught it!

The bailiff tapped me on the shoulder. "Come along, Cornell!"

And I was going to have ninety days to watch that patch grow at the inexorable rate of one sixty-fourth of an inch per hour!

CHAPTER SIXTEEN

The bailiff repeated, "Come along, Cornell." Then he added sourly, "Or I'll have to slip the cuffs on you."

I turned with a helpless shrug. I'd tried to lick 'em and I'd tried to join 'em and I'd failed both. Then, as of this instant when I might have been able to go join 'em, I was headed for the wrong side as soon as I opened my big yap. And if I didn't yelp, I was a dead one anyway. Sooner or later someone in the local jug would latch on to my condition and pack me off to Scholar Phelps' Medical Center.

Once more I was in a situation where all I could do was to play it by ear, wait for a break, and see if I could make something out of it.

But before I could take more than a step or two toward the big door, someone in the back of the courtroom called out:

"Your Honor, I have some vital information in this case."

His Honor looked up across the court with a great amount of irritation showing in his face. His voice rasped, "Indeed?"

I whirled, shocked.

Suavely, Dr. Thorndyke strode down the aisle. He faced the judge and explained who he was and why, then he backed it up with a wallet full of credentials, cards, identification, and so forth. The judge looked the shebang over sourly but finally nodded agreement. Thorndyke smiled self-confidently and then went on, facing me:

"It would be against my duty to permit you to incarcerate this miscreant," he said smoothly. "Because Mr. Cornell has Mekstrom's Disease!"

Everybody faded back and away from me as though he'd announced me to be the carrier of plague. They looked at me with horror and disgust on their faces, a couple of them began to wipe their hands with handkerchiefs; one guy who'd been standing where I'd dropped my little patch of Mekstrom Flesh backed out of that uncharmed circle. Some of the spectators left hurriedly.

His Honor paled. "You're certain?" he demanded of Dr. Thorndyke.

"I'm certain. You'll note the blood on his finger; Cornell recently picked off a patch of Mekstrom Flesh no larger than the head of a pin. It was his first sign." The doctor went on explaining, "Normally this early seizure would be difficult to detect, except from a clinical examination. But since I am telepath and Cornell has perception, his own mind told me he was aware of his sorry condition. One only need read his mind, or to dig at the tiny bit of Mekstrom Flesh that he dropped to your floor."

The judge eyed me nastily. "Maybe I should add a charge of contaminating a courtroom," he muttered. He was running his eyes across the floor from me to wherever I'd been, trying to locate the little patch. I helped him by not looking at it. The rest of the court faded back from me still farther. I could hardly have been less admired if I'd been made of pure cyanide gas.

The judge rapped his gavel sharply. "I parole this prisoner in the custody of Dr. Thorndyke, who as a representative of the Medical Center will remove the prisoner to that place where the proper treatment awaits him."

"Now see here—" I started. But His Honor cut me off.

"You'll go as I say," he snapped. "Unfortunately, the Law does not permit me to enjoy any cruel or unusual punishments, or I'd insist upon your ninety-day sentence and watch you die painfully. I—Bailiff! Remove this menace before I forget my position here and find myself in contempt of the law I have sworn to uphold. I cannot be impartial before a man who contaminates my Court with the world's most dangerous disease!"

I turned to Thorndyke. "All right," I grunted. "You win."

He smiled again; I wanted to wipe that smile away with a set of knuckles but I knew that all I'd get would be a broken hand against Thorndyke's stone-hard flesh. "Now, Mr. Cornell," he said with that clinical smoothness, "let's not get the old standard attitude."

"Nearly everybody who contracts Mekstrom's Disease," he said to the judge, "takes on a persecution complex as soon as he finds out he has it. Some of them have even accused me of fomenting some big fantastic plot against them. Please, Mr. Cornell," he went on facing me, "we'll give you the best of treatment that Medical Science knows."

"Yeah," I grunted.

His Honor rapped on the gavel once more. "Officer Gruenwald," he snapped, "you will accompany the prisoner and Dr. Thorndyke to the Medical Center and having done that you will return to report to me that you have accomplished your mission."

Then the judge glared around, rapped once more, and cried, "Case Finished. Next Case!"

I felt almost as sorry for the next guy coming in as I felt for myself. His Honor was going to be one tough baby for some days to come. As they escorted me out, a janitor came in and began to swab the floor where I'd been standing. He was using something nicely corrosive that made the icy, judicial eyes water, all of which discomfort was likely to be added to the next law-breaker's sorry lot.

I was in fine company. Thorndyke was a telepath and Officer Gruenwald was perceptive. They went as a team and gave me about as much chance to escape as if I'd been a horned toad sealed in a cornerstone. Gruenwald, of course, treated me as though my breath was deadly, my touch foul, and my presence evil. In Gruenwald's eyes, the only difference between me and Medusa the Gorgon was that looking at me did not turn him to stone. He kept at least one eye on me almost constantly.

I could almost perceive Thorndyke's amusement. With the best of social amenities, he could hardly have spent a full waking day in the company of either a telepath or a perceptive without giving away the fact that he was Mekstrom. But with me to watch over, Officer Gruenwald's mental attention was not to be turned aside to take an impolite dig at his companion. Even if he had, Thorndyke would have been there quickly to turn his attention aside.

I've read the early books that contain predictions of how we are supposed to operate. The old boys seemed to have the quaint notion that a telepath should be able at once to know everything that goes on everywhere, and a perceptive should be aware of everything material about him. There should be no privacy. There was to be no defense against the mental peeping Tom.

It ain't necessarily so. Had Gruenwald taken a dig at Thorndyke's hide, the doctor would have speared the policeman with a cold, indignant eye and called him for it. Of course, there was no good reason for Gruenwald to take a dig at Thorndyke and so he didn't.

So I went along with the status quo and tried to think of some way to break it up.

An hour later I was still thinking, and the bleeding on my finger had stopped. Mekstrom Flesh had covered the raw spot with a thin, stone-hard plate that could not be separated visually from the rest of my skin.

"As a perceptive," observed Dr. Thorndyke in a professional tone, "you'll notice the patch of infection growing on Mr. Cornell's finger.

The rate of growth seems normal; I'll have to check it accurately once I get him to the clinic. In fifty or sixty hours, Mr. Cornell's finger will be solid to the first joint. In ninety days his arm will have become as solid as the arm of a marble statue."

I interjected, "And what do we do about it?"

He moved his head a bit and eyed me in the rear view mirror. "I hope we can help you, Cornell," he said in a tone of sympathy that was definitely intended to impress Officer Gruenwald with his medical appreciation of the doctor's debt to humanity. "I sincerely hope so. For in doing so, we will serve the human race. And," he admitted with an entirely human-sounding selfishness, "I may be able to deliver a thesis on the cure that will qualify me for my scholarate."

I took a fast stab: "Doctor, how does my flesh differ from yours?"

Thorndyke parried this attention-getting question: "Mine is of no consequence. Dig your own above and below the line of infection, Cornell. If your sense of perception has been trained fine enough, dig the actual line of infection and watch the molecular structure rearrange. Can you dig that fine, Officer? Cornell, I hate to dwell at length upon your misfortune, but perhaps I can help you face it by bringing the facts to light."

#Like the devil you hate to dwell, Doctor Mekstrom!#

In the rear view mirror, his lips parted in a bland smile and one eyelid dropped in a knowing wink.

I opened my mouth to make another stab in the open but Thorndyke got there first. "Officer Gruenwald," he suggested, "you can help by putting out your perception along the road ahead and seeing how it goes. I'd like to make tracks with this crate."

Gruenwald nodded.

Thorndyke put the goose-pedal down and the car took off with a howl of passing wind. He said with a grin, "It isn't often that I get a chance to drive like this, but as long as I've an officer with me—"

He was above one forty by the time he let his voice trail off.

I watched the back of their heads. At this speed, Thorndyke would have both his mind and his hands full and the cop would be digging at the road as far ahead as his perception could dig a clear appreciation of the road and its hazards. Thorndyke's telepathy would be occupied in using this perception. That left me free to think.

I cast a dig behind me, as far behind me as my perception would reach. Nothing.

I thought furiously. It resulted in nothing.

I needed either a parachute or a full set of Mekstrom Hide to get out of this car now. With either I might have taken a chance and jumped. But as it was, the only guy who could scramble out of this car was Dr. James Thorndyke.

I caught his dropping eyelid in the rear view mirror again and swore at him under my breath.

Time, and miles, went past. One after the other, very fast. We hissed through towns where the streets had been opened for us and along broad stretches of highway and between cars and trucks running at normal speeds. One thing I must say for Thorndyke: He was almost as good a driver as I.

My second arrival at the Medical Center was rather quiet. I went in the service entrance, so to speak, and didn't get a look at the enamelled blonde at the front portal. They whiffed me in at a broad gate that was opened by a flunky and we drove for another mile through the grounds far from the main road. We ended up in front of a small brick building and as we went through the front office into a private place, Thorndyke told a secretary that she should prepare a legal receipt for my person. I did not like being bandied about like a hunk of merchandise, but nobody seemed to care what I thought. It was all very fast and efficient. I'd barely seated myself and lit a cigarette when the nurse came in with the document which Thorndyke signed, she witnessed, and was subsequently handed to Officer Gruenwald.

"Is there any danger of me—er—contracting—" he faltered uncertainly to Dr. Thorndyke.

"You'll notice that—" I started to call attention to Thorndyke's calmness at being in my presence and was going to invite Gruenwald to take a dig at the doctor's hide, but once more the doctor blocked me.

"None of us have ever found any factor of contagion," he said. "And we live among Mekstrom Cases. You'll notice Miss Clifton's lack of concern."

Miss Clifton, the nurse, turned a calm face to the policeman and gave him her hand. Miss Clifton had a face and a figure that was enough to make a man forget anything. She knew her part very well; together, the nurse and the policeman left the office together and I wondered just why a non-Mekstrom would have anything to do with an outfit like this.

Thorndyke smiled and said, "I won't tell you, Steve. What you don't know won't hurt anybody."

"Mind telling me what I'm slated for? The high jump? Going to watch me writhing in pain as my infection climbs toward my vitals? Going to amputate? Or are you going to cut it off inch by inch and watch me suffer?"

"Steve, some things you know already. One, that you are a carrier. There have been no other carriers. We'd like to know what makes you a carrier."

#The laboratory again?# I thought.

He nodded. "Also whether your final contraction of Mekstrom's Disease removes the carrier-factor."

I said hopefully, "I suppose as a Mekstrom I'll eventually be qualified to join you?"

Thorndyke looked blank. "Perhaps," he said flatly.

To my mind, that flat *perhaps* was the same sort of reply that Mother used to hand me when I wanted something that she did not want to give. I'd been eleven before I got walloped across the bazoo by pointing out to her that *we'll see* really meant *no*, because nothing that she said it to ever came to pass.

"Look, Thorndyke, let's take off our shoes and stop dancing," I told him. "I have a pretty good idea of what's been going on. I'd like an honest answer to what's likely to go on from here."

"I can't give you that."

"Who can?"

He said nothing, but he began to look at me as though I weren't quite bright. That made two of us, I was looking at him in the same manner.

My finger itched a bit, saving the situation. I'd been about to forget that Thorndyke was a Mekstrom and take a swing at him.

He laughed at me cynically. "You're in a very poor position to dictate terms," he said sharply.

"All right," I agreed reluctantly. "So I'm a prisoner. I'm also under a sentence of death. Don't think me unreasonable if I object to it."

"The trouble with your thinking is that you expect all things to be black or white and so defined. You ask me, 'am I going to live or die?'

and expect me to answer without qualification. I can only tell you that I don't know which. That it all depends."

"Depends upon exactly what?"

He eyed me with a cold stare. "Whether you're worthy of living."

"Who's to decide?"

"We will."

I grunted, wishing that I knew more Latin. I wanted to quote that Latin platitude about who watches the watchers. He watched me narrowly, and I expected him to quote me the phrase after having read my mind. But apparently the implication of the phrase did not appeal to him, and so he remained silent.

I broke the silence by saying, "What right has any man or collection of men to decide whether I, or anyone else, has the right to live or die?"

"It's done all the time," he replied succinctly.

"Yeah?"

"Criminals are—"

"I'm not a criminal; I've violated no man-made law. I've not even violated very many of the Ten Commandments. At least, not the one that is punishable by death."

He was silent for a moment again, then he said, "Steve, you're the victim of loose propaganda."

"Who isn't?" I granted. "The entire human race is lambasted by one form of propaganda or another from the time the infant learns to sit up until the elderly lays down and dies. We're all guilty of loose thinking. My own father, for instance, had to quit school before he could take any advanced schooling, had to fight his way up, had to collect his advanced education by study, application, and hard practice. He always swore that this long period of hardship strengthened his will and his character and gave him the guts to go out and do things that he'd never have thought of if he'd had an easy life. Then the old duck turns right around and swears that he'll never see any son of his take the bumps as he took them."

"That's beside the point, Steve. I know what sort of propaganda you've been listening to. It's the old do-good line; the everything for anybody line; the no man must die alone line."

"Is it bad?"

Dr. Thorndyke shrugged. "You've talked about loose propaganda," he said. "Well, in this welter of loose propaganda, every man had at least the opportunity of choosing which line of guff he intends to adhere to. I'm even willing to admit that there is both right and wrong on both sides. Are you?"

I stifled a sour grin. "I shouldn't, because it is a mistake in any political argument to even let on that the other guy is slightly more than an idiot. But as an engineer, I'll admit it."

"Now that's a help," he said more cheerfully. "You're objecting, of course, to the fact that we are taking the right to pick, choose, and select those people that we think are more likely to be of good advantage to the human race. You've listened to that old line about the hypothetical cataclysm that threatens the human race, and how would you choose the hundred people who are supposed to carry on. Well, have you ever eyed the human race in slightly another manner?"

"I wouldn't know," I told him. "Maybe."

"Have you ever watched the proceedings of one of those big trials where some conkpot has blown the brains out of a half-dozen citizens by pointing a gun and emptying it at a crowd? If you have, you've been appalled by the sob sisters and do-gooders who show that the vicious character was momentarily off his toggle. We mustn't execute a nut, no matter how vicious he is. We've got to protect him, feed him, and house him for the next fifty years. Now, not only is he doing Society absolutely no good while he's locked up for fifty years, he's also eating up his share of the standard of living. Then to top this off, so long as this nut is alive, there is the danger that some soft-hearted fathead will succeed in getting him turned loose once more."

"Agreed," I said. "But you're again talking about criminals, which I don't think applies in my case."

"Of course not," he said quickly. "I used it to prove that this is one way of looking at a less concrete case. Carry this soft-headed thinking a few steps higher. Medical science has made it possible for the human race to dilute its strength. Epileptics are saved to breed epileptics; haemophiliacs are preserved, neurotics are ironed out, weaknesses of all kinds are kept alive to breed their strain of weakness."

"Just what has this to do with me and my future?" I asked.

"Quite a lot. I'm trying to make you agree that there are quite a lot of undeserving characters here on Earth."

"Did I ever deny it?" I asked him pointedly, but he took it as not including present company.

But I could see where Thorndyke was heading. First eliminate the lice on the body politic. Okay, so I'm blind and can't see the sense of imprisoning a killer who is fed, clothed, and housed at my expense for the rest of his natural life. Then for the second step we get rid of weaklings, both physical and mental. I'll call Step Two passably okay, but—? Number Three includes grifters, beggars, bums, and guys out for the soft touch and here I begin to wonder. I've known some entertaining grifters, beggars, and bums; a few of them chose their way of life for their own, just as I became a mechanical engineer.

The trouble with this sort of philosophy is that it starts off with an appeal to justice and logic (I'm quoting myself), but it quickly gets dangerous. Start knocking off the bilge-scum. Then when the lowest strata of society is gone, start on the next. Carry this line of reasoning out to straight Aristotelian Logic and you come up with parties like you and me, who may have been quite acceptable when compared to the whole cross-section of humanity, but who now have no one but his betters to compete with.

I had never reasoned this out before, but as I did right there and then, I decided that Society cannot draw lines nor assume a static pose. Society must move constantly, either in one direction or the other. And while I object to paying taxes to support some rattlehead for the rest of his natural life, I'd rather have it that way than to have someone start a trend of bopping off everybody who has not the ability to absorb the educational level of the scholar. Because, if the trend turned upward instead of downward, that's where the dividing line would end.

Anarchy at one end, is as bad as tyranny at the other—

"I'm sorry you cannot come to a reasonable conclusion," said Dr. Thorndyke. "If you cannot see the logic of—"

I cut him off short. "Look, Doc," I snapped, "If you can't see where your line of thinking ends, you're in bad shape."

He looked superior. "You're sour because you know you haven't got what it takes."

I almost nipped. "You're so damned dumb that you can't see that in any society of supermen, you'd not be qualified to clean out ash trays," I tossed back at him.

He smiled self-confidently. "By the time they start looking at my level—if they ever do—you'll have been gone long ago. Sorry, Cornell. You don't add up."

Well, that was nothing I didn't know already. In his society, I was a nonentity. Yet, somehow, if that's what the human race was coming to under the Thorndyke's and the Phelps', I didn't care to stay around.

"All right," I snapped. "Which way do I go from here? The laboratory, or will you dispense with the preliminaries and let me take the high slide right now before this—" I held up my infected finger, "gets to the painful stages."

With the air and tone of a man inspecting an interesting specimen impaled on a mounting pin, Thorndyke replied:

"Oh—we have use for the likes of you."

CHAPTER SEVENTEEN

It would please me no end to report here that the gang at the Medical Center were crude, rough, vicious, and that they didn't give a damn about human suffering. Unfortunately for my sense of moral balance, I can't. They didn't cut huge slices out of my hide without benefit of anaesthesia. They didn't shove pipe-sized needles into me, or strap me on a board and open me up with dull knives. Instead, they treated me as if I'd been going to pay for my treatment and ultimately emerge from the Center to go forth and extol its virtues. I ate good food, slept in a clean and comfortable bed, smoked free cigarettes, read the best magazines—and also some of the worst, if I must report the whole truth—and was permitted to mingle with the rest of the patients, guests, victims, personnel, and so forth that were attached to my ward.

I was not at any time treated as though I were anything but a willing and happy member of their team. It was known that I was not, but if any emotion was shown, it was sympathy at my plight in not being one of them. This was viewed in the same way as any other accident of birth or upbringing.

In my room was another man about my age. He'd arrived a day before me, with an early infection at the tip of his middle toe. He was, if I've got to produce a time-table, about three-eights of an inch ahead of me. He had no worries. He was one of their kind of thinkers.

"How'd you connect?" I asked him.

"I didn't," he said, scratching his infected toe vigorously. "They connected with me."

"Oh?"

"Yeah. I was sleeping tight and not even dreaming. Someone rapped on my door and I growled myself out of bed and sort of felt my way. It was three a.m. Guy stood there looking apologetic. 'Got a message for you,' he tells me. 'Can't it wait until morning?' I snarl back. 'No,' he says. 'It's important!' So I invite him in. He doesn't waste any time at all; his first act is to point at an iron floor lamp in the corner and ask me how much I'd paid for it. I tell him. Then this bird drops twice the amount on the coffee table, strides over to the corner, picks up the lamp, and ties the iron pipe into a fancy-looking bowknot. He didn't even grunt. 'Mr. Mullaney,' he asks me, 'How would you like to be that strong?' I didn't have to think it over. I told him right then and there. Then we spent from three ayem to five thirty going through a fast question and answer routine, sort of like a complicated word-association test. At six o'clock I've packed and I'm on my way here with my case of Mekstrom's Disease."

"Just like that?" I asked Mr. Mullaney.

"Just like that," he repeated.

"So now what happens?"

"Oh, about tomorrow I'll go in for treatment," he said. "Seems as how they've got to start treatment before the infection creeps to the first joint or I'll lose the joint." He contemplated me a bit; he was a perceptive and I knew it. "You've got another day or more. That's because your ring finger is longer than my toe."

"What's the treatment like?" I asked him.

"That I don't know. I've tried to dig the treatment, but it's too far away from here. This is just a sort of preliminary ward; I gather that they know when to start and so on." He veiled his eyes for a moment. He was undoubtedly thinking of my fate. "Chess?" he asked, changing the subject abruptly.

"Why not?" I grinned.

My mind wasn't in it. He beat me three out of four. I bedded down about eleven, and to my surprise I slept well. They must have been shoving something into me to make me sleep; I know me very well and I'm sure that I couldn't have closed an eye if they hadn't been slipping me the old closeout powder. For three nights, now, I'd corked off solid until seven ack emma and I'd come alive in the morning fine, fit, and fresh.

But on the following morning, Mr. Mullaney was missing. I never saw him again.

At noon, or thereabouts, the end of the ring finger on my left hand was as solid as a rock. I could squeeze it in a door or burn it with a cigarette; I got into a little habit of scratching kitchen matches on it as I tried to dig into the solid flesh with my perception. I growled a bit at my fate, but not much.

It was about this time, too, that the slight itch began to change. You know how a deep-felt itch is. It can sometimes be pleasant. Like the itch that comes after a fast swim in the salty sea and a dry-out in the bright sun, when the drying salt water makes your skin itch with the vibrant pleasure of just being alive. This is not like the bite of any bug, but the kind that makes you want to take another dive into the ocean instead of trying to scratch it with your claws. Well, the itch in my finger had been one of the pleasant kinds. I could sort of scratch it away by taking the steel-hard part of my finger in my other hand and wiggle, briskly. But now the itch turned into a deep burning pain.

My perception, never good enough to dig the finer structure clearly, was good enough to tell me that my crawling horror had come to the boundary line of the first joint.

It was this pause that was causing the burning pain.

According to what I'd been told, if someone didn't do something about me right now, I'd lose the end joint of my finger.

Nobody came to ease my pain, nor to ease my mind. They left me strictly alone. I spent the time from noon until three o'clock examining my fingertip as I'd not examined it before. It was rock hard, but strangely flexible if I could exert enough pressure on the flesh. It still moved with the flexing of my hands. The fingernail itself was like a chip of chilled steel. I could flex the nail neither with my other hand nor by biting it; between my teeth it had the uncomfortable solidity of a sheet of metal that conveyed to my brain that the old teeth should not try to bite too hard. I tried prying on a bit of metal with the fingernail; inserting the nail in the crack where a metal cylinder had been formed to make a table leg. I might have been able to pry the crack wider, but the rest of my body did not have the power nor the rigidity necessary to drive the tiny lever that was my fingertip.

I wondered what kind of tool-grinder they used for a manicure.

At three-thirty, the door to my room opened and in came Scholar Phelps, complete with his benign smile and his hearty air.

"Well," he boomed over-cheerfully, "we meet again, Mr. Cornell."

"Under trying circumstances," I said.

"Unfortunately so," he nodded. "However, we can't all be fortunate."

"I dislike being a vital statistic."

"So does everybody. Yet, from a philosophical point of view, you have no more right to live at the expense of someone else than someone else has a right to live at your expense. It all comes out even in the final accounting. And, of course, if every man were granted a guaranteed immortality, we'd have one cluttered-up world."

I had to admit that he was right, but I still could not accept his statistical attitude. Not while I'm the statistic. He followed my thought even though he was esper; it wasn't hard to follow anyway.

"All right, I admit that this is no time to sit around discussing philosophy or metaphysics or anything of that nature. What you are interested in is you."

"How absolutely correct."

"You know, of course, that you are a carrier."

"So I've come to believe. At least, everybody I seem to have any contact with either turns up missing or comes down with Mekstrom's—or both."

Scholar Phelps nodded. "You might have gone on for quite some time if it hadn't been so obvious."

I eyed him. "Just what went on?" I asked casually. "Did you have a clean-up squad following me all the time, picking up the debris? Or did you just pick up the ones you wanted? Or did the Highways make you indulge in a running competition?"

"Too many questions at once. Most of which answers would be best that you did not know. Best for us, that is. Maybe even for you."

I shrugged. "We seem to be bordering on philosophy again when the important point is what you intend to do to me."

He looked unhappy. "Mr. Cornell, it is hard to remain unphilosophical in a case like this. So many avenues of thought have been opened, so many ideas and angles come to mind. We'll readily admit what you've probably concluded; that you as a carrier have become the one basic factor that we have been seeking for some twenty years and more. You are the dirigible force, the last brick in the building, the final answer. Or, and I hate to say it, were."

"Were?"

"For all of our knowledge of Mekstrom's we know so very little," he said. "In certain maladies the carrier is himself immune. In some we observe that the carrier results from a low-level, incomplete infection with the disease which immunizes him but does not kill the bugs. In others, we've seen the carrier become normal after he has finally contracted the disease. What we must know now is: Is Steve Cornell, the Mekstrom Carrier, now a non-carrier because he has contracted the disease?"

"How are you going to find out?" I asked him.

"That's a problem," he said thoughtfully. "One school feels that we should not treat you, since the treatment itself may destroy whatever unknown factor makes you a carrier. The other claims that if we don't treat you, you'll hardly live long enough to permit comprehensive research anyway. A third school believes that there is time to find out whether you are still a carrier, make some tests, and then treat you, after which these tests are to be repeated."

Rather bitterly, I said, "I suppose I have absolutely no vote."

"Hardly," his face was pragmatic.

"And to which school do you belong?" I asked sourly. "Do you want me to get the cure? Or am I to die miserably while you take tabs on my blood pressure, or do I merely lose an arm while you're sitting with folded hands waiting for the laboratory report?"

"In any case, we'll learn a lot about Mekstrom's from you," he said. "Even if you die."

As caustically as I could, I said, "It's nice to know that I am not going to die in vain."

He eyed me with contempt. "You're not afraid to die, are you, Mr. Cornell?"

That's a dirty question to ask any man. Sure, I'm afraid to die. I just don't like the idea of being not-alive. As bad as life is, it's better than nothing. But the way he put the question he was implying that I should be happy to die for the benefit of Humanity in general, and that's a question that is unfairly loaded. After all, everybody is slated to kick off. There is no other way of resigning from the universe. So if I have to die, it might as well be for the Benefit of Something, and if it happens to be Humanity, so much the better. But when the case is proffered on a silver tray, I feel, "Somebody else, not me!"

The next argument Phelps would be tossing out would be the one that goes, "Two thousand years ago, a Man died for Humanity—"

which always makes me sick. No matter how you look at us, there is no resemblance between Him and me.

I cut him short before he could say it: "Whether or not I'm afraid to die, and for good or evil, now or later, is beside the point. I have, obviously, nothing to say about the time, place, and the reasons."

We sat and glared at one another; he didn't know whether to laugh or snarl and I didn't care which he did. It seemed he was leading up to something that looked like the end. Then I'd get the standard funeral and statements would be given out that I'd died because medical research had not been able to save me and blah blah blah complete with lack of funds and The Medical Center charity drive. The result would mean more moola for Phelps and higher efficiency for his operations, and to the devil with the rest of the world.

"Let's get along with it," I snapped. "I've no opinion, no vote, no right of appeal. Why bother to ask me how I feel?"

Calmly he replied, "Because I am not a rough-shod, unhuman monster, Mr. Cornell. I would prefer that you see my point of view—or at least enough of it to admit that there is a bit of right on my side."

"Seems to me I went through that with Thorndyke."

"This is another angle. I'm speaking of my right of discovery."

"You're speaking of what?"

"Right of discovery. You as an engineer are familiar with the idea. If I were a poet I could write an ode to my love and no one would forbid me my right to give it to her and nobody else. If I were a cook with a special recipe no one could demand that I hand it over unless I was paid. He who discovers something new should be granted the right of control. If this Mekstrom business were some sort of physical patent or some new process, I could apply for a patent and have it for my exclusive use for a period of seventeen years. Am I not right?"

"Yes, but—"

"Except that my patent would be infringed upon and I'd have no control—"

I stood up suddenly and faced him angrily. He did not cower; after all he was a Mekstrom. But he did shut up for a moment.

"Seems to me," I snarled, "that any process that can be used to save human life should not be held secret, patentable, or under the control of any one man or group."

"This is an argument that always comes up. You may, of course, be correct. But happily for me, Mr. Cornell, I have the process and you have not, and it is my own conviction that I have the right to use it on those people who seem, in my opinion, to hold the most for the future advancement of the human race. However, I do not care to go over this argument again, it is tiresome and it never ends. As one of the ancient Greek Philosophers observed, you cannot change a man's mind by arguing with him. The other fact remains, however, that you do have something to offer us, despite your contrary mental processes."

"Do go on? What do I have to do to gain this benefit? Who do I have to kill?" I eyed him cynically and then added, "Or is it 'Whom shall I kill?' I like these things to be proper, you know."

"Don't be sarcastic. I'm serious," he told me.

"Then stop pussyfooting and come to the point," I snapped. "You know what the story is. I don't. So if you think I'll be interested, why not tell me instead of letting me find out the hard way."

"You, of course, were a carrier. Maybe you still are. We can find out. In fact, we'll have to find out, before we—"

"For God's Sake stop it!" I yelled. "You're meandering."

"Sorry," he said in a tone of apology that surprised me all the way down to my feet. He shook himself visibly and went on from there: "You, if still a carrier, can be of use to The Medical Center. Now do you understand?"

Sure I understand, but good. As a normal human type, they held nothing over me and just shoved me here and there and picked up the victims after me. But now that I was a victim myself, they could offer me their "cure" only if I would swear to go around the country deliberately infecting the people they wanted among them. It was that—or lie there and die miserably. This had not come to Scholar Phelps as a sudden flash of genius. He'd been planning this all along; had been waiting to pop this delicate question after I'd been pushed around, had a chance to torture myself mentally, and was undoubtedly soft for anything that looked like salvation.

"There is one awkward point," said Scholar Phelps suavely. "Once we have cured you, we would have no hold on you other than your loyalty and your personal honor to fulfill a promise given. Neither of us are naive, Mr. Cornell. We both know that any honorable promise is only as valid as the basic honor involved. Since your personal opinion is that this medical treatment should be used indiscriminately, and that our program to better the human race by competitive selection is foreign to your feelings, you would feel honor-bound to betray us. Am I not correct?"

What could I say to that? First I'm out, then I'm in, now I'm out again. What was Phelps getting at?

"If our positions were reversed, Mr. Cornell, I'm sure that you'd seek some additional binding force against me. I shall continue to seek some such lever against you for the same reason. In the meantime, Mr. Cornell, we shall make a test to see whether we have any real basis for any agreement at all. You may have ceased to be a carrier, you know."

"Yeah," I admitted darkly.

"In the meantime," he said cheerfully, "the least we can do is to treat your finger. I'd hate to have you hedge a deal because we did not deliver your cured body in the whole."

He put his head out of the door and summoned a nurse who came with a black bag. From the bag, Scholar Phelps took a skin-blast hypo and a small metal box, the top of which held a small slender, jointed platform and some tiny straps. He strapped my finger to this platform and then plugged in a length of line cord to the nearest wall socket. The little platforms moved; the one nearest my wrist vibrated rapidly across a very small excursion that tickled like the devil. The end platform moved in an arc, flexing the finger tip from straight to about seventy degrees. This moved fairly slow but regularly up and down.

"I'll not fool you," he said drily. "This is going to hurt."

He set the skin-blast hypo on top of the joint and let it go. For a moment the finger felt cold, numb, pleasant. Then the shock wore away and the tip of my finger, my whole finger and part of my hand shocked me with the most excruciating agony that the hide of man ever felt. Flashes and waves of pain darted up my arm to the elbow and the muscles in my forearm jumped. The sensitive nerve in my elbow sang and sent darting waves of zigzag needles up to my shoulder. My hand was a source of searing heat and freezing cold and the pain of being crushed and twisted and wrenched out of joint all at the same time.

Phelps wiped my wet face with a towel, loaded another hypo and let me have it in the shoulder. Gradually the stuff took hold and the awful pain began to subside. Not all the way, it just diminished from absolutely unbearable to merely terrible.

I knew at that moment why a trapped animal will bite off its own foreleg to get free of the trap.

From the depths of his bag he found a bottle and poured a half-tumbler for me; it went down like a whiskey-flavored soft drink. It had about as much kick as when you pour a drink of water into a highball glass that still holds a dreg of melted ice and diluted liquor. But it burned like fury once it hit my stomach and my mind began to wobble. He'd given me a slug of the pure quill, one hundred proof.

As some sort of counter-irritant, it worked. Very gradually the awful pain in my hand began to subside.

"You can take that manipulator off in an hour or so," he told me. "And in the meantime we'll get along with our testing."

I gathered that they could stop this treatment anywhere along the process if I did not measure up.

CHAPTER EIGHTEEN

Midnight. The manipulator had been off my hand for several hours, and it was obvious that my Mekstrom's was past the first joint and creeping up towards the next. I eyed it with some distaste; as much as I wanted to have a fine hard body, I was not too pleased at having agony for a companion every time the infection crossed a joint. I began to wonder about the wrist; this is a nice complicated joint and should, if possible, exceed the pain of the first joint in the ring finger. I'd heard tell, of course, that once you've reached the top, additional torture does not hurt any greater. I'd accepted this statement as it was printed. But now I was not too sure that what I'd just been through was not one of those exceptions that take place every now and then to the best of rules.

I was still in a dark and disconsolate mood. But I'd managed to eat, and I'd shaved and showered, and I'd hit the hay because it was as good a place to be as anywhere else. I could lie there and dig the premises with my esper.

There were very few patients in this building, and none were done up like the character in the Macklin place. They moved the patients to some other part of the grounds when the cure started. There weren't very many nurses, doctors, scholars, or other personnel around, either.

Outside along one side of a road was a small lighted house that was obviously a sort of guard, but it was casual instead of being formal and military in appearance. The ground, instead of being patrolled by human guards (which might have caused some comment) was carefully laid off into checkerboard squares by a complicated system of photobeams and induction bridges.

You've probably read about how the job of casing a joint should be done. I did it the same way. I dug back and forth, collecting the layout from the back door of my building towards the nearest puff of dead area. This coign of safety billowed outward from the pattern towards the building like an arm of cumulus cloud and the top of it rose like a column to a height above my range. It sort of leaned forward but it did not lean far enough to be directly above the building. The far side of the column was just like the rear side; even though I'm well trained, it always startles me when I perceive the far side of a smallish dead area. I'm inclined like everybody else to consider perception on a line-of-sight basis instead of on a sort of all-around grasp.

I let my thinker run free. If I could direct a breakout from this joint with a lot of outside help, I'd have a hot jetcopter pilot come down the dead-area column with a dead engine. The Medical Center did not have any radar, probably on the proposition that too high a degree of security indicated a high degree of top-secret material to hide. So I'd come down dead engine, land, and wait it out. Timing would have to be perfect, because I, the prisoner, would have to make a fast gallop across a couple of hundred yards of wide open psi area, scale a tall fence topped with barbed wire, cross another fifty yards into the murk, and then find my rescuer. The take off would be fast once I'd located the 'copter in the murk, and everything would depend upon a hot pilot who felt confident enough in his engine and his rotorjets to let 'em go with a roar and a lift without warmup.

During which time, unfortunately for all plans, the people at The Medical Center would have been reading my mind and would probably have that dead patch well patrolled with big, rough gentlemen armed with stuff heavy enough to stop a tank.

Lacking any sort of device or doodad that would conceal my mind from prying telepaths, about the only thing I could do was to lay here in my soft bed and daydream of making my escape.

Eventually I went to sleep and dreamed that I was hunting Mallards with a fly-rod baited with a stale doughnut. The only thing that bothered me was a couple of odd-looking guys who thought that the way to hunt Mallards was with shotguns, and their dress was just as out of taste as their equipment. Who ever hunted ducks from a canoe, dressed in windbreakers and hightopped boots? Eventually they bought some ducks from me and went home, leaving me to my slumbers.

About eight in the morning, there was a tentative tap on my door. While I was growling about why they should bother tapping, the door opened and a woman came in with my breakfast tray. She was not my nurse; she was the enamelled blonde receptionist.

She had lost some of her enamelled sophistication. It was not evident in her make-up, her dress, or her hair-do. These were perfection. In fact, she bore that store-window look that made me think of an automaton, triggered to make the right noises and to present the proper expression at the correct time. As though she had never had a thought of her own or an emotion that was above the level of very mild interest. As if the perfection of her dress and the characterless beauty of her face were more important than anything else in her life.

But the loss of absolute plate-glass impersonality was gone, and it took me some several moments to dig it out of her appearance. Then I saw it. Her eyes. They no longer looked glassily out of that clear oval face at a point about three inches above my left shoulder, but they were centered on me from no matter what point in the room she'd be as she went about the business of running open the blinds, checking the this and that and the other like any nurses' helper.

Finally she placed my tray on the bed-table and stood looking down at me.

From my first meeting with her I knew she was no telepath, so I bluntly said, "Where's the regular girl? Where's my nurse?"

"I'm taking over for the time," she told me. Her voice was strained; she'd been trying to use that too-deeply cultured tone she used as the professional receptionist but the voice had cracked through the training enough to let some of her natural tone come through.

"Why?"

Then she relaxed completely, or maybe it was a matter of coming unglued. Her face allowed itself to take on some character and her body ceased being that rigid window-dummy type. "What's your trouble—?" I asked her softly. She had something on her mind that was a bit too big for her, but her training was not broad enough to allow her to get it out. I hoped to help, if I could. I also wanted to know what she was doing here. If Scholar Phelps was thinking about putting a lever on me of the female type, he'd guessed wrong.

She was looking at me and I could see a fragment of fright in her face.

"Is it terrible?" she asked me in a whisper.

"Is what terrible?"

"Me—Me—Mekstrom's D—Disease—" The last word came out with a couple of big tears oozing from closed lids.

"Why?" I asked. "Do I look all shot to bits?"

She opened the eyes and looked at me. "Does it hurt?"

I remembered the agony of my finger and tried to lie. "A little," I told her. "But I'm told that it was because I'd waited too long for my first treatment." I hoped that I was correct; maybe it was wishful thinking, but I claim that right. I didn't want to go through the same agony every time we crossed a joint.

I reached over to the bedside table and found my cigarettes. I slipped two up and offered one of them to her. She put a tentative hand forward, slowly, a scared-to-touch reluctance in her motion. This changed as her hand came forward. It was the same sort of reluctance that you feel when you start out to visit the dentist for a roaring tooth. The closer you get to the dentist's office the less inclined you are to finish the job. Then at some indeterminate point you cross the place of no return and from that moment you go forward with increased determination.

She finally made the cigarette package but she was very careful not to touch my hand as she took out the weed. Then, as if she'd reached that point of no return, her hand slipped around the package and caught me by the wrist.

We were statue-still for three heartbeats. Then I lifted my other hand, took out the cigarette she'd missed, and held it forward for her. She took it. I dropped the pack and let my hand slip back until we were holding hands, practically. She shuddered.

I flipped my lighter and let her inhale a big puff before I put the next question: "Why are you here and what goes on?"

In a flat, dry voice she said, "I'm—supposed—to—" and let it trail away without finishing it.

"Guinea pig?" I blurted bluntly.

She collapsed like a deflated balloon. Next, she had her face buried in my shoulder, bawling like a hurt baby. I stroked her shoulder gently, but she shuddered away from my hand as though it were poison.

I shoved her upright and shook her a bit. "Don't blubber like an idiot. Sit there and talk like a human being!"

It took her a minute of visible effort before she said, "You're supposed to be a—carrier. I'm supposed to find out—whether you are—a carrier."

Well, I'd suspected something of that sort.

Shakily she asked me, "How do I get it, Mr. Cornell?"

I eyed her sympathetically.

Then I held up my left hand and looked at the infection. This was the finger that had been gummed to bits by the Mekstrom infant back in Homestead. With a shrug of uncertainty, I lifted her hand to my mouth. I felt with my tongue and dug with my perception until I had a tiny fold of her skin between my front teeth. Then sharply, I bit down, drawing blood. She jerked, stiffened, closed her eyes and took a deep breath but she did not cry out.

"That, if anything, should do it," I said flatly. "Now go out and get some iodine for the cut. Human-bite is likely to become infected with something bad. And I don't think antiseptic will hurt the Mekstrom Infection if it's taken place." They'd given me the antiseptic works in Homestead, I recalled. "Now, Miss Nameless, you sit over there and tell me how come this distressing tableau?"

"Oh—I can't," she cried. Then she left in a hurry sucking on her bleeding finger.

I didn't need any explanation; I'd just wanted my suspicions confirmed. Someone had a lever on her. Maybe someone she loved was a Mekstrom and her loyalty was extracted because of it. The chances were also high that she'd been given to understand that they'd accept her as a member if she ever caught Mekstrom's; and they'd taken my arrival as a fine chance to check me and get her at the same time.

I wondered about her; she was no big-brain. I couldn't quite see the stratified society outlined by Scholar Phelps as holding a position open for her in the top echelon. Except she was a woman, attractive if you like your women beautiful and dull-minded, and she probably would be happy to live in a little vacuum-type world bounded on all sides with women's magazines, lace curtains, TV soap opera, and a corral full of little Mekstrom kids. I grinned. Funny how the proponents of the stratified society always have their comeuppance by the need of women whose minds are bent on mundane things like homes and families.

Well, I hoped she caught it, if that's what she wanted. I was willing to bet my life that she cared a lot more for being with her man than she did for the cockeyed society he was supporting.

I finished my breakfast and went out to watch a couple of telepaths playing chess until lunch time and then gave up. Telepathic chess was too much like playing perceptive poker.

Then after lunch came the afternoon full of laboratory tests, inspections, experiments, and so forth; they didn't do much that hadn't been tried at Homestead, and I surprised them again by being able to help in their never-ending blood counts and stuff of that sort.

They did not provide me with a new room mate, so I wandered around after dinner hoping that I could avoid both Thorndyke and Phelps. I didn't want to get into another fool social-structure argument with them and the affair of the little scared receptionist was more than likely to make me say a few words that might well get me cast into the Outer Darkness for their mere semantic content.

Once more I hit the sack early.

And, once more, there came a tap on my door about eight o'clock. It was not a tentative little frightened tap this time, it was more jovial and eager sounding. My reaction was about the same. Since it was their show and their property, I couldn't see any reason why they made this odd lip-service to politeness.

It was the receptionist again. She came in with a big wistful smile and dropped my tray on the bed table.

"Look," she cried. She held up her hand. The bleeding had stopped and there was a thin film over the cut. I dug at it and nodded; it was the first show of Mekstrom Flesh without a doubt.

"That's it, kid."

"I know," she said happily. "Golly, I could kiss you."

Then before I could think of all the various ways in which the word "Golly" sounded out of character for her, she launched herself into my arms and was busily erasing every attempt at logical thought with one of the warmest, no-holds-barred smoocheroo that I'd enjoyed for what seemed like years. Since I'd held Catherine in my arms in her apartment just before we'd eloped, I'd spent my time in the company of Nurse Farrow who held no emotional appeal to me, and the rest of my female company had been Mekstroms whose handholding might twist off a wrist if they got a thrill out of it. About the time I began to respond with enthusiasm and vigor, she extricated herself from my clutch and slid back to the foot of the bed out of reach.

A little breathlessly she said, "Harry will thank you for this." *This* meant the infection in her finger.

Then she was gone and I was thinking, *Harry should drop dead!*

Then I grinned at myself like the Cheshire Cat because I realized that I was so valuable a property that they couldn't afford to let me die. No matter what, I'd be kept alive. And after having things go so sour for so long a time, things were about to take a fast turn and go my way.

I discounted the baby-bite affair. Even if the baby were another carrier, it would take a long time before the kid was old enough to be trusted in his aim.

I discounted it even more because I hadn't been roaring around the countryside biting innocent citizens. Mere contact was enough; if the bite did anything, it may have hastened the process.

So here I was, a nice valuable property, with a will of my own. I could either throw in with Phelps and bite only Phelps' Chosen Aristocrats, or I could go back to the Highways and bite everybody in sight.

I laughed at my image in the mirror. I am a democratic sort of soul, but when it comes to biting, there's some I'd rather bite than others.

I bared my teeth at my image, but it was more of a leering smile of the tooth-paste ad than a fierce snarl.

My image looked pensive. It was thinking, *Steve, old carnivore, ere you go biting anybody, you've first got to bite your way out of the Medical Center.*

CHAPTER NINETEEN

One hour later they pulled my fangs without benefit of anaesthesia.

Thorndyke came in to inspect the progress of my infection and allowed as how I'd be about ready for the full treatment in a few days. "We like to delay the full treatment as long as possible," he told me, "because it immobilizes the patient too long as it is." He pressed a call bell, waited, and soon the door opened to admit a nurses' helper pushing a trundle cart loaded with medical junk. I still don't know what was on the cart because I was too flabbergasted to notice it.

I was paying all my attention to Catherine, cheerful in her Gray Lady uniform, being utterly helpful, bright, gay, and relaxed. I was tongue tied, geflummoxed, beaten down, and—well, just speechless.

Catherine was quite professional about her help. She loaded the skin-blast hypo and slapped it into Thorndyke's open hand. Her eyes looked into mine and they smiled reassuringly. Her hand was firm as she took my arm; she locked her strength on my hand and held it immobile while Thorndyke shot me in the second joint. There was a personal touch to her only briefly when she breathed, "Steve, I'm so glad!" and then went on about her work. The irony of it escaped me; but later I did recall the oddity of congratulating someone who's just contracted a disease.

Then that wave of agony hit me, and the only thing I can remember through it was Catherine folding a towel so that the hem would be on the inside when she wiped the beads of sweat from my face. She cradled my head between her hands and crooned lightly to me until the depths of the pain was past. Then she got efficient again and waved Thorndyke aside to see to the little straps on the manipulator herself. She adjusted them delicately. Then she poured me a glass of ice water and put it where I could reach it with my other hand. She left after one long searching look into my eyes, and I knew that she would be back later to talk to me alone. This seemed all right with Dr. Thorndyke, the wily telepath who would be able to dig a reconstruction of our private talk with a little urging on his part.

After Catherine was gone, Thorndyke smiled down at me with cynical self-confidence. "There's your lever, Steve," he said.

The dope helped to kill all but the worst waves of searing pain; between them I managed to grind out, "How did you sell her that bill of goods, Thorndyke?"

His reply was scornful. "Maybe she likes your hide all in one piece," he grunted.

He left me with my mind a-whirl with thoughts and pain. The little manipulator was working my second finger joint up and down rhythmically, and with each move came pain. It also exercised the old joint, which had grown so rigid that my muscles hadn't been able to move it for several hours. That added agony, too.

The dope helped, but it also dimmed my ability to concentrate.

Up to a certain point everything was quite logical and easy to understand. Catherine was here because they had contacted her through some channel and said, "Throw in with us and we'll see that your lover does not die miserably." So much was reasonable, but after that point the whole thing began to take on a mad puzzle-like quality. Given normal circumstances, Catherine would have come to me as swiftly as I'd have gone to her if I'd known how. Not only that, but I'd probably have sworn eternal fealty to them for their service even though I could not stand their way of thinking.

But Catherine was smart enough to realize that I, as the only known carrier of Mekstrom's Disease, was more valuable live than dead.

Why, then, had Catherine come here to place herself in their hands? Alone, she might have gone off half-cocked in an emotional tizzy. But the Highways had good advisers who should have pointed out that Steve Cornell was one man alive who could walk with impunity among friend or foe. Why, they hadn't even tried to collect me until it became evident that I was in line for the Old Treatment. Then they had to take me in, because the Medical Center wanted any information they could get above and beyond the fact that I was a carrier. If someone from Homestead had been in that courtroom, I'd now be among friends.

Then the ugly thought hit me and my mind couldn't face it for some time.

Reorientation.

Catherine's cheerful willingness to help them must be reorientation and nothing else.

Now, although I've mentioned reorientation before, what I actually know about it is meager. It makes Dr. Jekylls out of former Mr. Hydes and the transformation is complete. It can be done swiftly; the rapidity depends upon the strength of the mind of the operator compared to the mind of the subject. It is slightly harder to reorient a defiant mind than a willing one. It sticks unless someone else begins to tinker again. It is easier to make a good man out of a bad one than the reverse, although the latter is eminently possible. This is too difficult a problem to discuss to the satisfaction of everybody, but it seems to go along with the old theory that "Good" does benefit the tribe of mankind in the long run, while "Bad" things cause trouble. I'll say no more than to point out that no culture based upon theft, murder, piracy, and pillage, has ever survived.

The thought of Catherine's mind being tampered with made me seethe with anger. I forgot my pain and began to probe around wildly, and as I probed I began to know the real feeling of helpless futility.

For here I was, practically immobilized and certainly dependent upon them for help. This was no time to attempt a rescue of my sweetheart—who would only be taken away kicking and screaming all the way from here to the first place where I could find a haven and have her re-reoriented. The latter would not be hard; among the other things I knew about reorientation was that it could be negated by some strong emotional ties and a personal background that included worthy objection to the new personality.

For my perceptive digging I came up with nothing but those things that any hospital held. Patients, nurses, interns, orderlies; a couple of doctors, a scholar presiding over a sheaf of files. And finally Catherine puttering over an autoclave. She was setting out a string of instruments under the tutelage of a superintendent of nurses who was explaining how the job should be done.

I took a deep, thankful breath. Her mind was occupied enough to keep her from reading the dark thoughts that were going through mine. I did not even want a loved one to know how utterly helpless and angry I felt.

And then, because I was preoccupied with Catherine and my own thoughts, the door opened without my having taken a dig at the opener beforehand. The arrival was all I needed to crack wide open in a howling fit of hysteria. It was so pat. I couldn't help but let myself go: "Well! This looks like Old Home Week!"

Miss Gloria Farrow, Registered Nurse, did not respond to my awkward joviality. Her face, if anything, was darker than my thoughts. I doubted that she had her telepathy working; people who get that wound up find it hard to even see and hear straight, let alone think right. And telepathy or perception goes out of kilter first because the psi is a very delicate factor.

She eyed me coldly. "You utter imbecile," she snarled. "You—"

"Whoa, baby!" I roared. "Slow down. I'm a bit less than bright, but what have I done now?"

I'd have slapped her across the face as an anodyne if she hadn't been Mekstrom.

Farrow cooled visibly, then her face sort of came apart and she sort of flopped forward onto the bed and buried her face in my shoulder. I couldn't help but make comparisons; she was like a hunk of marble, warm and vibrant. Like having a statue crying on my shoulder. She sagged against me like a loose bag of cement and her hands clutched at my shoulder blades like a pair of C-clamps. A big juicy tear dropped from her cheek to land on my chest, and I was actually surprised to find that a teardrop from a Mekstrom did not land like a drop of mercury. It just splashed like any other drop of water, spread out, and made my chest wet.

Eventually I held her up from me, tried to shake her gently, and said, "Now what's the shooting all about, Farrow?"

She shook her head as if to clear her thinking gear.

"Steve," she said in a quietly serious tone, "I've been such an utter fool."

"You're not unique, Farrow," I told her. "People have been doing damfool stunts since—"

"I know," she broke in. Then with an effort at light-heartedness, she added, "There must be a different version of that Garden of Eden story. Eve is always blamed as having tempted Adam. Somewhere, Old Adam must have been slightly to blame—?"

I didn't know what she was driving toward, but I stroked her hair and waited. She was probably right. It still takes two of a kind to make one pair.

"Steve—get out of here! While you're safe!"

"Huh?" I blurted. "What cooks, Farrow?"

"I was a nice patsy," she said. She sat up and wiped her eyes. "I was a fool. Steve, if James Thorndyke had asked me to jump off the roof, I'd have asked him 'what direction?' That's how fat-headed I am."

"Yes?" Something was beginning to form, now.

"I—led you on, Steve."

That blinkoed me. The phrase didn't jell. The half a minute she'd spent bawling on my shoulder with my arms around her had been the first physical contact I'd ever had with Nurse Farrow. It didn't seem—

"No, Steve. Not that way. I couldn't see you for Thorndyke any more than you could see me for Catherine." Her telepathy had returned, obviously; she was in better control of herself. "Steve," she said, "I led you on; did everything that Thorndyke told me to. You fell into it like a rock. Oh—it was going to be a big thing. All I had to do was to haul you deeper into this mess, then I'd disappear strangely. Then we'd be—tog—ether—we'd be—"

She started to come unglued again but stopped the dissolving process just before the wet and gooey stage set in. She seemed to put a set in her shoulders, and then she looked down at me with pity. "Poor esper," she said softly, "you couldn't really know—"

"Know what?" I asked harshly.

"He fooled me—too," she said, in what sounded like a complete irrelevancy.

"Look, Farrow, try and make a bit of sense to a poor perceptive who can't read a mind. Keep it running in one direction, please?"

Again, as apparently irrelevant, she said, "He's a top grade telepath; he knows control—"

"Control—?" I asked blankly.

"You don't know," she said. "But a good telepath can think in patterns that prevent lesser telepaths from really digging deep. Thorndyke is brilliant, of scholar grade, really. He—"

"Let's get back to it, Farrow. What's cooking?"

Sternly she tossed her head. It was an angry motion, one that showed her disdain for her own tears and her own weakness. "Your own sweet Catherine."

I eyed her, not coldly but with a growing puzzlement. I tried to formulate my own idea but she went on, briskly, "That accident of yours was one of the luckiest things that ever happened to you, Steve."

"How long have I been known to be a Mekstrom Carrier?" I asked bluntly.

"No more than three weeks before you met Catherine Lewis," she told me as bluntly. "It took the Medical Center that long to work her into a position to meet you, Steve."

That put the icing on the cake. If nothing else, it explained why Catherine was here willingly. I didn't really believe it because no one can turn one hundred and eighty degrees without effort, but I couldn't deny the fact that the evidence fits the claim. If what Farrow said were true, my marriage to Catherine would have provided them with the same lever as the little blonde receptionist. The pile-up must have really fouled up their plans.

"It did, Steve," said Farrow, who had been following my mental ramblings. "The Highways had to step in and help. This fouled things up for both sides."

"Both sides?" I asked, completely baffled.

She nodded. "Until the accident, the Medical Center did not know that the Highways existed. But when Catherine dropped completely out of sight, Thorndyke did a fine job of probing you. That's when he came upon the scant evidence of the Highway Sign and the mental impression of the elder Harrison lifting the car so that Phillip could get you out. Then he knew, and—"

"Farrow," I snapped, "there are a lot of holes in your story. For instance—"

She held up a hand to stop me. "Steve," she said quietly, "you know how difficult it is for a non-telepath to find someone he can trust. But I'm trying to convince you that—"

I stopped Farrow this time. "How can I believe you now?" I asked her pointedly. "You seem to have a part in this side of the quiet warfare."

Nurse Farrow made a wry face as though she'd just discovered that the stuff she had in her mouth was a ball of wooly centipedes. "I'm a woman," she said simply. "I'm soft and gullible and easily talked into complacency. But I've just learned that their willingness to accept women is based upon the fact that no culture can thrive without women to propagate the race. I find that I am—" She paused, swallowed, and her voice became strained with bitterness, "—useful as a breeding animal. Just one of the peasants whose glory lies in carrying their heirs. But I tell you, Steve—" and here she became strong and her voice rang out with a vigorous rejection of her future, "I'll be forever damned if I will let my child be raised with the cockeyed notion that he has some God-Granted Right to Rule."

My vigilant sense of perception had detected a change in the human-pattern in the building. People were moving—no, it was one person who was moving.

Down in the laboratory below, and at the other end of the building, Catherine was still working over the autoclave and instruments. The waspish-looking superintendent had taken off for somewhere else, and while Catherine was alone now, she was about to be joined by Dr. Thorndyke. Half afraid that my perception of them would touch off their own telepathic sense of danger, I watched deliberately.

The door opened and Thorndyke came in; Catherine turned from her work and said something, which of course I could not possibly catch.

#What are they saying, Farrow?# I snapped mentally.

"I don't know. They're too far for my range."

I swore, but I didn't really have to have a dialog script. Nor did they do the obvious; what they did was far more telling.

Catherine turned and patted his cheek. They laughed at one another, and then Catherine began handing Thorndyke the instruments out of the autoclave, which he proceeded to mix in an unholy mess in the surgical tray. Catherine saw what he was doing and made some remark; then threatened him with a pair of haemostats big enough to clamp off a three-inch fire hose. It was pleasant enough looking horseplay; the sort of intimacy that people have when they've been together for a long time. Thorndyke did not look at all frightened of the haemostats, and Catherine did not really look as though she'd follow through with her threat. They finally tangled in a wrestle for the instrument, and Thorndyke took it away from her. They leaned against a cabinet side by side, their elbows touching, and went on talking as if they had something important to discuss in the midst of their fun. It could have been reorientation or it could have been Catherine's real self. I still couldn't quite believe that she had played me false. My mind spinned from one side to the other until I came up with a blunt question that came to my lips without any mental planning. I snapped, "Farrow, what grade of telepath is Catherine?"

"Doctor grade," she replied flatly. "Might have taken some pre-scholar training if economics hadn't interfered. I'd not really call her Rhine Scholar material, but I'm prejudiced against her."

If what Farrow said was true, Catherine was telepath enough to control and marshall her mind to a faretheewell. She could think and plan to herself in the presence of another telepath without giving her plots away.

She was certainly smart enough to lead one half-trained perceptive around by a ring in my nose. Me? I was as big a fool as Farrow.

CHAPTER TWENTY

Nurse Farrow caught my hand. "Steve," she snapped out in a rapid, flat voice, "Think only one thought. Think of how Catherine is here; that she came here to protect your life and your future!"

"Huh?"

"Think it!" she almost cried. "She's coming!"

I nearly fumbled it. Then I caught on. Catherine was coming; to remove the little finger manipulator and to have a chit-chat with me. I didn't want to see her, and I was beginning to wish—then I remembered that one glimmer out of me that I knew the truth and everything would be higher than Orbital Station One.

I shoved my mind into low gear and started to think idle thoughts, letting myself sort of daydream. I was convincing to myself; it's hard to explain exactly, but I was play-thinking like a dramatist. I fell into it; it seemed almost truth to me as I roamed on and on. I'd been trapped and Catherine had come here to hand herself over as a hostage against my good behavior. She'd escaped the Highways bunch or maybe she just left them quietly. Somehow Phelps had seen to it that Catherine got word—I didn't know how, but that was not important. The important thing was Catherine being here as a means of keeping me alive and well.

I went on thinking the lie. Catherine came in shortly and saw what Nurse Farrow was doing.

"I was supposed to do that," said Catherine.

Nurse Farrow straightened up from her work of loosening the straps on the manipulator. "Sorry," she said in a cool, crisp voice. "I didn't know that. This is usually my job. It's a rather delicate proposition, you know." There was a chill of professional rebuff in Farrow's voice. It was the pert white hat and the gold pin looking down upon the gray uniform with no adornment. Catherine looked a bit uncomfortable but she apparently had to take it.

Catherine tried lamely, "You see, Mr. Cornell is my fiancée."

Farrow jumped on that one hard. "I'm aware of that. So let's not forget that scholars of medicine do not treat their own loved ones for ethical reasons."

Catherine took it like a slap across the face with an iced towel. "I'm sure that Dr. Thorndyke would not have let me take care of him if I'd not been capable," she replied.

"Perhaps Dr. Thorndyke did not realize at the time that Mr. Cornell would be ready for the Treatment Department. Or," she added slyly, "have you been trained to prepare a patient for the full treatment?"

"The full treatment—? Dr. Thorndyke did not seem to think—"

"Please," said Farrow with that cold crispness coming out hard, "As a nurse I must keep my own opinion to myself, as well as keeping the opinions of doctors to myself. I take orders only and I perform them."

That was a sharp shot; practically telling Catherine that she, as a nurses' helper, had even less right to go shooting off her mouth. Catherine started to reply but gave it up. Instead she came over and looked down at me. She cooed and stroked my forehead.

"Ah, Steve," she breathed, "So you're going for the treatment. Think of me, Steve. Don't let it hurt too much."

I smiled thinly and looked up into her eyes. They were soft and warm, a bit moist. Her lips were full and red and they were parted slightly; the lower lip glistened slightly in the light. These were lips I'd kissed and found sweet; a face I'd held between my hands. Her hair fluffed forward a trifle; threatened to cascade down over her shoulders. No, it was not at all hard to lie there and go on thinking all the soft-sweet thoughts I'd once hoped might come true—

She recoiled, her face changing swiftly from its mask of sweet concern to one of hard calculation. I'd slipped with that last hunk of thinking and given the whole affair away.

Catherine straightened up and turned to head for the door. She took one step and caved in like a wet towel.

Over her still-falling body I saw Nurse Farrow calmly reloading the skin-blast hypo, which she used to fire a second load into the base of Catherine's neck, just below the shoulder blades.

"That," said Farrow succinctly, "should keep her cold for a week. I just wish I'd been born with enough guts to commit murder."

"What—?"

"Get dressed," she snapped. "It's cold outside, remember?" I started to dress as Farrow hurled my clothing out of the closet at me. She went on in the meantime: "I knew you couldn't keep it entirely concealed from her. She's too good a telepath. So while you were holding her attention, I let her have a shot in the neck. One of the rather bad things about being a Mekstrom is that minor items like the hypo don't register too well."

I stopped. "Isn't that bad? Seems to me that I've heard that pain is a necessary factor for the preservation of the—"

"Stop yapping and dress," snapped Farrow. "Pain is useful when it's needed. It isn't needed in the case of a pin pricking the hide of a Mekstrom. When a Mekstrom gets in the way of something big enough to damage him physically, then it hurts him."

"Sort of when a locomotive falls on their head?" I grunted.

"Keep on dressing. We're not out of this jungle yet."

"So have you any plans?"

She nodded soberly. "Yes, Steve. Once you asked me to be your telepath, to complete your team. I let you down. Now I've picked you up again, and from here on—out—I—"

I nodded. "Sold," I told her.

"Good. Now, Steve, dig the hallway."

I did. There was no one there. I opened my mouth to tell her so, and then closed it foolishly.

"Dig the hallway down to the left. Farther. To the door down there—three beyond the one you're perceiving now—is there a wheelchair there?"

"Wheelchair?" I blurted.

"Steve, this is a hospital. They don't even let a man with an aching tooth walk to the toothache ward. He rides. Now, you keep a good esper watch on the hall and if anybody looks out while I'm gone, just cast a deep dig at their face. It's possible that at this close range I can identify them from the perceived image in your mind. Although, God knows, no two people ever *see* anything alike, let alone perceive it."

She slipped out, leaving me with the recumbent form of my former sweetheart. Her face had fallen into the relaxed expression of sleep, sort of slack and unbuttoned.

#Tough, baby,# I thought as I closed my eyes so that all my energy could be aimed at the use of my perception.

Farrow was going down the hall like a professional heading for the wheelchair on a strict order. No one bothered to look out; she reached the locker room and dusted the wheelchair just as if she'd been getting it for a real patient. (The throb in my finger returned for a parthian shot and I remembered that I *was* a real patient!) She trundled the chair back and into my room.

"In," she said. "And keep that perception aimed on the hallway, the elevator, and the center corridor stairs."

She packed me with a blanket, tucking it so that my shoes and overclothing would not show, doing the job briskly. Then she scooped Catherine up from the floor and dropped her into my bed, and then rolled Catherine into one of those hospital doodads that hospitals use for male and female alike as bedclothing.

"Anyone taking a fast dig in here will think she's a patient—unless the digger knows that this room is supposed to be occupied by one Steve Cornell, obviously male. Now, Steve, ready to steer?"

"Steer?"

"Steer by esper. I'll drive. Oh—I know the way," she told me with a chuckle. "You just keep your perception peeled for characters who might be over-nosy. I'll handle the rest."

We went along the hallway. I took fast digs at the rooms and hall ahead of us; the whole coast seemed clear. Waiting for the two-bit elevator was nerve wracking; hospitals always have such poky elevators. But eventually it came and we trundled aboard. The pilot was no big-dome. He smiled at Nurse Farrow and nodded genially at me. He was probably a blank, jockeying an elevator is about the top job for a non-psi these days.

But as the elevator started down, a doctor came out of one of the rooms on the floor below. He took a fast look at the indicator above the elevator door and made a dash to thumb the button. The elevator came to a grinding halt and he got on.

This bothered me, but Farrow merely simpered at the guy and melted him down to size. She made some remark to him that I couldn't hear, but from the sudden increase of his pulse rate, I gathered that she'd really put him off guard. He replied in the same unintelligible tone and reached for her hand. She held his hand, and if the guy was thinking of me, my name is Sing Hoy Low and I am a Chinese Policeman.

He held her hand until we hit the first floor, and he debarked with a calf-like glance at Nurse Farrow. We went on to the ground floor and down the lower corridor to the end, where Farrow spent another lifetime and a half filling out a white cardboard form.

The superintendent eyed me with a sniff. "I'll call the car," she said.

I half-expected Farrow to make some objection, but she quietly nodded and we waited for another lifetime until a big car whined to a stop outside. Two big guys in white coats came in, tripped the lever on back of the wheelchair and stretched me out flat and low-slung on the same wheels. It was a neat conversion from wheelchair to wheeled stretcher, but as Farrow trundled me out feet first into the cold, I felt a sort of nervous chill somewhere south of my navel. She swung me around at the last minute and I was shoved head first into the back of the car.

Car? This was a full-fledged ambulance, about as long as a city block and as heavy as a battleship. It was completely fitted for everything that anybody could think of, including a great big muscular turbo-electric power plant capable of putting many miles per behind the tail-pipe.

The door closed on my feet, and we took off with Farrow sitting right behind the two big hospital attendants, one of whom was driving and the other of whom was ogling Farrow in a calculating manner. She invited the ogle. Heck, she did it in such a way that I couldn't help ogling a bit myself. If I haven't said that Farrow was an attractive woman, it was because I hadn't really paid attention to her looks. But now I went along and ogled, realizing in the dimmer and more obscure recesses of my mind that if I ogled in a loudly lewd perceptive manner, I'd not be thinking of what she was doing.

So while I was pleasantly occupied in ogling, Farrow slipped two more hypos out from under her clothing. She slipped her hands out sidewise on the backs of their seats, put her face between them and said, "Anybody got a cigarette, fellows?"

The next that took place happened, in order of occurrence, as follows:

The driver grunted and turned his head to look at her. The other guy fumbled for a cigarette. Driver poked at the lighter on the dash, still dividing his attention between the road and Nurse Farrow. The man beside him reached for the lighter when it popped out and he held it for her while she puffed it into action. Farrow fingered the triggers on the skin-blast hypos. The man beside the driver replaced the lighter in its socket on the dash. The driver slid aside and to the floor, a second before the other hospital orderly flopped down like a deflated balloon.

The ambulance took a swoop to the right, nosed down into a shallow ditch and leaped like a shot deer out on the other side.

Farrow went over the back of the seat in a flurry and I rolled off of my stretcher into the angle of the floor and the sidewall. There was a rumble and then a series of crashes before we came to a shuddering halt. I came up from beneath a pile of assorted medical supplies, braced myself against the canted deck, and looked out the wind-shield. The trunk of a tree split the field of view as close to dead center as it could be.

"Out, Steve," said Farrow, untangling herself from the steering wheel and the two attendants. "Out!"

"What next?" I asked her.

"We've made enough racket to wake the statue of Lincoln. Out and run for it."

"Which way?"

"Follow me!" she snapped, and took off. Even in nurse's shoes with those semi-heels, Farrow made time in a phenomenal way. I lost ground steadily. Luckily it was still early in the afternoon, so I used my perception to keep track of her once she got out of sight. She was following the gently rolling ground, keeping to the lower hollows and gradually heading toward a group of buildings off in the near-distance.

I caught up with her just as we hit a tiny patch of dead area; just inside the area she stopped and we flopped on the ground and panted our lungs full of nice biting cold air. Then she pointed at the collection of buildings and said, "Steve, take a few steps out of this deadness and take a fast dig. Look for cars."

I nodded; in a few steps I could send my esper forward to dig the fact that there were several cars parked in a row near one of the buildings. I wasted no time in digging any deeper, I just retreated into the dead area and told her what I'd seen.

"Take another dig, Steve. Take a dig for ignition keys. We've got to steal."

"I don't mind stealing." I took another trip into the open section and gandered at ignition locks. I tried to memorize the ones with keys hanging in the locks but failed to remember all of them.

"Okay, Steve. This is where we walk in boldly and walk up to a couple of cars and get in and drive off."

"Yeah, but why—"

"That's the only way we'll ever get out of here," she told me firmly.

I shrugged. Farrow knew more about the Medical Center than I did. If that's the way she figured it, that's the way it had to be. We broke out of the dead area, and as we came into the open, Farrow linked her arm in mine and hugged it.

"Make like a couple of fatuous mushbirds," she chuckled. "We've been out walking and communing with nature and getting acquainted."

"Isn't the fact that you're Mekstrom and I'm human likely to cause some rather pointed comment?"

"It would if we were to stick around to hear it," she said. "And if they try to read our minds, all we have to do is to think nice mushy thoughts. Face it," she said quietly, "it won't be hard."

"Huh?"

"You're a rather nice guy, Steve. You're fast on the uptake, you're generally pleasant. You've got an awful lot of grit, guts and determination, Steve. You're no pinup boy, Steve, but—and this may come as a shock to you—women don't put one-tenth the stock in pulchritude that men do? You—"

"Hey. Whoa," I bubbled. "Slow down, before you—"

She hugged my arm again. "Steve," she said seriously, "I'm not in love with you. It's not possible for a woman to be in love with a man who does not return that love. You don't love me. But you can't help but admit that I am an attractive woman, Steve, and perhaps under other circumstances you'd take on a large load of that old feeling. I'll admit that the reverse could easily take place. Now, let's forget all the odd angles and start thinking like a pair of people for whom the time, the place, and the opposite sex all turned up opportunely."

I couldn't help thinking of Nurse Farrow as—Nurse Farrow. The name Gloria did not quite come out. I tried to submerge this mental attitude, and so I looked down at her with what I hoped to resemble the expression of a love-struck male. I think it was closer to the expression of a would-be little-theatre actor expressing lust, and not quite making the grade. Farrow giggled.

But as I sort of leered down at her, I had to admit upon proper examination of her charm that Nurse Farrow could very easily become Gloria, if as she said, we had the time to let the change occur. Another idea formed in my mind: If Farrow had been kicked in the emotions by Thorndyke, I'd equally been pushed in the face by Catherine. That made us sort of kindred souls, as they used to call it in the early books of the Twentieth Century.

Gloria Farrow chuckled. "Unlike the old torch-carriers of that day," she said, "we rebound a bit too fast."

Then she let my arm go and took my hand. We went swinging across the field in a sort of happy comradeship; it must have looked as though we were long-term friends. She was a good egg, hurt and beaten down and shoved off by Thorndyke, but she had a lot of the good old bounce. Of a sudden impulse I wanted to kiss her.

"Go ahead, Steve," she said. "But it'll be for the probable onlookers. I'm Mekstrom, you know."

So I didn't try. I just put an arm around her briefly and realized that any attempt at affection would be like trying to strike sparks off flint with a hunk of flannel.

We walked hand in hand towards the buildings, strolled up saucily towards two of the parked cars, made the sort of wave that lovers give one another in goodbye when they don't really want to demonstrate their affection before ten thousand people and stepped into two cars and took off.

Gloria Farrow was in the lead.

We went howling down the road, Farrow in the lead car by a hundred feet and me behind her. We went roaring around a curve, over a hill, and I had my perception out to its range, which was far ahead of her car. The main gate came into range, and we bore down upon that wire and steel portal like a pair of madmen.

Gloria Farrow plowed into the gate without letting up. The gate went whirling in pieces, glass flew and tires howled and bits of metal and plastic sang through the air. Her car weaved aside; I forgot the road ahead and put my perception into her car.

Farrow was fighting the wheel like a racing driver in a spin. Her hands wrenched the wheel with the swift strength of the Mekstrom Flesh she wore, and the wheel bent under her hands. Over and around she went, with a tire blown and the lower rail of the big gate hanging onto the fender like a dry-land sea-anchor. She juggled the wheel and made a snaky path off to one side of the road.

Out of the guardhouse came a uniformed man with a riot gun. He did not have time to raise it. Farrow ironed out her course and aimed the careening car dead center. She mowed the guard down and a half-thousandth of a second later she plowed into the guardhouse. The structure erupted like a box of stove-matches hit with a heavy-caliber soft-nosed slug, like a house of cards and an air-jet. There was a roar and a small gout of flame and then out of the flying wreckage on the far side came Farrow and her stolen car. Out of the mess of brimstone and shingles she came, turning end for end in a crazy, metal-crushing twist and spin. She ground to a broken halt before the last of the debris landed, and then everything was silent.

And then for the first and only time in my life I felt the penetrant, forceful impact of an incoming thought; a mental contact from another mind:

#Steve!# it screamed in my mind, #Get out! Get going! It's your move now——#

I put my foot on the faucet and poured on the oil.

CHAPTER TWENTY-ONE

My car leaped forward and I headed along the outside road towards the nearby highway. Through the busted gate I roared, past the downed guard and the smashed guardhouse, past the wreck of Farrow's car.

But Nurse Farrow was not finished with this gambit yet. As I drew even with her, she pried herself out of the messy tangle and came across the field in a dead run—and how that girl could run! As fast as I was going, she caught up; as fast as it all happened I had too little time to slow me down before Nurse Farrow closed the intervening distance from her wreck to my car and had hooked her arm in through one open window.

My car lurched with the impact, but I fought the wheel straight again and Farrow snapped, "Keep going, Steve!"

I kept going; Farrow snaked herself inside and flopped into the seat beside me. "Now," she said, patting the dashboard of our car, "It's up to the both of us now! Don't talk, Steve. Just drive like crazy!"

"Where—?"

She laughed a weak little chuckle. "Anywhere—so long as it's a long, long way from here."

I nodded and settled down to some fancy mile-getting. Farrow relaxed in the seat, opened the glove compartment and took out a first aid kit. It was only then I noticed that she was banged up quite a bit for a Mekstrom. I'd not been too surprised when she emerged from the wreck; I'd become used to the idea of the indestructibility of the Mekstrom. I was a bit surprised at her being banged up; I'd become so used to their damage-proof hide that the idea of minor cuts, scars, mars, and abrasions hadn't occurred to me. Yes, that wreck would have mangled a normal man into an unrecognizable mess of hamburger. Yet I'd expected a Mekstrom to come through it unscathed.

On the other hand, the damage to Farrow's body was really minor. She bled from a long gash on her thigh, from a wound on her right arm, and from a myriad of little cuts on her face, neck, and shoulders.

So as I drove crazy-fast away from the Medical Center Nurse Farrow relaxed in the seat and applied adhesive tape, compresses, and closed the gashes with a batch of little skin clips in lieu of sutures. Then she lit two cigarettes and handed one of them to me. "Okay now, Steve," she said easily. "Let's drive a little less crazily."

I pulled the car down to a flat hundred and felt the strain go out of me.

"As I remember, there's one of the Highways not far from here—"

She shook her head. "No, Steve. We don't want the Highways in Hiding, either."

At a mere hundred per I could let my esper do the road-sighting, so I looked over at her. She was half-smiling, but beneath the little smile was a firm look of self-confidence. "No," she said quietly, "We don't want the Highways. If we go there, Phelps and his outfit will turn heaven and earth to break it up, now that you've become so important. You forget that the Medical Center is still being run to look legal and aboveboard; while the Highways are still in Hiding. Phelps could make quite a bitter case out of their reluctance to come out into the open."

"Well, where do we go?" I asked.

"West," she said simply. "West, into New Mexico. To my home."

This sort of startled me. Somehow I'd not connected Farrow with any permanent home; as a nurse and later as one of the Medical Center, I'd come to think of her as having no permanent home of her own. Yet like the rest of us, Nurse Farrow had been brought up in a home with a mother and a father and probably some sisters and brothers. Mine were dead and the original home disbanded, but there was no reason why I should think of everybody else in the same terms. After all, Catherine had had a mother and a father who'd come to see me after her disappearance.

So we went West, across Southern Illinois and over the big bridge at St. Louis into Missouri and across Missouri and West, West, West. We parked nights in small motels and took turns sleeping with one of us always awake and alert with esper and telepath senses geared high for the first sight of any threat. We gave the Highways we came upon a wide berth; at no time did we come close to any of their way stations. It made our path crooked and much longer than it might have been if we'd strung a line and gone. But eventually we ended up in a small town in New Mexico and at a small ranch house on the edge of the town.

It is nice to have parents; I missed my own deeply when I was reminded of the sweet wonder of having people just plain glad to see their children again, no matter what they'd done under any circumstances. Even bringing a semi-invalid into their homes for an extended course of treatment.

John Farrow was a tall man with gray at the temples and a pair of sharp blue eyes that missed nothing. He was a fair perceptive who might have been quite proficient if he had taken the full psi course at some university. Mrs. Farrow was the kind of elderly woman that any man would like to have for a mother. She was sweet and gentle but there was neither foolish softness or fatuous nonsense about her. She was a telepath and she knew her way around and let people know that she knew what the score was. Farrow had a brother, James, who was not at home; he lived in town with his wife but came out to the old homestead about once every week on some errand or other.

They took me in as though I'd come home with their daughter for sentimental reasons; Gloria sat with us in their living room and went through the whole story, interrupted now and then by a remark aimed at me. They inspected my hand and agreed that something must be done. They were extremely interested in the Mekstrom problem and were amazed at their daughter's feats of strength and endurance.

My hand, by this time, was beginning to throb again. The infection was heading on a fine start down the pinky and middle fingers; the ring finger was approaching the second joint to that point where the advance stopped long enough for the infection to become complete before it crossed the joint. The first waves of that particular pain were coming at intervals and I knew that within a few hours the pain would become waves of agony so deep that I would not be able to stand it.

Ultimately, Farrow got her brother James to come out from town with his tools, and between us all we rigged up a small manipulator for my hand. Farrow performed the medical operations from the kit in the back of her car we'd stolen from the Medical Center.

Then after they'd put my hand through the next phase, Nurse Farrow looked me over and gave the opinion that it was now approaching the time for me to get the rest of the full treatment.

One evening I went to bed, to be in bed for four solid months.

I'd like to be able to give a blow by blow description of those four solid months. Unfortunately, I was under dope so much of the time that I know little about it. It was not pleasant. My arm laid like a log from the Petrified Forest, strapped into the machine that moved the joints with regular motion, and with each motion starting a dart of fire and mangling pain up to the shoulder. Needles entered the veins at the elbow and the armpit, and from bottles suspended almost to the ceiling to provide a pressurehead, plasma and blood-sustenance was trickled in to keep the arm alive.

Dimly I recall having the other arm strapped down and the waves of pain that blasted at me from both sides. The only way I kept from going out of my mind with the pain was living from hypo to hypo and waiting for the blessed blackness that wiped out the agony; only to come out of it hours later with my infection advanced to another point of pain. When the infection reached my right shoulder, it stopped for a long time; the infection rose up my left arm and also stopped at the shoulder. I came out of the dope to find James and his father fitting one of the manipulators to my right leg and through that I could feel the darting pains in my calf and thigh.

At those few times when my mind was clear enough to let me use my perception, I dug the room and found that I was lying in a veritable forest of bottles and rubber tubes and a swathe of bandages.

Utterly helpless, I vaguely knew that I was being cared for in every way. The periods of clarity were fewer, now, and shorter when they came. I awoke once to find my throat paralyzed, and again to find that my jaw, tongue, and lower face was a solid pincushion of darting needles of fire. Later, my ears reported not a sound, and even later still I awoke to find myself strapped into a portable resuscitator that moved my chest up and down with an inexorable force.

That's about all I know of it. When the smoke cleared away completely and the veil across my eyes was gone, it was Spring outside and I was a Mekstrom.

I sat up in bed.

It was morning, the sun was streaming in the window brightly and the fresh morning air of Spring stirred the curtains gently. It was quite warm and the smell that came in from the outside was alive with newborn greenery. It felt good just to be alive.

The hanging bottles and festoons of rubber hose were gone. The crude manipulators had been stowed somewhere and the bottles of medicine and stuff were missing from the bureau. There wasn't even a thermometer in a glass anywhere within the range of my vision, and frankly I was so glad to be alive again that I did not see any point to digging through the joint with my perception to find the location of the medical junk. Instead, I just wanted to get up and run.

I did take a swing at the clothes closet and found my stuff. Then I took a mild pass at the house, located the bathroom and also assured myself that no one was likely to interrupt me.

I was going to shave and shower and dress and go downstairs. I was just shrugging myself up and out of bed when Nurse Farrow came bustling up the stairs and into the room with no preamble.

"Hi!" I greeted her. "I was going to—"

"Surprise us," she said quickly. "I know. So I came up to see that you don't get into trouble."

"Trouble?" I asked, pausing on the edge of the bed.

"You're a Mekstrom, Steve," she told me unnecessarily. Then she caught my thought and went on: "It's necessary to remind you. You have to learn how to control your strength, Steve."

I flexed my arms. They didn't feel any different. I pinched my muscle with my other hand and it pinched just as it always had. I took a deep breath and the air went in pleasantly and come out again.

"I don't feel any different," I told her.

She smiled and handed me a common wooden lead pencil. "Write your name," she directed.

"Think I'll have to learn all over?" I grinned. I took the pencil, put my fist down on the top of the bureau above a pad of paper and chuckled at Farrow. "Now, let's see, my first initial is the letter 'S'

159

made by starting at the top and coming around in a sweeping, graceful curve like this—"

It didn't come around in any curve. As the lead point hit the paper it bore down in, flicked off the tip, and then crunched down, breaking off the point and splintering the thin, whittled wood for about an eighth of an inch. The fact that I could not control it bothered me inside and I instinctively clutched at the shaft of the pencil. It cracked in three places in my hand; the top end with the eraser fell down over my wrist to the bureau top and rolled in a rapid rattle to the edge where it fell to the floor.

"See?" asked Farrow softly.

"But—?" I blundered uncertainly.

"Steve, your muscles and your nervous system have been stepped up proportionately. You've got to re-learn the coordination between the muscle-stimulus and the feedback information from the work you are doing."

I began to see what she meant. I remembered long years ago at school, when we'd been studying some of the new alloys and there had been a sample of a magnesium-lithium-something alloy that was machined into a smooth cylinder about four inches in diameter and a foot long. It looked like hard steel. People who picked it up for the first time invariably braced their muscles and set both hands on it. But it was so light that their initial effort almost tossed the bar through the ceiling, and even long after we all knew, it was hard not to attack the bar without using the experience of our mind and sense that told us that any bar of metal *that* big had to be *that* heavy.

I went to a chair. Farrow said, "Be careful," and I was. But it was no trick at all to take the chair by one leg at the bottom and lift it chin high.

"Now, go take your shower," she told me. "But Steve, please be careful of the plumbing. You can twist off the faucet handles, you know."

I nodded and turned to her, holding out a hand. "Farrow, you're a brick!"

She took my hand. It was not steel hard. It was warm and firm and pleasant. It was—holding hands with a woman.

Farrow stepped back. "One thing you'll have to remember," she said cheerfully, "is only to mix with your own kind from now on. Now go get that shower and shave. I'll be getting breakfast."

Showering was not hard and I remembered not to twist off the water-tap handles. Shaving was easy although I had to change razor blades three times in the process. I broke all the teeth out of the comb because it was never intended to be pulled through a thicket of piano wire.

Getting dressed was something else. I caught my heel in one trouser leg and shredded the cloth. I broke the buckle on my belt. My shoelaces went like parting a length of wet spaghetti. The button on the top of my shirt pinched off and when I gave that final jerk to my necktie it pulled the knot down into something about the size of a pea.

Breakfast was very pleasant, although I bent the fork tines spearing a rasher of bacon and removed the handle of my coffee cup without half trying. After breakfast I discovered that I could not remove a cigarette from the package without pinching the end down flat, and after I succeeded in getting one into my mouth by treating both smoke and match as if they were made of tissue paper, my first drag on the smoke lit a howling furnace-fire on the end that consumed half of the cigarette in the first puff.

"You're going to take some school before you are fit to walk among normal people, Steve," said Gloria with amused interest.

"You're informing me?" I asked with some dismay, eyeing the wreckage left in my wake. Compared to the New Steve Cornell, the famous bull in the china shop was Gentle Ferdinand. I picked up the cigarette package again; it squoze down even though I tried to treat it gentle; I felt like Lenny, pinching the head off of the mouse. I also felt about as much of a bumbling idiot as Lenny, too.

My re-education went on before, through, and after breakfast. I manhandled old books from the attic. I shredded newspapers. I ruined some more lead pencils and finally broke the pencil sharpener to boot. I put an elbow through the middle panel of the kitchen door without even feeling it and then managed to twist off the door knob. Generally operating like a one-man army of vandals, I laid waste to the Farrow home.

Having thus ruined a nice house, Gloria decided to try my strength on her car. I was much too fast and too hard on the brakes, which of course was not too bad because my foot was also too insensitive on the go-pedal. We took off like a rocket being launched and then I tromped on the brakes (Bending the pedal) which brought us down sharp like hitting a haystack. This allowed our heads to catch up with the rest of us; I'm sure that if we'd been normal-bodied human beings we'd have had our spines snapped. Eventually I learned that everything had to be handled as if it were tissue paper, and gradually re-adjusted my reflexes to take proper cognizance of the feedback data according to my new body.

We returned home after a hectic twenty miles of roadwork and I broke the glass as I slammed the car door.

"It's going to take time," I admitted with some reluctance.

"It always does," smiled Farrow as cheerfully as if I hadn't ruined their possessions.

"I don't know how I'm going to face your folks."

Farrow's smile became cryptic. "Maybe they won't notice."

"Now look, Farrow——"

"Steve, don't forget for the moment that you're the only known Mekstrom Carrier."

"In other words your parents are due for the treatment next?"

"Oh, I was most thorough. Both of them are in the final stages right now. I'm sure that anything you did to the joint will only be added to by the time they get to the walking stage. And also anything you did they'll feel well repaid."

"I didn't do anything for them."

"You provided them with Mekstrom bodies," she said simply.

"They took to it willingly?"

"Yes. As soon as they were convinced by watching me and my strength. They knew what it would be like, but they were all for it."

"You've been a very busy girl," I told her.

She just nodded. Then she looked up at me with troubled eyes and asked, "What are you going to do now, Steve?"

"I'm going to haul the whole shebang down like Samson in the Temple."

"A lot of innocent people are going to get hurt if you do that."

"I can't very well find a cave in Antarctica and hide," I replied glumly.

"Think a bit, Steve. Could either side afford to let you walk into New Washington with the living proof of your Mekstrom Body?"

#Didn't stop 'em before,# I thought angrily. #And it seems to me that both sides were sort of urging me to go and do something that would uncover the other side.#

"Not deep enough," said Farrow. "That was only during the early phases. Go back to the day when you didn't know what was going on."

I grunted sourly, "Look, Farrow, tell me. Why must I fumble my way through this as I've fumbled through everything else?"

"Because only by coming to the conclusion in your own way will you be convinced that someone isn't lying to you. Now, think it over, Steve."

It made sense. Even if I came to the wrong conclusion, I'd believe it more than if someone had told me. Farrow nodded, following my thoughts. Then I plunged in:

#First we have a man who is found to be a carrier of Mekstrom's Disease. He doesn't know anything about the disease. Right?# (Farrow nodded slowly.) #So now the Medical Center puts an anchor onto their carrier by sicking an attractive dame on his trail. Um—# At this point I went into a bit of a mental whirly-around trying to find an answer to one of the puzzlers. Farrow just looked at me with a non-leading expression, waiting. I came out of the merry-go-round after six times around the circuit and went on:

#I don't know all the factors. Obviously, Catherine had to lead me fast because we had to marry before she contracted the disease from me. But there's a discrepancy, Farrow. The little blonde receptionist caught it in twenty-four hours—?#

"Steve," said Farrow, "this is one I'll have to explain, since you're not a medical person. The period of incubation depends upon the type of contact. You actually bit the receptionist. That put blood contact into it. You didn't draw any blood from Catherine."

"We were pretty close," I said with a slight reddening of the ears.

"From a medical standpoint, you were not much closer to Catherine than you have been to me, or Dr. Thorndyke. You were closer to Thorndyke and me, say, than you've been to many of the incidental parties along the path of our travels."

"Well, let that angle go for the moment. Anyway, Catherine and I had to marry before the initial traces were evident. Then I'd be in the position of a man whose wife had contracted Mekstrom's Disease on our honeymoon, whereupon the Medical Center would step in and cure her, and I'd be in the position of being forever grateful and willing to do anything that the Medical Center wanted me to do. And as a poor non-telepath, I'd probably never learn the truth. Right?"

"So far," she said, still in a noncommittal tone.

"So now we crack up along the Highway near the Harrison place. The Highways take her in because they take any victim in no matter what. I also presume from what's gone on that Catherine is a high enough telepath to conceal her thinking and so to become an undercover agent in the midst of the Highways organization. And at this point the long long trail takes a fork, doesn't it? The Medical Center gang did not know about the Highways in Hiding until Catherine and I barrelled into it end over end."

Farrow's face softened, and although she said nothing I knew I was on the right track.

#So at this point,# I went on silently, #Medical Center found themselves in a mild quandary. They could hardly put another woman on my trail because I was already emotionally involved with the missing Catherine—and so they decided to use me in another way. I was shown enough to keep me busy, I was more or less urged to go track down the Highways in Hiding for the Medical Center. After all, as soon as I'd made the initial discovery, Phelps and his outfit shouldn't have needed any more help.#

"A bit more thinking, Steve. You've come up with that answer before."

#Sure. Phelps wanted me to take my tale to the Government. About this secret Highway outfit. But if neither side can afford to have the secret come out, how come—?# I pondered this for a long time and admitted that it made no sense to me. Finally Farrow shook her head and said,

"Steve, I've got to prompt you now and then. But remember that I'm trying to make you think it out yourself. Now consider: You are running an organization that must be kept secret. Then someone learns the secret and starts heading for the Authorities. What is your next move?"

"Okay," I replied. "So I'm stupid. Naturally, I pull in my horns, hide my signs, and make like nothing was going on."

"So stopping the advance of your organization, which is all that Phelps really can expect."

I thought some more. #And the fact that I was carrying a story that would get me popped into the nearest hatch for the incipient paranoid made it all right?#

She nodded.

"And now?" she asked me.

"And now I'm living proof of my story. Is that right?"

"Right. And Steve, do not forget for one moment that the only reason that you're still alive is because you are valuable to both sides alive. Dead, you're only good for a small quantity of Mekstrom Inoculation."

"Don't follow," I grunted. "As you say, I'm no medical person."

"Alive, your hair grows and must be cut. You shave and trim off beard. Your fingernails are pared. Now and then you lose a small bit of hide or a few milliliters of blood. These are things that, when injected under the skin of a normal human, makes them Mekstrom. Dead, your ground up body would not provide much substance."

"Pleasant prospect," I growled. "So what do I do to avert this future?"

"Steve, I don't know. I've done what I can for you. I've effected the cure and I've done it in safety; you're still Steve Cornell."

CHAPTER TWENTY-TWO

"Look," I blurted with a sudden rush of brain to the head, "If I'm so all-fired important to both sides, how come you managed to sequester me for four months?"

"We do have the laws of privacy," said Farrow simply. "Which neither side can afford to flout overtly. Furthermore, since neither side really knew where you were, they've been busily prowling one another's camps and locking up the prowlers from one another's camps, and playing spy and counterspy and counter-counterspy, and generally piling it up pyramid-wise," she finished with a chuckle. "You got away with following that letter to Catherine because uppermost in your mind was the brain of a lover hunting down his missing sweetheart. No one could go looking for Steve Cornell, Mekstrom Carrier, for reasons not intrinsically private."

"For four months?" I asked, still incredulous.

"Well, one of the angles is that both sides knew you were immobilized somewhere, going through this cure. Having you a full Mekstrom is something that both sides want. So they've been willing to have you cured."

"So long as someone does the work, huh?"

"Right," she said seriously.

"Well, then," I said with a grim smile, "the obvious thing for me to do is to slink quietly into New Washington and to seek out some high official in secrecy. I'll put my story and facts into his hands, make him a Mekstrom, have him cured, and then we'll set up an agency to provide the general public with—"

"Steve, you're an engineer. I presume you've studied mathematics. So let's assume that you can—er—bite one person every ten seconds."

"That's six persons per minute; three-sixty per hour; and, ah, eighty-six-forty per day. With one hundred and sixty million Americans at the last census—um. Sixty years without sleep. I see what you mean."

"Not only that, Steve, but it would create a panic, if not a global war. Make an announcement like that, and certain of our not-too-friendly neighbors would demand their shares or else. So now add up your time to take care of about three billion human souls on this Earth, Steve."

"All right. So I'll forget that cockeyed notion. But still, the Government should know—"

"If we could be absolutely certain that every elected official is a sensible, honest man, we could," said Farrow. "The trouble is that we've got enough demagogues, publicity hounds, and rabble-rousers to make the secret impossible to keep."

I couldn't argue against that. Farrow was right. Not only that, but Government found it hard enough to function in this world of Rhine Institute with honest secrets.

"Okay, then," I said. "The only thing to do is to go back to Homestead, Texas, throw my aid to the Highways in Hiding, and see what we can do to provide the Earth with some more sensible method of inoculation. I obviously cannot go around biting people for the rest of my life."

"I guess that's it, Steve."

I looked at her. "I'll have to borrow your car."

"It's yours."

"You'll be all right?"

She nodded. "Eventually I'll be a way station on the Highways, I suppose. Can you make it alone, Steve? Or would you rather wait until my parents are cured? You could still use a telepath, you know."

"Think it's safe for me to wait?"

"It's been four months. Another week or two—?"

"All right. And in the meantime I'll practice getting along with this new body of mine."

We left it there. I roamed the house with Farrow, helping her with her parents. I gradually learned how to control the power of my new muscles; learned how to walk among normal people without causing their attention; and one day succeeded in shaking hands with a storekeeper without giving away my secret.

Eventually Nurse Farrow's parents came out of their treatment and we spent another couple of days with them.

We left them too soon, I'm sure, but they seemed willing that we take off. They'd set up a telephone system for getting supplies so that they'd not have to go into town until they learned how to handle their bodies properly, and Farrow admitted that there was little more that we could do.

So we took off because we all knew that time was running out. Even though both sides had left us alone while I was immobilized, both sides must have a time-table good enough to predict my eventual cure. In fact, as I think about it now, both sides must have been waiting along the outer edges of some theoretical area waiting for me to emerge, since they couldn't come plowing in without giving away their purpose.

So we left in Farrow's car and once more hit the big broad road.

We drove towards Texas until we came upon a Highway, and then turned along it looking for a way station. I wanted to get in touch with the Highways. I wanted close communication with the Harrisons and the rest of them, no matter what. Eventually we came upon a Sign with a missing spoke and turned in.

The side road wound in and out, leading us back from the Highway towards the conventional dead area. The house was a white structure among a light thicket of trees, and as we came close to it, we met a man busily tilling the soil with a tractor plow.

Farrow stopped her car. I leaned out and started to call, but something stopped me.

"He is no Mekstrom, Steve," said Farrow in a whisper.

"But this is a way station, according to the road sign."

"I know. But it isn't, according to him. He doesn't know any more about Mekstrom's Disease than you did before you met Catherine."

"Then what the devil is wrong?"

"I don't know. He's perceptive, but not too well trained. Name's William Carroll. Let me do the talking, I'll drop leading remarks for you to pick up."

The man came over amiably. "Looking for someone?" he asked cheerfully.

"Why, yes," said Gloria. "We're sort of mildly acquainted with the—Mannheims who used to live here. Sort of friends of friends of theirs, just dropped by to say hello, sort of," she went on, covering up the fact that she'd picked the name of the former occupant out of his mind.

"The Mannheims moved about two months ago," he said. "Sold the place to us—we got a bargain. Don't really know, of course, but the story is that one of them had to move for his health."

"Too bad. Know where they went?"

"No," said Carroll regretfully. "They seem to have a lot of friends. Always stopping by, but I can't help 'em any."

#So they moved so fast that they couldn't even change their Highway Sign?# I thought worriedly.

Farrow nodded at me almost imperceptibly. Then she said to Carroll, "Well, we won't keep you. Too bad the Mannheims moved, without leaving an address."

"Yeah," he said with obvious semi-interest. He eyed his half-plowed field and Farrow started her car.

We started off and he turned to go back to his work. "Anything?" I asked.

"No," she said, but it was a very puzzled voice. "Nothing that I can put a finger on."

"But what?"

"I don't know much about real estate deals," she said. "I suppose that one family could move out and another family move in just in this short a time."

"Usually they don't let farmlands lie fallow," I pointed out. "If there's anything off color here, it's the fact that they changed their residence without changing the Highway sign."

"Unless," I suggested brightly, "this is the coincidence. Maybe this sign is really one that got busted."

Farrow turned her car into the main highway and we went along it. I could have been right about the spoke actually being broken instead of removed for its directing purpose. I hoped so. In fact I hoped so hard that I was almost willing to forget the other bits of evidence. But then I had to face the truth because we passed another Highway Sign and, of course, its directional information pointed to that farm. The signs on our side of the highway were upside down; indicating that we were leaving the way station. The ones that were posted on the left hand side were rightside up, indicating that the drive was approaching a way station. That cinched it.

#Well,# as I told both Farrow and me, #one error doesn't create a trend. Let's take another look!#

One thing and another, we would either hit another way station before we got to Homestead, or we wouldn't. Either one could put us wise. So we took off again with determination and finally left that side of erroneous Highway Signs when we turned onto Route 66. We weren't on Route 66 very long because the famous U.S. Highway sort of trends to the Northeast and Homestead was in a Southern portion of Texas. We left Route 66 at Amarillo and picked up U.S. 87, which leads due South.

Not many miles out of Amarillo we came up another set of Highway Signs that pointed us on to the South. I tried to remember whether this section led to Homestead by a long route, but I hadn't paid too much attention to the maps when I'd had the chance and therefore the facts eluded me.

We'd find out, Farrow and I agreed, and then before we could think much more about it, we came upon a way station sign that pointed in to another farmhouse.

"Easy," I said.

"You bet," she replied, pointing to the rural-type mailbox alongside the road.

I nodded. The box was not new but the lettering on the side was. "Still wet," I said with a grunt.

Farrow slowed her car as we approached the house and I leaned out and gave a cheerful hail. A woman came out of the front door and waved at us.

"I'm trying to locate a family named Harrison," I called. "Lived around here somewhere."

The woman looked thoughtful. She was maybe thirty-five or so, clean but not company-dressed. There was a smudge of flour on her cheek and a smile on her face and she looked wholesome and honest.

"Why, I don't really know," she said. "That name sounds familiar, but it is not an uncommon name."

"I know," I said uselessly. Farrow nudged me on the ankle with her toe and then made a swift sign for "P" in the hand-sign code.

"Why don't you come on in?" invited the woman. "We've got an area telephone directory here. Maybe—?"

Farrow nudged me once more and made the sign of "M" with her swift fingers. We had hit it this time; here was a woman perceptive and a Mekstrom residing in a way station. I took a mild dig at her hands and there was no doubt of her.

A man's head appeared in the doorway above the woman; he had a hard face and he was tall and broad shouldered but there was a smile on his face that spread around the pipe he was biting on. He called, "Come on in and take a look."

Farrow made the sign of "T" and "M" and that told me that he was a telepath. She hadn't needed the "M" sign because I'd taken a fast glimpse of his hide as soon as he appeared. Parrying for time and something evidential, I merely said, "No, we'd hate to intrude. We were just asking."

The man said, "Oh, shucks, Mister. Come on in and have a cup of coffee, anyway." His invitation was swift enough to set me on edge.

I turned my perception away from him and took a fast cast at the surrounding territory. There was a mildly dead area along the lead-in road to the left; it curved around in a large arc and the other horn of this horseshoe shape came up behind the house and stopped abruptly just inside of their front door. The density of this area varied, the end in which the house was built was so total that I couldn't penetrate, while the other end that curved around to end by the road tapered off in deadness until it was hard to define the boundary.

If someone were pulling a flanking movement around through that horseshoe to cut off our retreat, it would become evident very soon.

A swift thought went through my mind: #Farrow, they're Mekstroms and he's a telepath and she's a perceptive, and they know we're friendly if they're Highways. If they're connected with Scholar Phelps and his—#

The man repeated, "Come on in. We've some mail to go to Homestead that you can take if you will."

Farrow made no sound. She just seesawed her car with three rapid back-and-forth jerks that sent showers of stones from her spinning wheels. We whined around in a curve that careened the car up on its outside wheels. Then we ironed out and showered the face of the man with stones from the wheels as we took off. The shower of dust and stones blinded him, and kept him from latching onto the tail of the car and climbing in. We left him behind, swearing and rubbing dirt from his eyes.

We whipped past the other end of the horseshoe area just as a jeepster came roaring down out of the thickened part into the region where my perception could make out the important things (Like three burly gents wearing hunting rifles, for instance.) They jounced over the rough ground and onto the lead-in road just behind us; another few seconds of gab with our friends and they'd have been able to cut us off.

"Pour it on, Farrow!"

I knew I was a bit of a cowboy, but Farrow made me look like a tenderfoot. We rocketed down the winding road with our wheels riding up on either side like the course in a toboggan run and Farrow rode that car like a test pilot in a sudden thunderstorm.

I was worried about the hunting rifles, but I need not have been concerned. We were going too fast to make good aim, and their jeepster was not a vehicle known for its smooth riding qualities. They lost one character over a rough bounce and he went tail over scalp into the grass along the way. He scared me by leaping to his feet, grabbing the rifle and throwing it up to aim. But before he could squeeze off a round we were out of the lead-in road and on the broad highway.

Once on the main road again, Farrow put the car hard down by the nose and we outran them. The jeepster was a workhorse and could have either pulled over the house or climbed the wall and run along the roof, but it was not made for chase.

"That," I said, "seems to be that."

"Something is bad," agreed Farrow.

"Well, I doubt that they'll be able to clean out a place as big as Homestead. So let's take our careful route to Homestead and find out precisely what the devil is cooking."

"Know the route?"

"No, but I know where it is on the map and we can figure it out from—"

"Steve, stop. Take a very careful and delicate view over to the right."

"Digging for what?"

"Another car pacing us along a road on the other side of that field."

I tried and failed. Then I leaned back in the seat and closed my eyes and tried again. On this second try I got a very hazy perception of a large moving mass that could only have been a car. In the car I received a stronger impression of weapons. It was the latter that cinched it.

I hauled out my roadmap and turned it to Texas. I thumbed the sectional maps of Texas until I located the sub-district through which we were passing and then I identified this section of U.S. 87 precisely. There was another road parallel and a half mile to the right, a dirt road according to the map-legend. It intersected our road a few miles ahead.

My next was a thorough covering of the road behind; as I expected another car was pacing us just beyond the range of my perception for anything but a rifle aimed at my hide.

Pacing isn't quite the word, I use it in the sense of their keeping up with us. Fact is that all of us were going about as fast as we could go, with safety of tertiary importance. Anyway, they were pacing us and closing down from that parallel road on the right.

I took a fast and very careful scanning of the landscape to our left but couldn't find anything. I spent some time at it then, but still came up with a blank.

#Turn left at that feeder road a mile ahead,# I thought at Farrow and she nodded.

There was one possibility that I did not like to face. We had definitely detected pursuit to our right and behind, but not to our left. This did not mean that the left-side was not covered. It was quite likely that the gang to the rear were in telepathic touch with a network of other telepaths, the end of which mental relay link was far beyond range, but as close in touch with our position and action as if we'd been in sight. The police make stake-out nets that way, but the idea is not exclusive. I recall hazing an eloping couple that way once.

But there was nothing to do but to take the feeder road to the left, because the devil we could see was more dangerous than the devil we couldn't.

Farrow whipped into the side road and we tore along with only a slight slowing of our headlong speed. I ranged ahead, worried, suspicious of everything, scanning very carefully and strictly on the watch for any evidence of attempted interception.

I caught a touch of danger converging up from the South on a series of small roads. This I did not consider dangerous after a fast look at my roadmap because this series of roads did not meet our side road for a long time and only after a lot of turning and twisting. So long as we went Easterly, we were okay from that angle.

The gang behind, of course, followed us, staying at the very edge of my range.

"You'll have to fly, Farrow," I told her. "If that gang to our South stays there, we'll not be able to turn down Homestead way."

"Steve, I'm holding this crate on the road by main force and awkwardness as it is."

But she did step it up a bit, at that. I kept a cautious and suspicious watchout, worrying in the back of my mind that someone among them might turn up with a jetcopter. So long as the sky remained clear—

As time went on, I perceived that the converging car to the South was losing ground because of the convolutions of their road. Accordingly we turned to the South, making our way around their nose, sort of, and crossing their anticipated course to lead South. We hit U.S. 180 to the West of Breckenridge, Texas and then Farrow really poured on the coal. The idea was to hit Fort Worth and lose them in the city where fun, games, and telepath-perceptive hare-and-hounds would be viewed dimly by the peaceloving citizens. Then we'd slope to the South on U.S. 81, cut over to U.S. 75 somewhere to the South and take 75 like a cannonball until we turned off on the familiar road to Homestead.

Fort Worth was a haven and a detriment to both sides. Neither of us could afford to run afoul of the law. So we both cut down to sensible speeds and snaked our way through the town, with Farrow and me probing the roads to the South in hope of finding a clear lane.

There were three cars pacing us, cutting off our retreat Southward. They hazed us forward to the East like a dog nosing a bunch of sheep towards pappy's barn.

Then we were out of Forth Worth and on U.S. 180. We whipped into Dallas and tried the same circumfusion as before and we were as neatly barred. So we went out of Dallas on U.S. 67 and as we left the city limits, we poured on the oil again, hoping to get around them so that we could turn back South towards Homestead.

"Boxed," I said.

"Looks like it," said Farrow unhappily.

I looked at her. She was showing signs of weariness and I realized that she'd been riding this road for hours. "Let me take it," I said.

"We need your perception," she objected. "You can't drive and keep a ranging perception, Steve."

"A lot of good a ranging perception will do once you drop for lack of sleep and we tie us up in a ditch."

"But—"

"We're boxed," I told her. "We're being hazed. Let's face it, Farrow. They could have surrounded us and glommed us any time in the past six hours."

"Why didn't they?" she asked.

"You ask that because you're tired," I said with a grim smile. "Any bunch that has enough cars to throw a barrier along the streets of cities like Forth Worth and Dallas have enough manpower to catch us if they want to. So long as we drive where they want us to go, they won't cramp us down."

"I hate to admit it."

"So do I. But let's swap, Farrow. Then you can use your telepathy on them maybe and find out what their game is."

She nodded, pulled the car down to a mere ramble and we swapped seats quickly. As I let the crate out again, I took one last, fast dig of the landscape and located the cars that were blocking out the passageways to the South, West, and North, leaving a nice inviting hole to the Easterly-North way. Then I had to haul in my perception and slap it along the road ahead, because I was going to ramble far and fast and see if I could speed out of the trailing horseshoe and cut out around the South horn with enough leeway to double back towards Homestead.

"Catch any plans from them?" I asked Farrow.

There was no answer. I looked at her. Gloria Farrow was semi-collapsed in her seat, her eyes closed gently and her breath coming in long, pleasant swells. I'd known she was tired, but I hadn't expected this absolute ungluing. A damned good kid, Farrow.

At that last thought, Farrow moved slightly in her sleep and a wisp of a smile crossed her lips briefly. Then she turned a bit and snuggled down in the seat and really hit the slumber-path.

A car came roaring at me with flashing headlamps and I realized that dusk was coming. I didn't need the lights, but oncoming drivers did, so I snapped them on. The beams made bright tunnels in the light and we went along and on and on and on, hour after hour. Now and then I caught a perceptive impression the crescent of cars that were corralling us along U.S. 67 and not letting us off the route.

I hauled out my roadmap and eyed the pages as I drove by perception. U.S. 67 led to St. Louis and from there due North. I had a hunch that by the time we played hide and seek through St. Louis and got ourselves hazed out to their satisfaction, I'd be able to give a strong guess as to our ultimate destination.

I settled down in my seat and just drove, still hoping to cut fast and far around them on my way to Homestead.

CHAPTER TWENTY-THREE

Three times during the night I tried to flip around and cut my way through their cordon, and each time I faced interception. It was evident that we were being driven and so long as we went to their satisfaction they weren't going to clobber us.

Nurse Farrow woke up along about dawn, stretched, and remarked that she could use a toothbrush and a tub of hot water and amusedly berated herself for not filling the back seat before we took off. Then she became serious again and asked for the details of the night, which I slipped her as fast as I could.

We stopped long enough to swap seats, and I stretched out but I couldn't sleep.

Finally I said, "Stop at the next dog wagon, Farrow. We're going to eat, comes anything."

"Won't that be dangerous?"

"Shucks," I grunted angrily. "They'll probably thank us. They're probably hungry too."

"We'll find out."

The smell of a roadside diner is usually a bit on the thick and greasy side, but I was so hungry that morning that it smelled like mother's kitchen. We went in, ordered coffee and orange juice, and then disappeared into the rest rooms long enough to clean up. That felt so good we ordered the works and watched the guy behind the fryplate handle the bacon, eggs, and home-fries with a deft efficient manner.

We pitched in fast, hoping to beat the flies to our breakfast. We were so intent that we paid no attention to the car that came into the lot until a man came in, ordered coffee and a roll, and then carried it over to our table.

"Fine day for a ride, isn't it?"

I eyed him; Farrow bristled and got very tense. I said, "I doubt that I know you, friend."

"Quite likely. But I know you, Cornell."

I took a fast dig; there was no sign of anything lethal except the usual collection of tire irons, screwdrivers, and other tools which, oddly enough, seldom come through as being dangerous because they're not weapons-by-design.

"I'm not heeled, Cornell. I'm just here to save us all some trouble."

#Telepath?#

He nodded imperceptibly. Then he said, "We'll all save time, gasoline, and maybe getting into grief with the cops if you take Route 40 out of St. Louis."

"Suppose I don't like U.S. 40?"

"Get used to it," he said with a crooked smile. "Because you'll take U.S. 40 out of St. Louis whether you like it or not."

I returned his crooked smile. I also dug his hide and he was a Mekstrom, of course. "Friend," I replied, "Nothing would convince me, after what you've said, that U.S. 40 is anything but a cowpath; slippery when wet; and impassible in the Early Spring, Late Summer, and the third Thursday after Michelmas."

He stood up. "Cornell, I can see your point. You don't like U.S. 40. So I'll help you good people. If you don't want to drive along such a lousy slab of concrete, just say the word and we'll arrange for you to take it in style, luxury, and without a trace of pain or strain. I'll be seein' you. And a very pleasant trip to you, Miss Farrow."

Then the character got up, went to the cashier and paid for our breakfast as well as his own. He took off in his car and I have never seen him since.

Farrow looked at me, her face white and her whole attitude one of fright. "U.S. 40," she said in a shaky voice, "runs like a stretched string from St. Louis to Indianapolis."

She didn't have to tell me any more. About sixty miles North of Indianapolis on Indiana State Highway 37 lies the thriving metropolis of Marion, Indiana, the most important facet of which (to Farrow and me) is an establishment called the Medical Research Center.

Nothing was going to make me drive out of St. Louis along U.S. 40. Period; End of message; No answer required.

Nothing, because I was very well aware of their need to collect me alive and kicking. If I could not roar out of St. Louis in the direction I selected, I was going to turn my car end for end and have at them. Not in any mild manner, but with deadly intent to do deadly damage. If I'd make a mild pass, they'd undoubtedly corral me by main force and carry me off kicking and screaming. But if I went at them to kill or get killed, they'd have to move aside just to prevent me from killing myself. I didn't think I'd get to the last final blow of that self-destruction. I'd win through.

So we left the diner after a breakfast on our enemy's expense account and took off again.

I was counting on St. Louis. The center of the old city is one big shapeless blob of a dead area; so nice and cold that St. Louis has reversed the usual city-type blight area growth. Ever since Rhine, the slum sections have been moving out and the new buildings have been moving in. So with the dead area and the brand-new, wide streets and fancy traffic control, St. Louis was the place to go in along one road, get lost in traffic, and come out, roaring along any road desirable. I could not believe that any outfit, hoping to work under cover, could collect enough manpower and cars to block every road, lane, highway and duckrunway that led out of a city as big as St. Louis.

Again they hazed us by pacing along parallel roads and behind us with the open end of their crescent aimed along U.S. 67. We went like hell; without slowing a bit we sort of swooped up to St. Louis and took a fast dive into that big blob-shaped dead area. We wound up in traffic and tied Boy Scout knots in our course. I was concerned about overhead coverage from a 'copter even though I've been told that the St. Louis dead area extends upward in some places as high as thirteen thousand feet.

The only thing missing was some device or doodad that would let us use our perception or telepathy in this deadness while they couldn't. As it was, we were as psi-blind as they were, so we had to go along the streets with our eyes carefully peeled for cars of questionable ownership. We saw some passenger cars with out-of-state licenses and gave them wide clearances. One of them hung on our tail until I committed a very neat coup by running through a stoplight and sandwiching my car between two whopping big fourteen-wheel moving vans. I'd have enjoyed the expression on the driver's face if I could have seen it. But then we were gone and he was probably cussing.

I stayed between the vans as we wound ourselves along the road and turned into a side street.

I stayed between them too long.

Because the guy in front slammed on his air-brakes and the big van came to a stop with a howl of tires on concrete. The guy behind did not even slow down. He closed in on us like an avalanche. I took a fast look around and fought the wheel of my car to turn aside, but he whaled into my tail and we went sliding forward. I was riding my brakes but the mass of that moving van was so great that my tires just wore flats on the pavement-side.

We were bearing down on that stopped van and it looked as though we were going to be driving a very tall car with a very short wheelbase in a very short time.

Then the whole back panel of the front van came tumbling towards me from the top, pivoting on a hinge at the bottom, making a fine ramp. The van behind me nudged us up the ramp and we hurtled forward against a thick, resilient pad that stopped my car without any damage either to the car or to the inhabitants.

Then the back panel closed up and the van took off.

Two big birds on each side opened the doors of our car simultaneously and said "Out!"

The tall guy on my side gave me a cocksure smile and the short guy said, "We're about to leave St. Louis on U.S. 40, Cornell. I hope you won't find this journey too rough."

I started to take a swing, but the tall one caught my elbow and threw me off balance. The short one reached down and picked up a baseball bat. "Use this, Cornell," he told me. "Then no one will get hurt."

I looked at the pair of them, and then gave up. There are odd characters in this world who actually enjoy physical combat and don't mind getting hurt if they can hurt the other guy more. These were the type. Taking that baseball bat and busting it over the head of either one would be the same sort of act as kids use when they square off in an alley and exchange light blows which they call a "cardy" just to make the fight legal. All it would get me was a sore jaw and a few cracked ribs.

So after my determination to take after them with murderous intent, they'd pulled my teeth by scooping me up in this van and disarming me.

I relaxed.

The short one nodded, although he looked disappointed that I hadn't allowed him the fun of a shindy. "You'll find U.S. 40 less rough than you expected," he said. "After all, it's like life; only rough if you make it rough."

"Go to hell and stay there," I snapped. That was about as weak a rejoinder as I've ever emitted, but it was all I could get out.

The tall one said, "Take it easy, Cornell. You can't win 'em all."

I looked across the nose of our trapped car to Farrow. She was leaning against the hood, facing her pair. They were just standing there at ease. One of them was offering a cigarette and the other held a lighter ready. "Relax," said the one with the smokes. The other one said, "Might as well, Miss Farrow. Fighting won't get nobody nowhere but where you're going anyway. Might as well go on your own feet."

Scornfully, Farrow shrugged. "Why should I smoke my own?" she asked nobody in particular.

Mentally I agreed: #Take 'em for all they're worth, Farrow!# And then I reached for one, too. Along the side of the van were benches. I sat down, stretched out on my back and let the smoke trickle up. I finished my cigarette and then found that the excitement of this chase, having died so abruptly, left me with only a desire to catch up on sleep.

I dozed off thinking that it wasn't everybody who started off to go to Homestead, Texas, and ended up in Marion, Indiana.

Scholar Phelps did not have the green carpet out for our arrival, but he was present when our mobile prison cell opened deep inside of the Medical Center grounds. So was Thorndyke. Thorndyke and three nurses of Amazon build escorted Farrow off with the air of captors collecting a traitor.

Phelps smiled superciliously at me and said, "Well, young sir, you've given us quite a chase."

"Give me another chance and we'll have another chase," I told him grumpily.

"Not if we can help it," he boomed cheerfully. "We've big plans for you."

"Have I got a vote? It's 'Nay!' if I do."

"You're too precipitous," he told me. "It is always an error, Mr. Cornell, to be opinionated. Have an open mind."

"To what?"

"To everything," he said with an expansive gesture. "The error of all thinking, these days, is that people do not think. They merely follow someone else's thinking."

"And I'm to follow yours?"

"I'd prefer that, of course. It would indicate that you were possessed of a mind of your own; that you weren't merely taking the lazy man's attitude and following in the footsteps of your father."

"Skip it," I snapped. "Your way isn't—"

"Now," he warned with a wave of a forefinger like a prohibitionist warning someone not to touch that quart, "One must never form an opinion on such short notice. Remember, all ideas are not to be rejected just because they do not happen to agree with your own preconceived notions."

"Look, Phelps," I snapped, deliberately omitting his title which I knew would bite a little, "I don't like your personal politics and I deplore your methods. You can't go on playing this way—"

"Young man, you err," he said quietly. He did not even look nettled that I'd addressed him in impolite (if not rough) terms. "May I point out that I am far ahead of your game? Thoroughly outnumbered, and in ignorance of the counter-movement against me until you so vigorously brought it to my attention; within a year I have fought the counter-movement to a standstill, caused the dispersement of their main forces, ruined their far-flung lines of communication, and have so consolidated my position that I have now made open capture of the main roving factor. The latter is you, young man. A very disturbing influence and so very necessary to the conduct of this private war. You prate of my attitude, Mr. Cornell. You claim that such an attitude must be defeated. Yet as you stand there mouthing platitudes, we are preparing to make a frontal assault upon their main base at Homestead. We've waged our war of attrition; a mere spearhead will break them and scatter them to the far winds."

"Nice lecture," I grunted. "Who are your writers?"

"Let's not attempt sarcasm," he said crisply. "It sits ill upon you, Mr. Cornell."

"I'd like to sit on you," I snapped.

"Your humor is less tolerable than your sarcasm."

"Can it!" I snapped. "So you've collected me. I'll still—"

"You'll do very little, Mr. Cornell," he told me. "Your determination to attack us tooth and nail was an excellent program, and with another type of person it might have worked. But I happen to know that your will to live is very great, young man, and that in the final blow, you'd not have the will to die great enough to carry your assault to its completion."

"Know a lot, don't you."

"Yes, indeed I do. So now if you're through trying to fence at words, we'll go to your quarters."

"Lead on," I said in a hollow voice.

With an air of stage-type politeness, he indicated a door. He showed me out and followed me. He steered me to a big limousine with a chauffeur and offered me cigarettes from a box on the arm rest as the driver started the turbine. The car purred with that muted sound of well-leashed power.

"You could be of inestimable value to us," he said in a conversational tone. "I am talking this way to you because you can be of much more value as a willing ally than you would be if unwilling."

"No doubt," I replied dryly.

"I suggest you set aside your preconceived notions and employ a modicum of practical logic," suggested Scholar Phelps. "Observe your position from a slightly different reign of vantage. Be convinced that no matter what you do or say, we intend to make use of you to the best of our ability. You are not entertaining any doubts of that fact, I'm sure."

I shrugged. Phelps was not asking me these things, the inquisitor was actually telling me. He went right on telling me:

"Since you will be used no matter what, you might consider the advisability of being sensible, Mr. Cornell. In blunt words, we are prepared to meet cooperation with certain benefits which will not be proffered otherwise."

"In blunter words you are offering to hire me."

Scholar Phelps smiled in a superior manner. "Not that blunt, Mr. Cornell, not that crude. The term 'hire' implies the performance of certain tasks in return for stipulated remuneration. No, my intention is to give you a position in this organization the exact terms of which are not clearly definable. Look, young man, I've indicated that your willing cooperation is more valuable to us than otherwise. Join us and you will enjoy the freedom of our most valued and trusted members; you will take part in upper level planning; you will enjoy the income and advantages of top executive personnel." He stopped short and eyed me with a peculiar expression. "Mr. Cornell, you have the most disconcerting way. You've actually caused me to talk as if this organization were some sort of big business instead of a cultural unit."

I eyed him with the first bit of humor I'd found in many days. "You seem to talk just as though a cultural unit were set above, beyond, and spiritually divorced from anything so sordid as money, position, and the human equivalent of the barnyard pecking order," I told him. "So now let's stop goofing off, and put it into simple terms. You want me to join you willingly, to do your job for you, to advance your program. In return for which I shall be permitted to ride in the solid gold cadillac, quaff rare champagne, and select my own office furniture. Isn't that about it?"

Scholar Phelps smiled, using a benign expression that indicated that he was pleased with himself, but which had absolutely nothing to do with his attitude towards me or any of the rest of the human race.

"Mr. Cornell, I am well aware of the time it may take for a man to effect a change in his attitude. In fact, I would be very suspicious if you were to make an abrupt reversal. However, I have outlined my position and you may have time to think it over. Consider, at the very least, the fact that while cooperation will bring you pleasure and non-cooperation will bring you pain, the ultimate result will be that we will make use of your ability in either case. Now—I will say no more for the present."

The limousine had stopped in front of a four story brick building that was only slightly different in general architecture than others in the Medical Center. I could sense some slight difference, but when I took a dig at the interior I found to my amazement that this building had been built deliberately in a dead zone. The dead area stood up in the clarity like a little blob of black ink at the bottom of a crystal clear swimming pool, seen just before the ink began to diffuse.

Scholar Phelps saw my look of puzzlement and said, suavely, "We've reversed the usual method of keeping unwilling guests. Here we know their frame of mind and attitude; therefore to build the place in a dead area keeps them from plotting among themselves. I trust that your residence herein will be only temporary, Mr. Cornell."

I nodded glumly. I was facing those last and final words: *Or Else!*

Phelps signed a register at a guard's station in the lobby. We took a very fast and efficient elevator to the third floor and Phelps escorted me along a hallway that was lined with doors, dormitory style. In the eye-level center of each door was a bull's eye that looked like one-way glass and undoubtedly was. I itched to take a look, but Phelps was not having any; he stopped my single step with a hand on my arm.

"This way," he said smoothly.

I went this way and was finally shown into one of the rooms. My nice clean cell away from home.

CHAPTER TWENTY-FOUR

As soon as Phelps was gone, I took a careful look at my new living quarters. The room itself was about fourteen by eighteen, but the end in which I was confined was only fourteen by ten, the other eight feet of end being barred off by a very efficient-looking set of heavy metal rods and equally strong cross-girdering. There was a sliding door that fit in place as nicely as the door to a bank vault; it was locked by heavy keeper-bars that slid up from the floor and down from the ceiling and they were actuated by hidden motors. In the barrier was a flat horizontal slot wide enough to take a tray and high enough to pass a teacup. The bottom of this slot was flush with a small table that extended through the barrier by a couple of feet on both sides so that a tray could be set down on the outside and slipped in.

I tested the bars with my hands, but even my new set of muscles wouldn't flex them more than a few thousandths of an inch.

The walls were steel. All I got as I tried them was a set of paint-clogged fingernails. The floor was also steel. The ceiling was a bit too high for me to tackle, but I assumed that it, too, was steel. The window was barred from the inside, undoubtedly so that any visitor from the outside could not catch on to the fact that this building was a private calaboose.

The—er—furnishings of this cold storage bin were meager of minimum requirements. A washstand and toilet. A bunk made of metal girders welded to the floor. The bedding rested on wide resilient straps fixed to the cross-bars at top and bottom of the bed. A foam-rubber mattress, sheets, and one blanket finished off the bed.

It was a cell designed by Mekstroms to contain Mekstroms and by wiseacres to contain other wiseacres. The non-metallic parts of the room were, of course, fireproof. Anything I could get hold of was totally useless as a weapon or lever or tool; anything that might have been useful to a prisoner was welded down.

Having given up in the escape department, I sat on my bunk and lit a cigarette. I looked for tell-tales, and found a television lens set above the door of the room eight feet outside of my steel barrier. Beside the lens was a speaker grille and a smaller opening that looked like a microphone dust cover.

With a grunt, I flipped my cigarette at the television lens. I hit just above the hole, missing it by about an inch. Immediately a tinny-sounding voice said,

"That is not permitted, Mr. Cornell. You are expected to maintain some degree of personal cleanliness. Since you cannot pick up that cigarette butt, you have placed an unwelcome task upon our personnel. One more infraction of this nature and you will not be permitted the luxury of smoking."

"Go to the devil!" I snapped.

There was no reply. Not even a haughty chuckle. The silence was worse than any reply because it pointed out the absolute superiority of their position.

Eventually I dozed off, there being nothing else to do. When I awoke they'd shoved a tray of food in on my table. I ate unenthusiastically. I dozed again, during which time someone removed the tray. When I woke up the second time it was night and time to go to bed, so I went. I woke up in the morning to see a burly guy enter with a tray of breakfast. I attempted to engage him in light conversation but he did not even let on that I was in the cell. Later he removed the tray as silently as he'd brought it, and I was left with another four hours of utter boredom until the same bird returned with a light lunch. Six hours after lunch came a slightly more substantial dinner, but no talk.

By bedtime the second night I was getting stir-crazy.

I hit the sack at about nine thirty, and tossed and turned, unable to drop off because I was not actually tired. I was also wondering when they'd come around with their brain-washing crew, or maybe someone who'd enter with an ultimatum.

On the following morning, the tray-bearer was Dr. Thorndyke, who sat on the chair on the outside of my bars and looked at me silently. I tried giving him stare for stare, but eventually I gave up and said, "So now where do we go?"

"Cornell, you're in a bad spot of your own making."

"Could be," I admitted.

"And yet, really, you're more of a victim of circumstances."

"Forgetting all the sideplay, I'm a prisoner," I told him curtly. "Let's face a few facts, Thorndyke, and stop tossing this guff."

"All right," he said shortly, "The facts are these: We would prefer that you help us willingly. We'd further prefer to have you as you are. That is, un-reoriented mentally."

"You couldn't afford to trust me," I grunted.

"Maybe we can. It's no secret that we've latched on to quite a number of your friends. Let's assume that they will all be well-treated if you agree to join us willingly."

"I'm sure that the attitude of any of my friends is such that they'd prefer me to stand my ground rather than betray their notions of right and wrong." I told him.

"That's a foolish premise," he replied. "You could no more prevail against us than you could single-handedly overthrow the Government. Having faced that fact, it becomes sound and sensible to accept the premise and then see what sort of niche you can carve out of the new order."

"I don't like your new order," I grunted.

"Many people will not," he admitted. "But then, people do not really know what's good for them."

I almost laughed at him. "Look," I said, "I'd rather make my own ignorant mistakes than to have some Great Father supervise my life. And speaking of fathers, we've both got to admit that God Himself permits us the complete freedom of our wills."

Thorndyke sneered at me. "If we're to quote the Scripture," he said sourly, "I'll point out that 'The Lord Thy God is a jealous God, visiting His wrath even upon seven generations of those who hate Him.'"

"Granted," I replied calmly, "But whether we love Him or hate Him is entirely up to our own particular notion. Now—"

"Cornell, stop talking like an idiot. Here, too, you can take your choice. I'm not ordering you. I'm just trying to point out that whether you go on suffering or enjoying life is entirely up to your own decision. And also your decision will help or hinder others."

"You're entirely too Godlike," I told him.

"Well," he said, "think it over."

"Go to the devil!"

"Now, that's a very weak response," he said loftily, "Doing nobody any good or harm. Just talk. So stop gabbing and think."

Thorndyke left me with my thoughts. Sure, I had bargaining power, but it was no good. I'd be useful only until they discovered some method of inoculating normal flesh with Mekstrom's Disease, and once that was taken care of, Steve Cornell would be a burden upon their resources.

So that was the morning of my third day of incarceration and nothing more took place all day. They didn't even give me anything to read, and I almost went nuts. You have no idea of how long fourteen hours can be until you've been sitting in a cell with absolutely nothing to do. I exercised by chinning myself on the bars and playing gymnastics. I wanted to run but there was not enough room. The physical thrill I got out of being able to chin myself with one hand wore off after a half hundred pull-ups because it was no great feat for a Mekstrom. I did push-ups and bridges and other stunts until I was bored again. And all the while, my thinking section was going around and around. The one main point that I kept coming back to was a very unpleasant future to face:

It was certain that no matter what I did, nor how I argued, I was going to help them out. Either I would do it willingly or they'd grow tired of the lecture routine and take me in for a mental re-evaluation, after which (Being not-Steve Cornell any more) I'd join their ranks and do their bidding. About the only thing I could look at with self-confidence was my determination to hold out. If I was going to join them, it would be after I were no longer the man I am, but reoriented into whatever design they wanted. And that resolve was weakened by the normal human will to live. You can't make a horse drink water, but you can lead a human being to a well and he will drink it dry if you keep a shotgun pointed in his direction.

And so it ended up with my always wondering if, when the cards were all dealt out face up, whether I would have the guts to keep on saying 'No' right up to the point where I walked into their department of brain-washing. In fact, I was rather afraid that in the last moment I'd weaken, just to stay being me.

That uncertainty of mine was, of course, just the idea they wanted to nourish in my mind. They were doing it by leaving me alone with my mental merry-go-round.

Again I hit the sack out of sheer boredom and I turned and tossed for what seemed like hours before I dropped off to sleep, wondering and dreaming about who was to be the next visitor with a bill of goods to sell.

The next visitor came in about midnight, or thereabouts. I woke up with the realization that someone had come in through the outer door and was standing there in the semi-dark caused by a bright moon shining in through my barred window.

"Steve," she said, in a near whisper.

"Go away," I told her. "Haven't you done enough already?"

"Oh, please, Steve. I've got to talk to you."

I sat on the edge of my bunk and looked at her. She was fully dressed; her light printed silk was of the same general pattern and fit that she preferred. In fact, Catherine looked as I'd always seen her, and as I'd pictured her during the long hopeless weeks of our separation.

"You've got something to add?" I asked her coldly.

"I've got to make you understand, Steve," she pleaded.

"Understand what?" I snapped. "I know already. You deliberately set out to marry, or else-how tie some emotional cable onto me. God knows that you succeeded. If it hadn't been for that accident, I'd have been nailed down tight."

"That part is true," she whispered.

"Naturally, you've got justification."

"Well, I have."

"So has any burglar."

She shook her head at me. "Steve, you don't really understand. If only you could read my mind and know the truth—"

She let this trail off in a helpless awkwardness. It was one of those statements that are meaningless because it can be said by either friend or foe and cannot be checked.

I just looked at her and suddenly remembered something:

This was the first time in my life that I was in a position to do some verbal fencing with a telepath on even terms. I could say 'Yes' and think 'No' with absolute impunity. In fact, I might even have had an edge, since as a poor non-telepath I did have some training in subterfuge, falsehood, and diplomatic maneuver that the telepath couldn't have. Catherine and I, at long last, were in the position of the so-called good old days when boys and girls couldn't really know the truth about one another's real thoughts.

"So what's this truth?" I demanded.

"Steve, answer me truly. Have you ever been put on an odious job, only to find that the job is really pleasant?"

"Yes."

"Then hear me out. I—in fact, no woman—takes kindly to being directed to do what I did. I was told to meet you, to marry—" Her face looked flustered and it might have been a bit flushed for all I knew. I couldn't see color enough in the dim light to be sure. "—And then I met you, Steve, and I found out that you were really a very nice sort of guy."

"Well, thanks."

"Don't be bitter. Hear the truth. If Otto Mekstrom had not existed, if there were no such thing as Mekstrom's Disease, and I had met you freely and openly as men and women meet, I'd have come to feel the same, Steve. I must make you understand that my emotional attachment to you was not increased nor decreased by the fact that my physical actions were directed at you. If anything, my job was just rendered pleasantly easier."

I grunted. "And so you were made happy."

"Yes," she whispered. "And I was going to marry you and live honestly with you—"

"Heck of a marriage with the wife in the Medical Center for Mekstrom's Disease and our first child—"

"Steve, you poor fool, don't you understand? If our child came as predicted, the first thing I'd do would be to have the child inoculate the father? Then we'd be—"

"Um," I grunted. "I hadn't thought of that." This was a flat lie. I'd considered it a-plenty since my jailing here. Present the Medical Center with a child, a Mekstrom, and a Carrier, and good old pappy would be no longer needed.

"Well, after I found out all about you, Steve, that's what I had in mind. But now—"

"Now what?" I urged her gently. I had a hunch that she was leading up to something, but ducking shy about it until she managed to find out how I thought. It would have been all zero if we'd been in a clear area, but as it was I led her gently on.

"But now I've failed," she said with a slight wail.

"What do they do with failures?" I asked harshly. "Siberia? Or a gunny sack weighted down with an anvil? Or do they drum you out of the corps?"

"I don't know."

I eyed her closely. I was forced to admit that no matter how Catherine thought, she was a mighty attractive dish from the physical standpoint. And regardless of the trouble she'd put me through, I could not overlook the fact that I had been deep enough in love to plan elopement and marriage. I'd held her slender body close, and either her response had been honestly warm or Catherine was an actress of very rare physical ability. Scholar Phelps could hardly have picked a warmer temptress in the first place; putting her onto me now was a stroke of near-genius.

I got up from the edge of my bunk and faced her through my bars. She came close, too, and we looked into each other's faces over a cross-rail of the heavy fence.

I managed a wistful grin at her. "You're not really a failure yet, are you, kid?"

"I don't quite know how to—to—" she replied.

I looked around my little cell with a gruesome gesture. "This isn't my idea of a pleasant home. And yet it will be my home until someone decides that I'm too expensive to keep."

"I know," she breathed.

Taking the bit in my teeth, I said, "Catherine even though—well, heck. I'd like to help you."

"You mean that?" she asked in almost an eager voice.

"It's not impossible to forget that we were eloping when all this started."

"It all seems so long ago," she said with a thick voice. "And I wish we were back there—no, Steve, I wish Mekstrom's Disease had never happened—I wish—"

"Stop wishing and think," I told her half-humorously. "If there were no Mekstrom's Disease, the chances are that we'd never have met in the first place."

"That's the cruel part of it all," she cried. And I mean *cried*.

I rapped on the metal bars with a fist. "So here we are," I said unhappily. "I can't help you now, Catherine."

She put her hands through the bars and held my face between them. She looked searching into my eyes, as if straining to force her blocked telepath sense through the deadness of the area. She leaned against the steel but the barrier was very effective; our lips met through the cold metal. It was a very unsatisfactory kiss because we had to purse our lips like a pair of piccolo players to make them meet. It was like making love through a keyhole.

This unsatisfactory lovemaking did not last long. Unsteadily, Catherine said, "I want you, Steve."

Inwardly I grinned, and then with the same feeling as if I'd laughed out loud at a funeral, I said, "Through these steel bars?"

She brought out a little cylindrical key. Then went to a brass wall plate beside the outer door, inserted the key, and turned. The sliding door to my cell opened on noiseless machined slides.

Then with a careful look at me, Catherine slipped a little shutter over the glass bull's eye in the door. Her hand reached up to a hidden toggle above the door and as she snapped it, a thick cover surged out above the speaker, television lens, and microphone grille, curved down and shut off the tell-tales with a cushioned sound. Apparently the top management of the joint used these cells for other things than mere containment of unruly prisoners. I almost grinned; the society that Scholar Phelps proposed was not the kind that flourished in an atmosphere of trust, or privacy—except for the top brass.

Catherine turned from her switch plate and came across the floor with her face lifted and her lips parted.

"Hold me, Steve."

My hand came forward in a short jab that caught her dead center in the plexus below the ribs. Her breath caught in one strangled gasp and her eyes went glassy. She swayed stiffly in half-paralysis. My other hand came up, closing as it rose, until it became a fist that connected in a shoulder-jarring wallop on the side of her jaw. Her head snapped up and her knees caved in. She folded from the hips and went down bonelessly. From her throat came the bubbly sound of air being forced painfully through a flaccid wet tube.

I jumped outside of the cell barrier because I was certain that they had some means of closing the cell from a master control center. I don't know much about penology, but that's the way I'd do it. I was half-surprised that I'd been able to get away with this much.

Catherine stirred and moaned, and I stopped long enough to take the key out of the wall plate. The cell door closed on its silent slides.

I had hardly been able to more than run the zipper up my shirt when the door opened and I had to dance like a fool to get behind it. The door admitted a flood of bright light from the corridor, and Dr. James Thorndyke. The cell door must have been bugged.

Thorndyke came in behind a large automatic clutched in one nervous fist. He strained his eyes at the gloom that was not cut by the ribbon of light.

And then I cut him down with a solid slice of my right hand to the base of his neck. I remembered to jump off the ground as the blow went home; there was a crunch of bone and muscle as Thorndyke caved forward to the floor. He dropped the gun, luckily, as his body began to twitch and kick spasmodically as the life drained out of him.

I re-swallowed a mouthful of bitter bile as I reached down to pick up his gun. Then the room got hot and unbearably small and I felt a frantic urge to leave, to close the door upon that sight.

CHAPTER TWENTY-FIVE

I was yards away from my door before my panic left me. Then I remembered where and who I was and took a fast look around. There was no one else in the corridor, of course, or I would not have been able to cut and run as I had. But I looked around anyway until my reasoning power told me that I had done little to help my position.

Like the canary, my plans for escape ended once I was outside of my cage. I literally did not know what to do with my new-found freedom. One thing was becoming painfully obvious: I'd be pinned down tight once I put a foot outside of the dead area in which this building was constructed. What I needed was friends, arms, ammunition, and a good, solid plan of escape. I had neither; unless you call my jailed friends such help. And there I could not go; the tell-tales would give me away to the master control center before I could raise my small—and unarmed—army.

So I stood there in the brightly lighted corridor and tried to think. I got nowhere, but I was driven to action again by the unmistakable sound of the elevator at the end of the corridor.

I eyed the various cell doors with suspicion; opening any but an empty room would cause some comment from the occupant, which again would give me away. Nor did I have time to canvass the joint by peeking into the one-way bull's eyes, peering into a semi-gloom to see which room was empty.

So instead of hiding in the corridor, I sloped towards the elevator and the stairwell that surrounded it, hoping that I could make it before the elevator rose to my floor.

I know that my passage must have sounded like a turbojet in full flight, but I made the stairway and took a headlong leap down the first short flight of stairs just as the elevator door rolled open. I hit the wall with a bumping crash that jarred my senses, but I kept my feet and looked back up the stairs.

I caught a flash of motion; a guard sauntering past the top of the well, a cigarette in one hand and a lazy-looking air about him. He was expecting no trouble, and so I gave him none.

I crept up the stairs and poked my head out just at the floor level.

The guard, obviously confident that nothing, but nothing, could ever happen in this welded metal crib, jauntily peered into a couple of the rooms at random, took a long squint at the room I'd recently vacated, and then went on to the end of the hall where he stuck a key in a signal-box. On his way back he paused again to peer into my room, straining to see if he could peer past the little shutter over the bull's eye. Then he shrugged unhappily, and started to return.

I loped down the stairs to the second floor and waited. The elevator came down, stopped, and the guard repeated his desultory search, not stopping to pry into any darkened rooms.

Just above the final, first-floor flight, I stopped and sprawled on the floor with only my head and the nose of my gun over the top step.

Below was the guard's desk and standing beside the desk with anger in every line of his ugly face was Scholar Phelps!

The elevator came down, stopped, and the guard walked out, to be nailed by Phelps.

"Your job," snapped the good Scholar coldly, "says you are to walk."

"Well, er—sir—it's—"

"Walk!" stormed Phelps angrily. "You can't cover that stairway in the elevator, you fumbling idiot."

"But, sir—"

"Someone could easily come down while you go up."

"I know that, sir, but—"

"Then why do you disobey?" roared Phelps.

"Well, you see, sir, I know how this place is built and no one has ever made it yet. Who could?" The guard looked mystified.

Phelps had to face that fact. He did not accept it gracefully. "My orders are orders," he said stiffly. "You'll follow them. To the last letter."

"Yes sir. I will."

"See that you do. Now, I'm going up. I'll ride and you walk. Meet me on the fourth and bring the elevator down with you."

"Yessir."

I sloped upstairs like a scared rabbit. Up to the third again where I moved down the corridor and slipped into the much-too-thin niche made by a door. Stolidly the guard came up the stairs, crossed in front of the elevator with his back to me, turned the far corner and went on up to the fourth.

As his feet started up the stairs, I was behind him; by the time he reached the top, I was half way up.

Phelps said, "Now, from this moment on, Waldron, you'll follow every order to the absolute letter. And when I ring, don't make the error of bringing the elevator. Send it. It'll come up and stop without a pilot."

"Yes sir. I'm sorry sir. But you understand, sir, there isn't really much to guard, sir."

"Then guard nothing. But guard it well, because a man in your position is gauged in success by the amount of boredom he creates for himself."

The guard started down and I darted up to poke my head out to see where Phelps was going. As I neared the floor level, I had a shock like someone hurling twenty gallons of ice water in my face. The top floor was the end of the dead area, and I—

—pulled my head down into the murk like a diver taking a plunge.

So I stood there making like a guppy with my head, sounding out the boundary of that deadness, ducking down as soon as the mental murk gave me a faint perception of the wall and ceiling above me. Then I'd move aside and sound it again. Eventually I found a little billowing furrow that rose above the floor level and I crawled out along the floor, still sounding and moving cautiously with my body hidden in the deadness that rose and fell like a cloud of murky mental smoke to my sense of perception.

I would have looked silly to any witness; wallowing along the floor like a porpoise acting furtive in the bright lights.

But then I couldn't go any farther; the deadness sank below the floor level and left me looking along a bare floor that was also bare to my sense of perception.

I shoved my head out of the dead zone and took a fast dig, then dropped back in again and lay there re-constructing what I'd perceived mentally. I did it the second time and the third, each time making a rapid scan of some portion of that fourth floor.

In three fast swings, I collected a couple of empty offices, a very complete hospital set-up operating room, and a place that looked like a consultation theatre.

On my fourth scan, I whipped past Scholar Phelps, who was apparently deep in some personal interest.

I rose at once and strode down the hall and snapped the door open just as Phelps' completely unexpecting mind grasped the perceptive fact that someone was coming down his hallway wearing a great big forty five automatic.

"Freeze!" I snapped.

"Put that weapon down, Mr. Cornell. It, nor its use, will get your freedom."

"Maybe all I want out of life is to see you leave it," I told him.

"You'd not be that foolish, I'm sure," he said.

"I might."

He laughed, with all the self-confidence in the world. "Mr. Cornell, you have too much will to live. You're not the martyr type."

"I might turn out to be the cornered-rat type," I told him seriously. "So play it cagey, Phelps."

"Scholar Phelps, please."

"I wouldn't disgrace the medical profession," I told him. "So—"

"So what do you propose to do about this?"

"I'm getting out."

"Don't be ridiculous. One step out of this building and you'll return within a half minute. How did you get out?"

"I was seduced out. Now—"

"I'd advise you to surrender; to stop this hopeless attempt; to put that weapon down. You cannot escape. There are, in this building, your mental and intellectual superiors whose incarceration bear me witness."

I eyed him coldly and quietly. "I'm not convinced. I'm out. And if you could take a dig below you'd see a dead man and an unconscious woman to bear me witness. I broke your Dr. Thorndyke's neck with a chop of my bare hand, Phelps; I knocked Catherine cold with a fist. This thing might not kill you, but I'm a Mekstrom, too, and so help me I can cool you down but good."

"Violence will get you nothing."

"Try my patience. I'll bet my worthless hide on it." Then I grinned at him. "Oh, it isn't so worthless, is it?"

"One cry from me, Mr. Cornell, and—"

"And you'll not live to see what happens. I've killed once tonight. I didn't like it. But the idea is not as new now as it was then. I'll kill you, Phelps, if for no other reason than merely to keep my word."

With a sneer, Phelps turned to his desk and I stabbed my perception behind the papers and stuff to the call button; then I launched myself across the room like a rocket, swinging my gun hand as I soared. The steel caught him on the side of the head and drove him back from his call button before his finger could press it. Then I let him have a fist in the belly because the pistol swat hadn't much more than dazed him. The fist did it. He crumpled in a heap and fought for breath unconsciously.

I turned to the wall he'd been eyeing with so much attention.

There was row upon row of small kine tubes, each showing the dark interior of a cell. Below each was a row of pilot lights, all dark.

On his desk was a large bank of push buttons, a speaker, and a microphone. And beside the push button set-up was a ledger containing a list of names with their cell numbers.

I found Marian Harrison; pushed her button, and heard her ladylike snore from the speaker. A green lamp winked under one of the kine tubes and I walked over and looked into the darkened cell to see her familiar hair sprawled over a thick pillow.

I went to the desk and snapped on the microphone.

"Marian," I said. "MARIAN! HEY! MARIAN HARRISON!"

In the picture tube there was a stir, then she sat up and looked around in a sort of daze.

"Marian, this is Steve Cornell, but don't—"

"Steve!"

"—cry out," I finished uselessly.

"Where are you?" she asked in a whisper.

"I'm in the con room."

"But how on Earth—?"

"No time to gab. I'll be down in a rush with the key. Get dressed!"

"Yes, Steve."

I took off in a headlong rush with the 'Hotel Register' in one hand. I made the third floor and Marian's cell in slightly more than nothing flat, but she was ready when I came barging into her room. She was out of the cell before it hit the backstop and following me down the hall towards her brother's room.

"What happened?" she asked breathlessly.

"Later," I told her. I opened Phillip Harrison's cell. "You go wake up Fred Macklin and tell him to come here. Then get the Macklin girl—Alice, it says here—and the pair of you wake up others and start sending 'em up stairs. I'll call you on the telltale as soon as I can."

Marian took off with the key and the register and I started to shake Phillip Harrison's shoulder. "Wake up!" I cried. "Wake up, Phillip!"

Phillip made a noise like a baby seal.

"Wake up!"

"Wha—?"

"It's Steve Cornell. Wake up!"

With a rough shake of his head, Phillip groaned and unwound himself out of a tangle of bedclothing. He looked at me through half-closed glassy eyes. Then he straightened and made a perilous course to the washstand where he sopped a towel in cold water and applied it to his face, neck, and shoulders. When he dropped the towel in the sink, his expression was fresher and his eyes were mingled curiosity and amazement.

"What gives?" he asked, starting to dress in a hurry.

"I busted out, slugged Scholar Phelps, and took over the master control room. I need help. We can't keep it long unless we move fast."

"Yeah man. Any moving will be fast," he said sourly. "Got any plans?"

"We've—"

The door opened to let Fred Macklin enter. He carried his shirt and had been dressing on the run. "What goes on?" he asked.

"Look," I said quickly. "If I have to stop and give anybody a rundown, we'll have no time to do what has to be done. There are a couple of sources of danger. One is the guard down at the bottom of the stairway. The other is the possible visitor. You get a couple of other young, ambitious fellows and push that guard post over, but quick."

"Right. And you?"

"I've got to keep our hostage cold," I snapped. "And I'm running the show by virtue of being the guy that managed to bust loose."

In the hallway there was movement, but I left it to head back to Scholar Phelps. I got there in time to hear him groan and make scratching noises on the carpet. I took no chances; I cooled him down with a short jab to the pit of the stomach and doubled him over again.

He was sleeping painfully but soundlessly when Marian came in.

I turned to her. "You're supposed to be waking up—"

"I gave the key and the register to Jo Anne Tweedy," she said. "Jo Anne's the brash young teenager you took a bump with in Ohio. She's competent, Steve. And she's got the Macklin twins to help her. Waking up the camp is a job for the junior division." She eyed the recumbent Phelps distastefully. "What have you in mind for him?"

"He's valuable," I said. "We'll use him to buy our freedom."

The door opened again, interrupting Marian. It was Jonas Harrison. He stood there in the frame of the door and looked at us with a sort of grim smile. I had never met the old patriarch of the Harrison Family before, but he lived up to my every expectation. He stood tall and straight; topped by a wealth of snow white hair, white eyebrows, and the touch of a white moustache. His eyes contrasted with the white; a rich and startling brown.

This was a man to whom I could hand the basic problem of engineering our final escape; Jonas Harrison was capable of plotting an airtight getaway.

His voice was rich and resonant; it had a lift in its tone that sounded as though his self-confidence had never been in danger of a set-back: "Well, son, you seem to have accomplished quite a job this night. What shall we do next?"

"Get the devil out of here," I replied—

—wondering just exactly how I'd known so instantly that this was Jonas Harrison. The rich and resonant voice had flicked a subsurface recollection on a faint, raw spot and now something important was swimming around in the mire of my mind trying to break loose and come clear.

I turned from the sword-sharp brown eyes and looked at Marian. She was almost as I had first seen her: Not much make-up if any at all, her hair free of fancy dressing but neat, her legs were bare and healthy-tanned.

I looked at her, and for a half dozen heartbeats her image faded from my sight, replaced by the well remembered figure of Catherine as I had known her first. It was a dizzy-making montage because my perception senses the real figure of Marian, superimposed on the visual memory-image of Catherine. Then the false sight faded and both perception and eyesight focused upon the true person of Marian Harrison.

Marian stood there, her face softly proud. Her eyes were looking straight into mine, as if she were mentally urging me to fight that hidden memory into full recollection.

Then I both saw and perceived something that I had never noticed before. A fine golden chain hung around her throat, its pendant hidden from sight beneath the edge of her bodice. But my sense of perception dug a modest diamond, and I could even dig the tiny initials engraved in the metal circlet:

SC-MH

To dig anything that fine, I knew that it must be of importance to me. And then I knew that it had once been so very personally my own business, for the submerged recollection came bursting up to the top of my mind. Marian Henderson had been mine once long ago!

Boldly I stepped forward and took the chain between my fingers. I snapped it, and held the ring. "Will you wear it again, my dear?"

She held up her left hand for me to slip it on. "Steve," she breathed, "I've never stopped wearing it, not really."

"But I didn't see it until now—"

Jonas Harrison said, "No, Steve, you couldn't see it until you remembered."

"But look—"

"Blame me," he said in his firm determined voice. "The story begins and ends with you, Steve. When Marian contracted Mekstrom's Disease, she herself insisted that you be spared the emotional pain that the rest of us could not avoid. So I erased her from your mind, Steve, and submerged any former association. Then when the Highways in Hiding came to take us in, I left it that way because Marian was still as unattainable to you as if she were dead. If an apology is needed, I'll only ask that you forgive my tampering with your mind and personality."

"Apologize?" I exploded. "I'm here, we're here, and you've just provided me with a way out of this mousetrap!"

"A way out?" he murmured, in that absent way that telepaths have when they're concentrating on another mind. Fast comprehension dawned in the sharp brown eyes and he looked even more self-confident and determined. Marian leaned back in my arms to look into my eyes. "Steve," she cried, "it's simply got to work!" Gloria Farrow merely said, "He'll have to have medication, of course," and went briskly to a wall cabinet and began to fiddle with medical tools. Howard Macklin and Jonas Harrison went into a deep telepathic conference that was interrupted only when Jonas Harrison turned to Phillip to say, "You'll have to provide us with uninterrupted time, somehow."

Marian disengaged herself reluctantly and started to propel me out of the room. "Go help him, Steve. What we are going to do is not for any non-telepath to watch."

Outside, Phillip threatened me with the guard's signal-box key. "Mind telling a non-telepath what the devil you cooked up?"

I smiled. "If your father has the mental power to erase Marian from my mind, he also has the power to do a fine reorientation job on

Scholar Phelps. Once we get the spiderwebs cleaned out of the top dog, we start down the pyramid, line by line and echelon by echelon, with each reoriented recruit adding to our force. Once we get this joint operating on the level, we can all go to work for the rest of the human race!"

There is little left to tell. The Medical Center and the Highways in Hiding are one agency dedicated to the conquest of the last and most puzzling of the diseases and maladies that beset Mankind. We are no closer to a solution than we ever were, and so I am still a very busy man.

I have written this account and disclosed our secret because we want no more victims of Mekstrom's Disease to suffer.

So I will write finish with one earnest plea and one ray of hope:

Please do not follow one of our Highways unless you are already infected. Since I cannot hope to inoculate the entire human race, and will not pick or choose certain worthy types for special attention, I will deal only with those folks who find Mekstrom's Disease among their immediate family. Such people need never be parted from their loved ones. The rest of you will have to wait your turn.

But we'll get to it sooner or later. Thirty days ago, Steve, Junior, was born. He's a healthy little Mekstrom, and like his pappy, Steve Junior is a carrier, too.

THE END